1.

In deepest Munich, ~~~~~~~~~~~~~~~~~~~~ as falling and there was a chill ~~~~~~~~~~~~~~~~~~~~ il was present. The streets were empt~ ~~~~~~~~~~~~~~~~~ e street lights caused shadows to stretch ~~~~~~~~~~~~~~~~~ ~ nis office, Dietmarr Schultz sat in a large ~~~~~~~~~~~ . behind a pristine desk, where files were stacked as hi~ ~~~~~~~~ .. A large glass of whisky sat on the table, begging to be drun~ ~t it merely sat there forlornly as its drinker twitched in deep sleep. Dietmarr Schultz was a leading light in the Abwehr, the secret German intelligence service, and under pressure from his superiors for his alleged troublesome personality. Mr. Schultz knew very well that those at the top of the tree in German politics disliked him and in recent times he had been suspended from official duties, accused of losing a high-profile weapon smuggler in Northern Africa.

The papers gathered in front of him were several pages of evidence as he prepared for the beginning of his hearing in the morning. The clock had just ticked past midnight when Dietmarr Schultz juddered awake from his sleep. The papers, gathered in a neat pile on his desk flew in all directions.

"For God's sake!" shouted Dietmarr as he began to pick up the vast array of documents, evidence and statements from the floor. Placing the piles of paper back on to his desk, Dietmarr noticed movement outside his window. Walking slowly toward the glass, he peered outside to see four gentlemen with guns patrolling the streets. He was in no doubt they had been sent to keep an eye on his actions, as the power of the increasingly popular National Socialist German Workers' Party rocketed. There had been rumours that its protagonist, Adolf Hitler, was planning a Europe wide invasion but this was merely hearsay that Dietmarr had yet to hear from official lines. Strolling back to his desk to stack the last of the scattered papers on to it, Dietmarr yawned profusely, downed the whisky that had been gathering dust and promptly went to bed. Tomorrow was to be a big day.

At 7am, the sun arose to show the depth of the snowfall from the night before. The guards who had been strolling the street hours earlier were still present, gathered in a tight-knit group around a small bin that was producing a tiny fire. Dietmarr awoke, with brief feelings of success, before the thoughts of his impending hearing drowned his ideas. His suit sat hung up on the wardrobe, looking perfectly neat amongst the rest of Dietmarr's bedroom that was as disorganised as the messiest teenager's. As Dietmarr gazed out of the window, wondering what the day ahead would bring, his phone rang.

"Hello?"

"Dietmarr, its Johan". Johan Muller was Dietmarr's lawyer and had been working solely on his case for the past six months.

"I'm so sorry to tell you this, but the time of the hearing has been moved from 10am to 8.30am this morning. You need to get to the Justizpalast by 8am."

Dietmarr's face was a picture of horror.

"Are you kidding?! It takes me 40 minutes to get to the other side of the city! Are you trying to make me look stupid?!" Dietmarr's voice was raised as he panicked at the pace at which he would have to move. "Okay, fine, put the phone down I need to hurry up!"

"Sorry again, see you soon", Johan said abruptly as Dietmarr threw the phone down and hurriedly got changed into his suit. His hair was also a mess as he rushed to the bathroom to make it look tidy and professional. The German government made a habit of changing the times of hearings and trials to suit their agenda, but Dietmarr had never considered that they would do it to a member of the Abwehr, regardless of the tensions between the two parties. Running around his house now, Dietmarr gathered all of the papers he had collected from his floor the night before and stuffed them into his battered brown briefcase.

Twenty minutes later he ran outside the door, flagged down a taxi almost immediately and jumped inside.

"Justizpalast please", gasped Dietmarr as the taxi driver pulled away with no real speed or urgency. "And put your foot down please, I'm running late!"

"I'll drive at my own speed thanks very much", said the driver slowly as a smile spread across his face, as if he was pleased at making a client unhappy.

As the car rumbled along the Autobahnen of Munich, Dietmarr was going through his final preparations as well as rehearsing his initial speech in his head. Dietmarr knew that the odds were stacked against him, but he was determined to fight his corner. As well as being accused of losing a weapon smuggler, Dietmarr had also been outed as opposing the rising influence of Adolf Hitler, popular among his colleagues. It was true, he staunchly disagreed with the haste at which Hitler was planning to change the face of his country and his attitude towards minorities, but he had not been vocal in his dissent. He had discussed his feelings with a couple of close colleagues, but no further.

It had just gone 8 o'clock as the car came to a halt outside the Justizpalast, and as Dietmarr paid the required thirty Deutschmarks to the driver, who merely grunted in acknowledgement, the voice of Johan Muller was in Dietmarr's ear.

"You're late." said Johan firmly.

"It isn't my fault the time was changed, what's all that about?" questioned Dietmarr. "Isn't it your job to stop this kind of shit?" Dietmarr shook his head and walked past Johan towards the towering steps to the courthouse.

"Give it a rest!" shouted Johan, following his client up the stairs.

The Justizpalast sat in the centre of the city, with grand pillars either side of a huge oak door that opened inwards into a magnificent entrance hallway. Imposing portraits of former leaders adorned the walls, surrounded by bulky golden borders. A chandelier graced the ceiling, casting a shadow over the winding staircases that took its occupants to different parts of the building. The floor was decorated with beautiful artwork and there were hundreds of doors leading to countless courtrooms.

"This place freaks me out..." whispered Dietmarr as he strolled towards the nearest manned desk to ask for his pass.

"There you go", said the man on the desk. "Good luck. You're going to need it." He spoke without raising his head to acknowledge Dietmarr's existence and his tone was cold and spiteful, suggesting hatred and annoyance.

"Charming", said Dietmarr loudly, taking the pass out of the receptionist's hand and putting it in his inner lined jacket pocket.

Without delay, he made his way to Courtroom Six, the venue of the hearing which was to last for the entirety of the day.

"Dietmarr". Johan was sat outside the main door, sorting his way through the morning's agenda. "They're going to open up with an initial statement from the prosecution and then your statement. You need to deliver your speech with confidence and without hesitation. Are you sure you don't want me to talk on your behalf?"

"No, I'm fine." Dietmarr had wanted to express his own confidence in his position with passion without it being diluted by lawyer's talk. His trust in Johan's judgement had wavered ever since he had heard from inside the Abwehr that he had represented Hermann Goering in a case the previous year. Goering was a striking force in the National Socialist German Workers' Party, an organisation that was rumoured to trample over anyone who got in its way. Dietmarr was pacing the corridors and sweat was beginning to drip from his brow as the nerves of the situation began to play on his mind. His whole career in the Intelligence Service hinged on the outcome of today. He knew full well the loss of his target in North Africa had nothing to do with him, but he had been made a scapegoat by the German government due to the influence of the rising opposition parties outside of the Weimar Republic.

"It's time." Johan stood up abruptly from his seat and lead Dietmarr into the courtroom. As he walked in through the front door, the first thing he noticed were the public galleries, eerily empty and ghost-like. Court ushers sat in the front row, pens in hand, scribbling intently on the notepads in front of them. Two elaborately dressed judges sat either side of a grand silver throne. However, looking to the right of the room, Dietmarr noticed his trusted colleagues from the Abwehr sitting side-by-side with leading politicians from the German Democratic Party and the President himself, Paul Von Hindenburg.

The sight of friends sitting hand-in-hand with the government in the opposition ranks left Dietmarr feeling as if he had been stabbed in the back by his own family. His colleagues gazed down at their feet, unable to look him in the eye, as Dietmarr sat down next to Johan on the opposite side of the benches, along with Johan's junior associates.

"I can't wait for this to start!" exclaimed one of the younger looking associates. "Such a high profile case for me to get my teeth into, it really is a dream come true!"

Dietmarr stared at him with daggers in his eyes as the childish-looking associate's smile vanished from his face with a flash.

How had he not known about the two-faced nature of his colleagues? Did they despise him as much as the government did? It was true, he had sacrificed some friendships to be promoted in the Abwehr, but he didn't think revenge was on the cards. Dietmarr looked forward, without any expression on his face, as the fluid gown of the head judge appeared from the top table.

"All rise!" shouted the head usher, as everyone stood to welcome the entrance of the judge. Old in his appearance, the judge was Albert Pelscher, a thirty-year veteran of the German courtrooms. His face looked gaunt and tired, as his black gown followed him gracefully to the throne that stood menacingly at the top of the room. He turned towards the front and sat down, followed by the ushers and then the two sides of the argument. Dietmarr was last to take his seat, still reeling from the shock of seeing his friends sitting in the opposition ranks.

"Welcome to the hearing of Mr Dietmarr Schultz, accused of Unprofessional Behaviour." Mr. Pelscher did not hang around in the delivery of his opening words, but Dietmarr was focused solely on his opening statement, which was sat on his wobbling knees. All of a sudden, he felt as if the life was being sucked out of his soul. The betrayal of his friends and colleagues had hit him hard, and he felt as if the whole world was against him. Dietmarr knew he had his opponents, because of his strong opinions, but today he had learnt that this group was larger than first thought.

"Firstly, I ask the prosecution to stand and deliver their opening sentiments. Mr. Leitner."

The judge sat down with a thud and almost immediately, Mr. Leitner, glasses in hand, stood to address the courtroom.

"Ladies and Gentlemen, this is a country of conservatism. We are steadily growing to be one of the strongest and most influential countries in the world, and the safety and security of this great country needs to keep pace with our growing stature."

Dietmarr was not listening. He was reading and re-reading his own statement, making changes on a whim to match his growing anger at the resentment shown towards him. Johan Muller was listening intently to Mr. Leitner's opening words, which had opened with stunning strength and powers of persuasion.

"The security of this country is absolutely paramount to the ideas of future governments", Leitner continued. "This is why our Intelligence Service personnel need to be the very best and deliver perfection every single time. On this occasion, the defendant in question has let his country down."

Dietmarr's head shot up at the strongly delivered final line by

Mr. Leitner. In truth, Dietmarr had made a minor error in keeping tabs on his target, but in reality, he could do nothing to stop him leaving for Hamburg. He had been given false information on his whereabouts by his superiors at Abwehr headquarters and ultimately lost him. In initial questioning, the Abwehr had denied all responsibility, claiming Dietmarr had been out drinking in an Italian bar on a crucial night of the operation. Dietmarr knew this was a lie.

Leitner continued.

"On the night in question, the defendant chose to socialise with the locals, along with a woman he had met in Milan a few days before. Looking at the statements provided from witnesses, Mr. Schultz was flirting with an unnamed Italian lady when he was supposed to be following his target to Rome Ciampino Airport. It is quite clear that Mr. Schultz is more interested in being a womaniser than a serious secret agent for this country."

Dietmarr sat in shocked silence. He was not expecting the prosecution to tell the court he was a womaniser. He knew he should not have been drinking on the night he was supposed to follow his target, but his personality and his commitment to his job left no doubt that he simply did not have time to pursue sexual interests.

Leitner was finishing his ten minute opening speech.

"We will argue to the court that Dietmarr Schultz committed a dereliction of duty and jeopardised the security of this country by allowing a known weapon smuggler to bring a large number of weapons into this country illegally."

Leitner sat down and received a hearty slap on the back by President von Hindenburg, who was sat directly behind him with a gratifying smile on his face.

"Thank you Mr. Leitner". Judge Pelscher was again upstanding, outlining to the court that it was his decision and his decision alone on whether to find Dietmarr Schultz guilty. Dietmarr knew his opportunity to tell his side of the story was coming, and a steely determination laced with underlying anger had returned to his heart.

Judge Pelscher continued to stand. He was still explaining to everyone inside courtroom number six that only the evidence given would be examined and considered and not any of the opinions created by people not involved in the trial. All of this was preamble for Dietmarr who was getting fidgety in his chair as he was desperate to tell his side of the story for the first time.

"I will now move the proceedings on to our first prosecution witness, General Kurt van Easting. Mr. Leitner, if you will."

The elderly judge took his seat without any hint of sarcasm, but Johan Muller stood up with alarming pace.

"Your Honour, you have given the prosecution a chance to outline their initial feelings, and in line with statutory guidelines, you must give the defence the same opportunity".

Dietmarr had stood up with him, a look of pure fire spread across his startled face. Already, this trial stank of undiluted farce and theatre, and if he was not going to be given the chance to give his initial thoughts, he feared he wouldn't be able to throughout the whole trial.

"Mr Muller, as you have already been told, the court does not have sufficient time to hear from both sides, therefore you will sit down and we shall continue." Judge Pelscher was final in his statement, and Johan Muller sat down uncomfortably. However, Dietmarr remained standing.

"You cannot be serious!" he shouted to gasps from the opposition ranks. "You mean to say I can't have my say against these outrageous allegations from the beginning?! What kind of court is this?"

"Sit down Mr. Schultz or I will have you prosecuted for contempt of court." Judge Pelscher was unflinchingly calm in shooting down Dietmarr's protestations but Dietmarr was not going to lie down.

"This is outrageous, Your Honour, you simply cannot be so openly biased!"

"This is your final chance Mr. Schultz, take a seat." said Judge Pelscher with a little more force, and with that, Johan Muller dragged Dietmarr down to his bench.

"Why didn't you put up more of a fight?!" hissed Dietmarr to Johan.

"Arguing with the judge will help no one, you're just going to have to get on with it!" whispered Johan back, but Dietmarr was beyond infuriated.

"I demand to have my initial say in this courtroom!" Dietmarr stood up again to repeated gasps. Out of the corner of his eye, he could see President von Hindenburg shaking his head with comedic velocity.

"That's enough!" Judge Pelscher stood up quickly and leaned forward towards the upstanding Dietmarr. "We're going to take a ten minute break. Muller. With me".

With that, he strode out of the door to his left-hand side, and the courtroom stood with him. Dietmarr, in deep shock at the opening events of his hearing, threw a cursed look towards Johan, who disquietingly shuffled past him to follow the judge. Dietmarr followed with the speed of a cheetah out of one of the side doors of the courtroom. His face was a frightening shade of dark red as he skimmed behind Johan, seething under his breath. He slammed the door behind him and instantly made a move to the shocked looking Johan.

"What the hell was that?!" enquired Dietmarr. "You KNEW I wasn't going to get a chance to speak so why didn't you tell me?!"

"It was only going to make you angry before the start which wouldn't have helped anyone!" exclaimed Johan. "Why did you make a scene right at the start of the hearing?!" It's going to set a precedent!" Johan seemed embarrassed at the altercation but Dietmarr was unwavering in his insistance.

"If this was a fair trial, I'd have been given a chance to speak!" seethed Dietmarr just as the door opened to reveal the bolstering frame of Judge Pelscher.

"If this was a fair trial, which it is, you wouldn't stand up and accuse this court of bias, Mr Schultz. Mr Muller, you will have to control your client in future, is that clear?"

Mr Pelscher sounded slightly arrogant as he passed judgement on the opening exchanges.

"Your Honour, why am I not allowed to speak and the prosecution are?! It's insane!" shouted Dietmarr as Judge Pelscher held his hand up to silence him.

"Mr Schultz, there is protocol to follow and I have no choice but to abide by it. I do not need a lecture from a failed agent on how to do my job!" Mr Pelscher's face was turning a darker shade of red as he slammed his hand down on the table in front of him.

Dietmarr's jaw dropped to the floor.

"What do you mean, FAILED agent?! Have you made your mind up that I'm guilty already have you?!"

Judge Pelscher stood wide-eyed behind his desk, slowly realising that he may have said something wrong. Johan Muller was standing to one side, looking intently at Judge Pelscher and seemed as embarrassed as him. Dietmarr was stood in the middle of the room, his stature suggesting he was about to get involved in a fist fight.

"Fine, if I grant you five minutes to speak in that courtroom, will you cease in publicly criticising my judgement in future?"

Judge Pelscher had a look of exasperation on his face as he questioned Dietmarr.

"That will suffice." said Dietmarr sternly.

"Fine. Five minutes. But then we continue. We've only been given one day to settle this nonsense. Is that understood?" asked Judge Pelscher.

"Yes sir", said Dietmarr.

"And if I hear another word out of you criticising me, you'll be facing more than the unemployment line!" exclaimed Judge Pelscher as he stormed out of the room.

It seemed to Dietmarr that the Judge's mind was already made up, but Dietmarr had little choice but to ignore what he presumed and continue.

Dietmarr was relieved he would have a chance to speak but he would have to cut down his speech dramatically to fit in with the new guidelines. He was still annoyed that he was getting less time, but chose not to argue against the Judge's offer.

Five minutes later, the courtroom had gathered again, with Judge Pelscher seated in his winged silver throne. As the hustle and bustle of everyone taking their seats quietened down, Judge Pelscher stood up.

"In a slight change to the order of proceedings, the defence has been granted five minutes to deliver an opening statement. Mr Muller."

Mr Muller stood.

"Your Honour, my client would like to deliver his opening statement in person before passing on the speaking duties to myself, so I would invite Mr Schultz to deliver."

"So be it. Mr Schultz." sighed Judge Pelscher, as if the words that Dietmarr were about to deliver meant little to the hearing.

Dietmarr's hands were shaking slightly, as he held his statement in front of him. He could feel the eyes of important people on him as a deathly silence fell across the courtroom.

"Ladies and Gentlemen, Your Honour, I have done nothing wrong. I have been made a scapegoat for a serious breach of misjudgement by my colleagues at the Abwehr in relation to the disappearance of Alberto Inganio. I was told he was heading south towards Palermo, when instead he was travelling north towards Rome. I was given wrong information in revenge for being a top-class secret agent and as an act of jealousy after being promoted three years ago."

An audible groan spread fast across the courtroom at the last statement, which Dietmarr just about heard. He was slightly perturbed at some of the whispered comments coming from opposition benches, spoken just loud enough to reach his ears, but he continued regardless.

"Ever since that time, the agency has worked to undermine my position and has resorted to acts of treachery to displace me."

Dietmarr's voice was beginning to shake and the confidence on which he prided himself was vanishing as he listened to his own words. His mouth was getting dry and his voice croaky, as Johan stared up at him with worry in his eyes.

"For it is true I was in a bar in Milan, it was for a matter of minutes as I was talking to a potential alibi. To suggest that I was fraternising with the locals is a total fabrication of the facts, and an exaggeration to the extreme. I am always completely and totally thorough in my job and I am certain that if I was given the correct information from headquarters, I would not have lost Alberto Inganio and there would be less illegal weaponry in this country as a result. I plead with you, Your Honour, to not believe the outrageous lies that the prosecution present and let me continue with my work as one of the country's best secret agents."

With that, Dietmarr took his seat and there was a silence in the room that seemed to last an eternity. Dietmarr could feel the burning eyes of Johan next to him, but he continued to look forward towards Judge Pelscher, who got to his feet once more.

"Thank you Mr Schultz. Intriguing words for sure", said Judge Pelscher in a questioningly sarcastic tone.

"We shall now continue on schedule with the first witness for the prosecution, the Abwehr Head of Operations, General Kurt Van Easting. Mr Leitner, please."

Kurt Van Easting was Dietmarr's boss, a huge mustachioed

beast of a man, who boasted countless medals on his breast as he took to the stand. He was the first person that Dietmarr noticed sitting in the opposition ranks, and he suspected that Van Easting would spend his entire time on the stand lying through his teeth. General Van Easting's voice was bold and deep as he read out his oath and stood before the room.

"I, General Kurt Van Easting, will give evidence in front of this court in the full knowledge that false statements and evidence could lead to prosecution."

"Fat chance...", whispered Dietmarr under his breath, as the court usher sat back down in his seat and Mr. Leitner, with the glinting of the ceiling lights in his eyes, briefly browsed his notes before facing Van Easting.

"General, please give us an overview of what it is like working with Mr. Schultz."

"Well...", Van Easting threw Dietmarr a nervous look before continuing. "Mr. Schultz came into the Abwehr as an extremely efficient and intelligent man. Straight out of university, he showed a rare talent for espionage rarely seen in this country. His fitness was world-class and his decision-making almost faultless". Van Easting, sweating under the gaze of the President, emphasised the word 'almost', as if he feared he was praising the under fire spy too much. He continued.

"However, as the years went on, his actions became a worry. He would be given a mission to complete, but then go off and do his own thing, without a care in the world. His mission commander would regularly come to me expressing his grave concerns." Upon those words, Van Easting guided the court to a well-dressed man sitting in the very far corner of the courtroom, almost as if he was attempting to hide.

Dietmarr did not need to look up to see who Van Easting was talking about. His mission commander was a small, bespectacled man called Oliver Hoffman, who was cowered in the corner of the courtroom, face behind the local newspaper as if he was scared of the entire episode that was taking place before him.

Dietmarr never had a problem with his mission commander. They were polar opposites in terms of personality, but while Dietmarr was outspoken and opinionated, Hoffman merely bumbled through his job with the ability of a lower school student. However, they were always pleasant towards each other. Meanwhile, Van Easting was taking a lengthy sip of water as the questioning continued.

"Please give us an example of when Mr. Schultz absconded from his duties", asked Mr. Leitner snidely.

"Back at the turn of the decade..." began Van Easting before being interrupted.

"Please be more specific General." Judge Pelscher was looking ruefully towards Van Easting, imploring him to be ruthless.

"I'd say right at the beginning of 1930, January or February, Mr. Schultz was stationed in Russia on an observatory mission. He was to keep tabs on a Russian conman, the name of whom escapes me..."

Van Easting was seen hastily crawling through his notes, before holding a piece of paper up in the air.

"Aha!", cheered Van Easting. "Here we are. 6th February 1930. A direct quote from Oliver Hoffman. 'Dietmarr Schultz has not reported for four whole days and we don't know whether he is alive or dead. He may have been killed by his target, Alexandr Kirischenko.' It turns out he was cavorting with Russian girls in St. Petersburg!"

Kurt Van Easting's face painted a picture of pleasure and triumph. However, this was a lie. Not only was Van Easting lying about Dietmarr meeting the girls, he was lying about Dietmarr being in Russia at all. Dietmarr was on compassionate leave during this time due to the untimely death of his father, knowledge that everyone in the room knew apart from Judge Pelscher.

"Is this the act of a committed agent or a lost soul?" continued Kurt Van Easting. "Do we deserve to be treated to half-arsed attempts to keep track of the world's most dangerous people? NO WE DO NOT!" Van Easting bellowed out the last few words with his trademark booming voice. Dietmarr merely sat glumly, looking downwards and shaking his head.

"Thank you General." Judge Pelscher was upstanding once more as he requested Johan Muller to begin his questioning.

"Thank you your honour." Johan stood up, knees wobbling slightly as he opened his assault on Van Easting.

"General Van Easting, we are told by reliable sources that Oliver Hoffman isn't very good at his job. Care to elaborate?"

Dietmarr's eyes shot up to the scene in front of him. Johan was stood hunched over a large pile of papers, while Kurt Van Easting stood proudly at the top of the room, his chest puffed out, showing off his countless medals.

"I can confirm Mr. Hoffman is a brilliant asset to the Abwehr." announced Van Easting curtly.

There was a silence and a series of sighs from Johan Muller as he mulled over his next question. To Dietmarr's eyes, his confidence looked shot and he didn't know what he was doing. This was unravelling into a total disaster.

"Mr Muller? Surely you must have more questions?" enquired Judge Pelscher.

"Er, yes Your Honour, just bear with me for one moment." squeaked Johan as he quickly ran his fingers through his notes.

"You are aware that this hearing is a one-day hearing only, Mr Muller?" Judge Pelscher appeared restless in his throne.

"I am aware, Your Honour", claimed Johan as he appeared from the mass of paper, holding one piece that was adorned with countless scribbles.

"Mr. Van Easting, General Sir", breathed Johan in a rushed tone. "On this piece of paper, I have a quote from your predecessor, General Joachim Kiln that Oliver Hoffman is an, "inadequate agent and should not be promoted", while he praises my client for his exceptional work. What do you have to say to that?"

Dietmarr was shocked. How had Johan not known? He quickly jumped up to where Johan was standing to ask him to retract the question, but before he could, Van Easting, grinning from ear to ear, was ready to answer.

"Mr. Muller, if you had done your research, you'd have known that General Kiln was sacked for gross misconduct after siphoning Abwehr funds to his own bank account. His opinion on the Abwehr is irrelevant and probably incorrect".

Dietmarr had his head in his hands. How had Johan made such a basic error? Johan's face was a picture of horror and shock as he stood down from his position.

"That's all", he whispered as he sheepishly sat down on the benches.

"What the fuck are you playing at?" hissed Dietmarr.

"I'm so sorry, I genuinely didn't know", whispered Johan disconsolately as Judge Pelscher was addressing the courtroom once more.

"Due to the unscheduled delay, there is no more time to hear from anymore witnesses this morning. Therefore, we shall break for one hour, before reconvening at 1pm. Please be reminded that this process must be completed today."

With that, Judge Pelscher walked out of the room via the door to his left and with him, the courtroom rose. President Von Hindenburg could be heard enthusiastically chatting to his associates. Meanwhile, Dietmarr sat staring straight ahead.

What was going on here? It almost seemed as if Johan was on their side. Johan had shuffled out as soon as Judge Pelscher had called time, looking worn out from the morning's events.

After a few minutes, Dietmarr got to his feet wearily and made his way to the front reception for a cigarette. Despite everything, he was still confident that the hearing, the result of which would be heard in a few days, would still go his way. Oliver Hoffman, the bumbling commander, was still to take to the stand along with Dietmarr himself. If life had taught him anything, it was never to give up until there was nothing more he could do. His Father, himself a war veteran, taught him that lesson. Dietmarr's father was always proud of his son's work, although the pair rarely saw each other before his passing. His Mother had died when Dietmarr was a young boy, after their home was ambushed by a group of unruly tearaways. Mrs. Schultz was murdered by one of them when Dietmarr was only seven years old. With his father away on active duty, Dietmarr was taken into care and lived an independent adolescence, opting to take care of himself from the age of fourteen. He largely spent his time as a young man studying hard and learning new languages. Dietmarr was fluent in six languages, which came in handy during his time as a secret agent for the Abwehr.

After half an hour, Johan strolled back into the building, with a surprisingly smug look across his face as his gaze met Dietmarr's.

"I've just been doing a bit of digging", claimed Johan before he was interrupted by an angry Dietmarr.

"Bit late for that isn't it? You've fucked this up already..." slated Dietmarr.

"No, listen, listen. It turns out General Kiln wasn't sacked. He resigned after being threatened by Van Easting. I will bring it up in the afternoon session."

Dietmarr was sceptical, but nodded in agreement as they walked back into Courtroom Six for the afternoon session. Mr. Leitner had not moved since the morning exchanges as he scurried through his notes. Dietmarr took his seat, next to Johan.

"We'll have them this afternoon, don't you worry kid." Johan seemed dangerously optimistic about their chances and Dietmarr's mood had picked up after the disastrous opening session.

Within ten minutes, Judge Pelscher was seated once more and the courtroom had re-assembled. Oliver Hoffman, due to take to the stand next, was still hidden away under his newspaper, as if his contribution to the hearing would be forgotten about if he was hiding.

"Welcome back gentlemen. We shall continue with the second of three witnesses, Commander Oliver Hoffman. Thank you, Mr. Leitner."

Judge Pelscher sat down, took a sip of his coffee and gestured for Commander Hoffman to take to the stand. Gingerly, Hoffman put down his newspaper and stodgily walked up the small staircase to the stand.

"I, Commander Oliver Thomas Hoffman, will give evidence in front of this court in the full knowledge that false statements and evidence could lead to prosecution."

Hoffman sounded unbelievably nervous, as if his words could lead to his own downfall. Mr. Leitner was stood menacingly as he gesticulated towards Hoffman to hurry up and put the declaration away.

"In your own time Commander..." exclaimed Leitner, in such a way that he was greeted with a stern look from Judge Pelscher.

"Sorry Your Honour. I mean, Mr. Leitner, sir."

"Yes Commander, I am not the judge in this case. Let's get on with it. Mr. Hoffman, describe Dietmarr Schultz as an agent. Was he successful?"

Oliver Hoffman looked towards Dietmarr with a sense of remorse strewn across his face. He looked sad and unbelievably worn.

"He was unreliable..." said Hoffman quietly.

"Please speak louder Commander, and project your voice to the courtroom. How was Dietmarr Schultz as an agent?"

Mr. Leitner's tone was stern and seemed to put Hoffman under pressure. Commander Hoffman took a huge gulp of water and wiped his brow that was profusely sweating.

"Erm... Mr. Schultz was rather unreliable in his duties."

Hoffman seemed uneasy speaking his words, but was continued to be put under pressure by Leitner.

"Please give us an example Mr. Hoffman". Leitner stood impatiently, holding a particularly thick file in his hands.

Again, Hoffman threw a concerned look towards Dietmarr, but once again began to attack Dietmarr's capabilities.

"When Dietmarr first joined the Abwehr in 1924, he was an enthusiastic and capable agent. Within three years, he had killed three fellow colleagues in a friendly fire incident and risked a world war after altercations with Britain."

Hoffman looked down at his feet, as Dietmarr merely sat in another shocked silence. Hoffman, inadequate as he was at his job, was at least one of the most honest men Dietmarr had met. Yet here he was, lying through his teeth under oath. Dietmarr was left confused and hurt.

Leitner continued.

"This was the famed incident in Cannes, France where..." Leitner turned the pages of his file confidently, "Sargeant Peter Closiva, Private Lukas Olahm and Private Oliver Schmidt were shot dead, correct?"

"Correct", said Hoffman quietly.

"Excuse me?" implored Leitner.

"That is correct", stated Hoffman in a slightly louder tone.

"So, simply put Commander Hoffman, would you say Mr. Schultz, after the incidents you have provided with us and other situations you have heard, is a capable agent?"

There was a silence. Once again, Oliver Hoffman gazed in the direction of Dietmarr, who was sat intently on the edge of his bench.

"No, I would not." said Hoffman.

"Thank you, that is all Your Honour".

Leitner sat down, slapped on the back by President von Hindenburg while Dietmarr sat staring directly at Oliver Hoffman, who wiped the sweat from his forehead with a small towel he had produced from his inside pocket.

"Mr. Muller, do you have any questions for Commander Hoffman?" asked Judge Pelscher.

"I do Your Honour.", said Johan as he stood proudly and more confidently than he had done previously.

"Commander Hoffman, did you have any knowledge of the reasoning behind the sacking of the previous General?"

Oliver Hoffman threw a look to the opposite side of the courtroom this time, where Kurt Van Easting was sat next to the President, slowly but noticeably shaking his head.

"No", stated Hoffman.

"You've just been instructed to say no by HIM!" Dietmarr couldn't control his anger. He was upstanding again, but Judge Pelscher was quick to stamp his authority.

"Mr. Schultz, please resist your temptations to throw this courtroom into disarray. General Van Easting knows the rules only too well, and I did not see any form of communication between Van Easting and Hoffman. Muller, please continue."

Dietmarr was seething and breathing heavily, but reluctantly sat down.

Johan was eager to continue.

"So you mean to say that, despite being the Commander alongside Van Easting at the time, that you did not know he was threatening General Kiln to stand down?"

"I had no knowledge of the incident." Hoffman said quickly, not looking across to the benches this time, as he knew he was under strict instruction.

"Well, I can tell you with complete confidence Your Honour, that this is the case, and I have a copy of the exchanges to prove it."

Dietmarr turned round with enough velocity to crick his neck, but was amazed that Johan had managed to get his hands on something so lucrative. For the first time, the opposite benches shuffled uncomfortably in their seats as Judge Pelscher invited the court usher to take the pages from Muller, who looked both proud and triumphant in equal measure. Dietmarr's eyes were wide in shock as Judge Pelscher took the pages and scoured them with brutal detail.

The silence in the courtroom was deafening. Dietmarr knew that these conversations could prove that Van Easting was in the wrong and throw the whole case into suspicion. However, Johan had not talked to him about it, so he was unsure what the exchanges actually included.

Still, Judge Pelscher was reading the exchanges, to increased murmuring in the courtroom. As he finished reading the final page, Pelscher rose his head to the expectant crowd in front of him.

"These exchanges, though interesting, have no relevance to the case of Dietmarr Schultz and the weapons smuggler. Anything else Mr. Muller?"

Dietmarr's brief optimism vanished as quickly as the smile on Johan's face.

"But, didn't you read the part where General Kiln specifically tells Van Easting that Schultz is on compassionate leave, when Van Easting told this courtroom this morning that he was in Russia?"

"Yes", stated Judge Pelscher simply.

"So doesn't that prove that General Van Easting is a compulsive liar?" asked Johan to raised eyebrows from the opposite benches.

"Maybe. But it still doesn't prove that Schultz is a capable agent. It doesn't prove he didn't shoot dead three of his own colleagues or indeed, as the subject of this case, prove that he was at no fault of losing Alberto Ingenio in Northern Africa."

Judge Pelscher's ruling sounded final and absolute.

"Anything else Mr. Muller?" enquired Judge Pelscher.

"No Your Honour, that is all..." said Johan quietly as he slumped down to his bench.

There were two hours remaining in the specified time, with just one witness to give evidence, Dietmarr himself. Although he would give it his all, Dietmarr felt the optimism leave his being and he felt the result of this hearing was only going one way.

Judge Pelscher was upstanding.

"We shall take a brief interlude of twenty minutes before resuming with our final witness, Mr. Dietmarr Schultz. Thank you."

With that, he once again walked out of the door to his left. Dietmarr sat slouched in his seat, deflated, next to an equally sad-looking Johan. President von Hindenburg sat successfully on his bench, talking in loud, brash tones to his fellow government officials and Mr. Leitner, while Oliver Hoffman had resumed hiding behind his newspaper in the corner. Kurt Van Easting had left the room, probably to let out a huge sigh of relief that Judge Pelscher hadn't incriminated him. Dietmarr however, had made his mind up. This case was corrupt.

After the brief break, Judge Pelscher strolled into the room to retake his seat ahead of an expectant and baying crowd.

"The final witness, Mr. Dietmarr Schultz", announced Pelscher.

Dietmarr almost hopped up to the stand and took the piece of paper with his oath written on it in italic black ink.

"I, Dietmarr Schultz, will give evidence in front of this court in the full knowledge that false statements and evidence could lead to prosecution. As if that's not going to happen anyway".

Johan closed his eyes at the saying of the last sentence and shook his head ashamedly. Judge Pelscher was upstanding once more.

"Mr. Schultz, please repeat the oath without the sarcastic undertones."

Dietmarr sighed and repeated the oath, without the final sentence and handed the piece of paper back to the usher, who was silently laughing under his breath.

"Mr. Leitner", said Judge Pelscher as he nodded in the direction of the arrogant lawyer who knew victory was around the corner.

"Mr Schultz, please tell us about your career in the Abwehr", asked Mr. Leitner in a confident tone.

Dietmarr nodded.

"Certainly Mr Leitner, but first, please allow me to read a statement."

Johan Muller looked confused as Dietmarr drew a single piece of paper from his blazer pocket and opened it up.

"I have been a secret agent for this country for 8 years, dedicating my entire life to the safety and security of Deutschland. I have risked my life, thrown myself into perilous situations and cavorted with the enemy all in order to keep this great country safe from unwanted invasions. Today, I turned up to this hearing with the sole intention of outlining my intentions to continue to serve for the Abwehr. Instead, I have been greeted with complete disdain, ranging from cold-hearted colleagues to blatant lying. I am of the firm belief that this hearing is corrupt and staged to such a degree that I even question if my own attorney is on my side. It is therefore with deep regret that I resign from the Abwehr with immediate effect. Let me add my final thoughts. This country will go to the dogs if you allow certain members of society to take power. Your Honour, I look forward to your final verdict that has been promised within the coming week."

The room was shocked into silence as Dietmarr placed his statement back in his pocket and proceeded to stroll straight out of Courtroom number six.

Johan sat stunned on his bench, while the opposite side laughed with derision, high-fiving each other with happiness etched across their faces. Judge Pelscher, seemingly glad that the hearing was over, was upstanding for the final time.

"Well, that was unexpected. Gentlemen, thank you for your attendance today. I shall deliberate with my fellow colleagues and advise of the verdict within seven days."

With that statement, he walked out of the door to his left for the final time, laughing and joking with his junior colleagues who were following him. Johan Muller, isolated with his piles of papers, began packing them away into his black briefcase as President von Hindenburg strolled over to him. Kurt Van Easting quickly followed in his wake after shaking the hand of a government official.

President Hindenburg coughed politely to get the attention of Johan, who looked up from his briefcase.

"Well played Johan", stated President Hindenburg, hand outstretched.

"Thank you Mr. President", replied Johan courtly. In Hindenburg's hand lay a cheque that Johan Muller took with haste and pocketed.

"I like how you tried to incriminate me to seem genuine Johan! We could make a secret agent out of you yet!", beamed Van Easting as he too shook Johan's hand.

"Just as long as you keep your half of the bargain and keep my family safe?", enquired Johan inquisitively.

"I will make sure of it Muller", exclaimed Kurt Van Easting as he made his way back to his associates.

"Talk to you soon Muller!" boomed Hindenburg as he followed Van Easting back to the opposite benches. Johan looked briefly at the cheque, the total of 2.3 million Deutschmarks scrawled in black with his name alongside it.

As he continued to pack his briefcase, he smiled. Job done.

2.

"Fifty-one, fifty-two, fifty-three, fifty-four..."

Henry could hold on for no longer. He forced his way up out of the pool of water and gasped for air.

"One minute and fifty four seconds is not good enough Irthing!" The rasping sounds of Lieutenant Arthur Pooley echoed around the marble chamber as MI6 agent, Henry Irthing breathed heavily and towelled himself down. He was in the middle of rigorous training for a new mission, the briefing of which would take place that very evening. Lieutenant Pooley had been recruited to put him through his paces.

"Again. Now!" shouted Pooley as he grabbed Henry's head and forced it back into the water. Bubbles surfaced as Henry attempted to breathe.

"Don't you dare come up now, Irthing, you'd be useless being water boarded!" screamed Lieutenant Pooley as Henry took a firm grip of the handles in the pool and held tight.

One minute later, he once again forced his head out of the water, unable to take the strain any longer.

"Shit effort!" screamed Lieutenant Pooley as he walked out. "We'll start again in the morning!"

As soon as Pooley left the room, Henry collapsed to a heap on the ground. He had been put through his paces for three straight hours without a break and was exhausted. He had been through this process before, as was normal before any mission, but it never got any easier.

Just as he was catching his breath, Henry's commander, Alfred Pursey, walked into the room.

"Brutal isn't he?" said Alfred in a caring tone. "Unfortunately, you'll have another three hours with him tomorrow but that'll be it."

"Thank fuck for that", blurted out Henry, still gasping for air. "The guy is a monster, Brian never used to be this hard on me."

"Well Brian was lenient." claimed Alfred. "This guy isn't. We need to be on top of our game with new dangers hovering around the corner. Talking of which, do you know what this evening is about?"

Henry looked up from his crouched position on the floor.

"Not a dickie bird. Something about Germany?" asked Henry inquisitively.

"Indeed", stated Alfred. The new boss will tell you more this evening, but in short, you're in for a long, hard chase my boy! See you later!" With that, he promptly walked out and left Henry to get changed into dry clothes.

Henry Irthing, a Cambridge graduate, had been working for the British intelligence services for fourteen years, starting in domestic security before transferring to Her Majesty's MI6 in 1928. Since then, he had been on missions in France, the Caribbean islands and China, with varying success. He was considered by some to be a bumbling, indecisive agent.

Henry got changed into his spare clothes, a pristine white shirt with a dark blue tie and matching tie clip. Black shoes complimented the jet black blazer that completed a professional look, as he walked outside to be greeted by a brand new Lincoln limousine, which was his chauffeur driven choice of car. Climbing in, he asked the driver to take him to MI6 headquarters, where he would wait for an hour before his briefing with the big bosses of the corporation.

"Would you like to stop off anywhere to dine, sir?" enquired the driver, closing his own door and looking in the rear view mirror.

"No thank you, Miles. Straight to Headquarters", stated Henry as he sat back and looked out of the window. London painted a picture of hustle and bustle, with important looking businessmen walking past with faces of anger and frustration. Upon turning the corner, a different side of London was presented, with market traders attempting to sell their goods to the baying public, who were scouring the stalls for the cheapest food. Cyclists sped through the market, avoiding people by swerving in and out of the stalls. One particular market trader threw a particularly expletive-ridden tirade at one such cyclist, who had knocked over his stall.

However, Henry's mind had switched to the mission that lay ahead. He had overheard concerns from his superiors that Germany was planning something but he was unable to hear what from his own office. In an hour or so, he was going to hear exactly what Germany were up to.

Thirty minutes later, the Lincoln limousine had pulled up outside a grey-looking decrepit building, which was the home of MI6. Walking in through the front door, Henry held his arms out to be searched by the armed guards.

"Don't get a hard on now will you!", said Bill jokingly.

Henry laughed nervously.

"I'll try not to mate!" as Bill moved on to another visitor waiting at the doorway.

Henry laughed along and proceeded to the front desk to sign in.

"Evening Phillip, how are you?" asked Henry politely.

"Not so bad squire, thanks for asking. Here for the briefing?", enquired Phillip, the receptionist, not bothering to wait for an answer.

"Through the double doors, up the stairs, second door on your right. Alfred and Mike are up there already".

"Ta Phil", said Henry as he made his way through the doors and up the winding staircase to the upper reaches of the building.

A knock on the door was greeted by a welcome from a smart-looking Commander Alfred Pursey, dressed in an all black suit, with medals spread across his chest proudly.

"Evening Irthing. Recovered yet?" asked Alfred Pursey, pouring a glass of whiskey for the three present gentlemen.

"Just about..." said Henry, looking tentatively at the other man in the room, sat staring at a file on the main table, spectacles in hand.

"Ah, I see you've noticed our brand new Governor, Mr Michael Langley. Michael, meet our top secret agent, Henry Irthing. Henry, meet Mike."

"Good evening sir, nice to meet you", said Henry with a smile, holding his outstretched hand to Michael.

"Yes yes, nice to meet you, take a seat", said Michael abruptly, refusing the handshake offered by Henry. Henry, baffled, sat down opposite Michael and next to Commander Pursey.

"I hear you're one our best agents?" enquired Michael, still peering down at the file sat in front of him. "Henry Irthing, son of your run-of-the-mill butcher, can be considered to be slightly soft and indecisive." Michael Langley looked up from his file. "Indecisive?"

It was an odd way to start a meeting, but Henry, well versed in facing tough questioning answered with aplomb.

"When I first started sir, maybe. Nowadays, I'm one of the best agents this country has" stated Henry, with confidence.

"And what about killing people? Doesn't it put you off?" asked Michael.

"It's all part of the job. I will kill if necessary." replied Henry unnervingly.

"And the wife?" questioned Michael, in a tone that suggested it was a normal question to ask.

Henry looked sideways towards an equally confused looking Commander Pursey before turning back to Michael Langley, who was looking directly at him, eyebrows raised.

"I'm not sure I understand your meaning Governor?" asked Henry.

"The wife. Would you kill the wife if needs must?" enquired Michael, who was not startled by the amazed look he was receiving from Henry.

"I'm not married Governor, so I suppose I wouldn't have to", replied Henry, sheepishly.

"Oh great, we've got a puff as our greatest agent", joked Michael who stood up and offered a hand to Henry. "Great to meet you Henry!"

Commander Pursey offered a wry smile as Henry held his hand out and shook Michael's hand vigorously.

"Very nice to meet you Governor", replied Henry courteously.

"Now, let's get down to business. Another whiskey please, Alf". Michael was holding his glass out expectedly and Commander Pursey, taken aback by the request, took it from him.

"Certainly sir. Henry?"

"I'm fine sir, thank you", replied Henry. He wanted a clear head for the briefing which would outline his work for the coming months.

"How much do you know of Germany, my boy?" asked Michael, accepting the glass of whiskey offered by Commander Pursey.

"A fair bit. I speak fluent German, my father fought against the Germans in the Great War and I have visited both Munich and Hamburg socially." said Henry, as if he was reading from his personal resume.

"Great, great, I really want to know about the German females you've seen to." said Michael sarcastically. "I wasn't expecting such an amateurish answer, Mr. Irthing. Now. Tell me what you know of the real Germany?"

Henry had to consider his thoughts for a while, wondering what the Governor meant by, "the real Germany". He gathered all he knew of the German political system and replied politely.

"Currently under the jurisdiction of the Weimar Republic, I've heard President von Hindenburg is corrupt and that another party are looking to take over?" Henry looked to Michael for a nod but received nothing but a glare in response.

"Go on..." implored Michael, holding out a hand, gesturing for Henry to continue.

"The only other party I can imagine taking over are the National Socialist German Worker's Party... run by Adolf Hitler?"

Again, Henry was looking to Michael for a response and this time, he received one.

"Bingo!" shouted Michael, slamming his hand on the table. "Hitler! Adolf Hitler, Great War veteran turned "great" politician." Michael gesticulated wildly at the suggestion that Adolf Hitler was great.

"He is our target. We have reason to believe that he is planning a Europe-wide invasion and a plot to force President von Hindenburg to appoint him Chancellor. From there, the next step is the Presidency. Let's face it, Hindenburg is about to pack his bags. It is of my firm belief, that however bad von Hindenburg is, he isn't half as bad as this Adolf Hitler. We must stop him."

Henry could sense the temperature rise in the room with the excitement of Michael's voice. He sensed that Michael was genuinely looking forward to ridding the world of this Adolf Hitler.

"So you want me to kill him?" asked Henry.

"Ha!" scoffed Michael incessantly. "Good luck with that. The man has every single security personnel tracking him twenty-four seven. No, going straight for the jugular is too dangerous. It would be a suicide mission."

"So what exactly do you suggest Langley?" Commander Pursey had listened intently to the opening exchanges, but was known to be impatient.

"Easy tiger, I'm getting to it!" said Michael cheerily. "Hitler has a command below him. Senator Hermann Goering, his second in command, although not officially. He is equally as dangerous and equally protected by security. Joseph Goebbels, who is quite frankly, an imbecile whom you needn't worry about at the moment. And then there is a man who goes by the name of Erich von Manstein." Michael pushed a photograph of a clean shaven, bespectacled man towards Henry.

"This chap is Hitler's head strategist. Without him, Hitler would be clueless. Unlike the main men however, he is not tracked night and day."

Henry was listening intently, writing down the names that had been given to him.

Michael continued.

"Henry, it is von Manstein who must be eliminated. This will cause considerable disruption to Hitler's plans and although it may not completely stop him, it will delay them to such a degree that we can get our forces sorted. Talking of which, any update on that twat Pollard?" asked Michael, turning towards Commander Pursey.

Coughing slightly on his whiskey, Alfred Pursey replied, "Err, no sir, I believe he is still on a recruitment drive."

"That guy is as slow as my Aunt Mary in a 100 yard dash", exclaimed Michael as he pointed towards a map of Europe he had laid out on his desk.

"Come over here Irthing. Pursey, I'll have another whiskey."

Commander Pursey looked ahead in disdain as he snatched Michael's glass out of his hand and walked over to a globe that housed a whole variety of spirits.

"Now, to begin with, we're going to drop you here." Michael had grabbed a metal pointer from below his desk and pointed to Germany.

Henry gazed down at the map and saw the pointer on top of a small town.

"Potsdam?" asked Henry.

"Wonderful town. It has a high-class brothel that you could check out", joked Michael, before he was shot down by Commander Pursey.

"Michael, really?" shouted Pursey from the drinks globe, before being ushered to calm down by the laughing Governor.

"I'm kidding Alf! Really, what's life without a laugh or two?!" stated Michael. "In all seriousness Henry, Potsdam is a cosy little town, but also happens to be the birthplace of our primary target, Mr von Manstein. He regularly commutes from his home in Potsdam to Berlin, which is 35 miles away. He still lives at home with his parents would you believe!"

Michael grabbed the whiskey that had been disquietingly

delivered to his desk by an irate Commander Pursey and downed it in one.

"Corrr, that's good stuff!" claimed Michael. Henry threw Alfred a concerned look but his attention was quickly drawn back to the map as Michael continued his brief.

"You will be stationed at a motel in the town, run by a yank", at which point Commander Pursey interrupted.

"Please Governor, can we try and be at least a little bit official?"

"Give it a rest Alf, it doesn't matter as long as the job is done." Henry looked perplexed at the ease at which his new Governor was delivering his brief but listened intently none the less.

Michael continued.

"You will be stationed at a motel run by an AMERICAN", Michael nodded in the direction of Commander Pursey who stood shaking his head.

"He will look after you while you keep tabs on von Manstein. All we want from you are mannerisms, what he does in Potsdam and a firm description of his abode. Just for the first week or so. After that, we want you to regularly follow him to Berlin to investigate what he does for Hitler. Got it?

Henry looked confused.

"Got what?" he asked tentatively.

"Have you got the mission?! Do you understand your mission?! God help me, I thought you were intelligent!" Michael poked Henry with his pointer in frustration.

"Right. Yes sir", said Henry, slightly embarrassed.

"After you've gained the relevant information, we want you to eliminate him. Is that clear?", asked Michael.

"Yes sir", replied Henry with a nod of the head.

"Grand. Whiskey?" enquired Michael.

"Do you drink anything else?!" implored Commander Pursey, picking up Michael's glass without prompt.

"Kid?" gesturing towards Henry with his empty glass.

"Okay, I'll have one for the road" said Henry, as he strolled over to the globe with Commander Pursey.

"Quite a character isn't he, the new General", claimed Henry.

"Quite the understatement lad. He's a madman. We don't see eye to eye. He's too relaxed about the whole thing. We are on the brink of something extremely dangerous here and all he can think is about is bloody whiskey!"

Commander Pursey was letting his frustrations out in hushed tones as Michael Langley continued to pore over the map, dragging miniature soldiers across the face of it, like a war strategist.

"If he ends up being drunk on the job, I'm going to absolutely slaughter him." whispered Commander Pursey as he walked back across to Michael's desk.

"Your mission will begin exactly a week from today. In a few months, Hitler will be without a strategist. I'll say cheers to that", chanted Michael.

"Cheers", stated Henry, who was joined in a toast by Commander Pursey who still looked mildly annoyed at his role of the servant.

"Go get 'em kid", said Michael triumphantly, once again downing his whiskey and planting the glass on the table. Henry was staring into the distance, through the only window in the room and out into the night sky. Another mission lay ahead of him and he could feel the concoction of excitement and butterflies building up in his stomach. His thoughts flew back to his time at Harrow and at Cambridge. All those nights spent holed up in his room researching and studying while his peers went out drinking and chasing girls. It was all worth it. For this was the life he was promised.

...

"Agent Snake to Control. Landed safely. Housed in confirmed location. Target spotted and logged in local address. This is my first correspondence, expect another in two days. Over and out. H."

It was a cold night in Potsdam in Northern Germany, with light snow glistening the pavement as Henry walked back to the motel where he was staying. His breath visible in the night air, he knocked on the front door three times to notify the owner it was him. The door opened and Henry waltzed inside quicker than a gazelle.

"Any luck finding him?" An American drawl could be heard from the drawing room, that of Brock Weston, the owner of the motel.

"Thank you for your hospitality Mr Weston, but I can't discuss my mission with you. My apologies". Henry was under strict instruction to work alone and to not discuss his work with anyone not involved with MI6.

"Ahh, a proper spy, hey. 'If I told you, I would have to kill you' and all that jazz hey!" said Brock cheerily as he took the kettle off the stove. Henry had just got back from delivering his first letter back to headquarters. He had seen Erich von Manstein within an hour of arriving, tending to the garden at the front of his small cottage on the outskirts of the town. His parents' cottage looked dilapidated and beaten. Two of the upper windows were boarded up and the others were dirty and cracked. Outside the house sat a moderately sized pushbike and an old-fashioned cart which housed bricks and odd pieces of wood. Henry, covered by a huge fur coat, went unnoticed by the German strategist as he walked past to get an initial look at the house and his mannerisms, just as he had been instructed to do so.

"Tea?" asked Brock politely, as Henry replaced his boots with a pair of slippers that he had brought with him.

"Yes please, sir", responded Henry as he took a seat next to the window.

"Please, call me Brock. None of this posh English talk with you! No sirs and ma'ams in this place, do you hear me?"

"Yes si... I mean, Brock. Sorry, force of habit". Henry had been brought up to respect people and his elders by calling them 'Sir' and 'Madam'. It was one of the very first things he learnt at Harrow, and if he didn't talk to his seniors correctly, he would be caned in the Headmaster's office.

"So what's it like working as a spy. Killed many people hey?" enquired Brock as he took the seat next to Henry's.

Henry looked across to Brock and once again signalled that he wasn't allowed to talk about his work.

"Ahh, not even general chat hey!", exclaimed Brock. "Never mind. I'm gonna call it a night, see you in the morning." With that, he took off up the stairs and to bed.

Henry was left to gaze out of the window. He could von Manstein's cottage on the horizon, sitting lonely on a crest on the edge of town. A small fire could be seen burning in the front garden, with the silhouette of a man crouched over it, throwing in planks of wood and coal.

"It's probably nothing", Henry whispered to himself, before

seeing off the remainder of his tea and dragging himself up to bed. It had been a long day.

Over the next week, Henry kept strict tabs on von Manstein, noting that he was out of town from very early morning to late at night. When he came home, he was always greeted by his father who waited intently out on the road every evening for the arrival of his son. During the times when von Manstein was out of town, Henry strolled around Potsdam, learning about the local trade and speaking to local people in German, in which Henry was perfectly fluent. Only a single conversation was of any use, as he found out more about the von Manstein family from a local butcher:

Henry: Guten Morgen! Nettes Hackfleisch haben Sie hier. Ich hätt' gerne ein halbes Dutzend Frankfurter und ein halbes Kilo von Ihrem besten Rumpsteak.

Butcher: Morgen! Sechs Frankfurter und Steak kommen sofort! Hab' Sie noch nie hier gesehen! Sind Sie neu hier?

Henry: Jap, ich bin grade erst mit meinem amerikanischen Onkel hergezogen, bin erst letzte Woche hier angekommen.

Butcher: Ahh, es ist echt ein nettes Städtchen, es wird Ihnen hier gefallen.

Henry: Ja das hoffe ich doch.

Butcher: Hatten Sie schon das Vergnügen die Manstein's zu treffen?

Henry: Nein, das hatte ich noch nicht. Warum fragen Sie?

Butcher: Ihr Sohn, der Erich, ist eine interessante Persönlichkeit. Er fährt jeden Morgen um vier aus der Stadt und kommt immer erst spät abends wieder. Ich glaube der führt irgendwas im Schilde!

Henry: Zum Beispiel was?

Butcher: Also das Gerücht geht um er würde irgendwas für die

Regierung arbeiten, als Spion oder so. Die Leute reden immer viel über sowas. Sein Vater wartet jeden Abend draußen auf ihn.

Henry: Oh, das ist komisch.

Butcher: Ich glaube er arbeitet in Berlin, irgendwo im Stadtzentrum. Ich hab' nur neulich zufällig eine Unterhaltung zwischen ihm und seiner Mutter in der Kneipe überhört.

Henry: Haben Sie noch irgendwas anderes gehört?

Butcher: Nein, ich war gerade im Gehen. Warum denn? Kennen Sie ihn etwa?

Henry: Nein, ich will mich bloß ein bisschen unterhalten. Ich lerne die Stadt noch kennen, verstehen Sie?

Butcher: Na gut. Sechs Frankfurter und ein halbes Kilo Rumpsteak. Das macht dann… 23 Deutschmarks 80.

Henry: So, hier. Behalten Sie den Rest.

Butcher: Sehr vielen Dank. Passen Sie auf sich auf.

From tomorrow, he was to follow the curious von Manstein to Berlin to learn more about what he did for Adolf Hitler. He was excited yet nervous in equal measure about the next stage of the operation. Truth be told, he had grown bored of walking around the same hot spots for a week. He was looking forward to spreading his wings.

Henry was awake extremely early the next day. The snow was falling once more as the clock ticked over to 3:30am. Getting dressed in many layers to combat the cold, Henry needed to be in the proximity of the von Manstein cottage so he could follow Erich from his cottage to wherever he spent the majority of his days. Over the past week, Henry hadn't noticed a single motor car enter or leave the cottage, so presumed the pushbike was Erich's. He borrowed Brock's own pushbike so he could keep pace with von Manstein on his commute.

Half an hour later, wrapped up in a thick black coat, scarf and his driving gloves, Henry found himself stationed not far from the cottage entrance. Right on cue, Erich von Manstein emerged from the building, strolled over to his bicycle and rode off. Henry did not know how far it was to the German capital, but he climbed on to Brock's pushbike and set off in pursuit.

Cycling on the bumpy roads was difficult, but Henry had to keep so far behind as not to attract attention to himself. The route from Potsdam to Berlin consisted of carefully selected back roads, most of which were full of potholes. The snow continued to fall, covering the ground, making cycling tough.

It was four hours later, as the sun was rising, when the outline of the capital became visible. Henry had accompanied von Manstein the entire way, holding back just enough to keep out of plain sight. Only once did he fear his cover would be blown after slipping on a particularly hidden piece of black ice.

Von Manstein had parked his bicycle outside a grand looking building on the outskirts of Berlin. The building was dark, suggesting no one was inside, as von Manstein made his way inside. Henry loitered on the opposite side of the street, leaving his pushbike in an alleyway next to a cafe that was just opening its doors.

"Guten morgen!" cried the cafe owner, as Henry replied joyfully. His eyes were fixed on the building opposite, waiting for more faces to turn up.

It was an hour and a half later, with the sounds of the city filling the morning sky, when more characters arrived. Henry, still stationed outside the cafe, had taken a seat with a coffee keeping him warm. He looked intently as cars pulled up outside the building, releasing important looking members, before driving off at high speed.

Rising to his feet, Henry casually crossed the road, hands in his pocket to protect him from the bitter wind. Walking round the side of the building, he noticed an open gate leading into what looked like the kitchens. Avoiding the chef who had his back turned to him smoking a cigarette, Henry slid inside the gate and into the building via the kitchen door.

"Who are you?"

Another chef was stood by a raging stove just inside the door, ladle in hand, serving hot soup into countless bowls stationed on a huge oak table in the middle of the room.

"Sorry. First day. I didn't know how to get in, so saw this open door", Henry said calmly as he walked past the chef, who merely looked confused and shrugged his shoulders.

Henry, wanting to avoid needless conversations, walked straight out of the kitchens and into the hallway. He was greeted by a number of serious looking officials, all in deep discussions ranging from their journey to their mistresses. Henry took out a file from his briefcase, in order to mix into the crowds, and stood intently in the corner, perusing it. Occasionally, he would look up to keep an eye on the situation, but von Manstein was nowhere to be seen.

After a small while, the soup that was being made in the kitchen came out in separate bowls for the ravenous government officials who strode up to the tables to help themselves. Henry joined the back of the queue, not wanting to draw attention to himself. He received a couple of odd looks from others, who obviously didn't recognise him, but otherwise he was left to his own devices.

"I wonder what von Manstein is up to?"

A voice could be heard from the front of the queue, roughly fifteen places in front of Henry, whose ears pricked up at the name of his target.

"No idea", replied a colleague. "Word is that he's meeting Poland's foreign team this afternoon, but obviously we don't know about that!"

The first man laughed cautiously in return.

"Any idea where that meeting is?" he replied.

"Gortemburg Room according to Mr. Lichstein", said the second voice as they both turned round, soup in hand.

"Excuse me Gentlemen", asked Henry, as he stepped out of the queue to approach the two smartly dressed men.

"I couldn't help but overhear your conversation. I'm von Manstein's new junior and I have no idea where he is. Any ideas?"

"His office is literally just down there", the first man pointed down a long, narrow corridor at the end of the room. "Right to the end, door on the right."

"Thank you sir", replied Henry as he re-joined the queue for the soup. He didn't want to appear too eager in his chase.

After ten minutes of queuing and drinking his vegetable soup, he made his way down the corridor. He could hear raised voices coming from the office at the end, of which he soon discovered was von Manstein's. Backtracking slightly, Henry stationed himself in the office next door, which was completely empty apart from a broken desk that looked as if it had been thrown in with disgruntlement.

"You really think Poland are just going to sit back and just let us roll over them?!" An angry voice emanated from the office as Henry listened intently.

"Threaten them with violence and Pilsudski will roll over. He's a coward!" The second voice sounded much harsher than the first, but it seemed the two men were in a heated argument.

"Adolf, you simply cannot go barging into Poland and start killing their people, there will be uproar! Not to mention, it's highly illegal!"

"Shut up Erich, I don't plan to be legal about anything. The Jews of that country must be wiped out, do you hear?"

"I understand Adolf, but we need to be clear about what we're going to do once we're in power", replied von Manstein hurriedly.

"What do you mean, WE?" questioned Hitler. "There's no 'WE' about it. I will run this country, and you will be my associate. Is that clear?" Hitler's tone was brutally cold as he addressed von Manstein.

"Yes sir, I understand" replied von Manstein quietly.

"Right. Don't get too big for your boots, von Manstein. You are my strategist, not my equal." Hitler's footsteps could be heard pacing the room next door, as Henry could feel his heart beating out of his chest.

Hitler continued.

"This time next year, I will be Chancellor of this great country. Von Hindenburg will be too knackered to carry out Presidential duties all by himself and I will offer my services. We need a plan to eliminate that bastard if he insists on carrying on, got it?" Hitler's tone was once again aggressive as von Manstein replied.

"Yes sir. I've got it. I'll work on a contingency plan to eliminate the President with Goering. I'm sure he'll revel in taking him out."

"Don't be ridiculous Erich, we'll get a soldier to do it. How many times have I told you, we do not get involved in front line action!"

Hitler was shouting now, as he was heard to slam his fist on the wall that Henry was listening through.

"Yes sir, sorry sir." said von Manstein, just loud enough for Henry to hear. Henry was scribbling on a piece of paper, taking down the main bulk of the conversation.

"Right." exclaimed Hitler. "The second thing I wanted to talk to you about was your parents."

There was a brief silence that cut through the air, before von Manstein replied nervously.

"My parent, sir?"

"Your father especially", said Hitler. "Why am I hearing stories that he waits outside every time you get home, von Manstein? Are you still a kid?"

"No sir, I am not sir, but as you can imagine he gets nervous about my wellbeing in the position I am in." Von Manstein's voice was shaking slightly as Hitler's dominance in the conversation quickly took hold.

"Why would he have reason to be nervous, Erich?" exclaimed Hitler. "Do you think you are in danger?"

"No sir, but he gets anxious very easily", responded von Manstein quickly.

"Nonsense!" shouted Hitler. "You are one of the safest people in this whole country Erich!" Hitler was once again pacing the room with the weight of an elephant as he addressed Erich von Manstein.

"However, the presence of your dear father every night when you get home from work is a risk. People will get suspicious of your actions Erich. Do you understand what I'm saying?" Hitler's tone had slowed to a menacing, low pitch.

"I think so, sir", replied von Manstein quietly.

"Tell him to stop with this childish parenting!" shouted Hitler once more, as the sound of a glass smashing against the same wall made Henry jump.

"I will not have this operation sabotaged by an over-cautious jumped up little coward, do you understand von Manstein?!" Hitler's voice reached increased volumes once more.

"Yes sir, I understand sir", replied von Manstein quickly.

"Good." declared Hitler. "I don't want to get rid of you von Manstein, but if needs must, I will do whatever it takes." Hitler said with a calm demure. "We must be patient. This has to be perfect."

"Can I ask what the hell you think you are doing?"

Henry jumped back from the wall, letting the glass he was holding to the wall fall to the floor, causing it to smash into pieces. A tall, muscly beast of a man stood at the doorway, a machine gun strapped across his chest and looking intently at Henry, who confidently stood up straight.

"I'm von Manstein's new junior but I was sent out of the room by Mr. Hitler and I decided to wait in this room. Is there a problem?" Henry stated with aplomb.

"Why were you holding that glass to the wall sir?" asked the guard as he pointed to the decimated glass on the floor.

"I was listening wasn't I!" seethed Henry in a quiet a voice as possible. "I'm new, I want to know what's going on!"

The guard looked suspicious. "There is surely a reason why they didn't want you in the room, Mister?"

"Muller", responded Henry quickly.

"Mr Muller.", said the guard. "I'm afraid I'm going to have to ask you to stand against that wall. As I'm sure you understand, we are on high alert and I need to search you. Can I see your pass please?"

The guard's hand was outstretched towards Henry, imploring him to hand over his pass. Henry walked over slowly, reaching into his blazer pocket to act like he was looking for it.

As Henry reached within touching distance of the guard, he quickly took his hand out of his pocket, grabbed the guard's arm and with the strength of an ox, tossed him over his shoulder on to the floor. The guard quickly went to get to his feet, but Henry, needing to act quickly, kicked the guard in the head repeatedly. Blood flowed from the head of the security guard like a river as he wailed in pain. Henry went into his blazer pocket once more, drawing a small pen knife which he proceeded to nail straight into the heart of the guard, who let out a piercing scream.

With that, the door to the room opened once more, with guards, equal in stature and build flowed into the room. Quicker than a sprinter, Henry fled out of the room, barging past the guards and into the corridor.

"Stop that man!" cried one of the guards, as Henry stormed through the corridor which was still full with officials and dignitaries. None of them was quick enough to stop Henry as he stormed through the crowds and out through the front door of the building. Four guards were on his tail as Henry sprinted through the streets of Berlin, attempting to escape. Passers-by stood nonplussed as Henry barged through streets' stalls and knocked over chairs, attempting to halt the progress of the guards who were not giving up the chase.

The cold air gripped Henry's lungs with force as he continued to run. The guards were gaining, as a couple of others were coming up behind him on bikes. Henry changed his course, running down an alleyway and into a small restaurant that was nearly empty apart from an elderly gentleman sat at the bar, talking to the owner.

They both jumped as Henry smashed his way in through the door and ran towards the back of the bar. He knocked over barrels and chairs in his wake, in a panic to get to a safe place. Henry could hear the loud voices of the guards who had followed him in to the bar.

"The bastard is in here somewhere!" shouted one of them, as the ever-increasing number of footsteps got closer to Henry's location. There was nowhere for him to hide, as there was no visible doorway out of the building. His only choice was the cellar, but that would leave him cornered. Henry had no choice.

As the voices of the guards got ever louder, Henry ran down the staircase into the cellar that smelt of rotten eggs and ale. He had drawn his pen knife in preparation, although he was sure he would be overpowered. An otherwise faultless career in espionage was about to end at the first hurdle of his most important mission.

"He's out the back!" shouted one of the guards as they began to run in the direction of the cellar. Henry's heart was once again beating out of his chest, as he prepared for the door to be beaten down. This could be the end.

"Hey! You! Down here!"

A dishevelled looking man, covered in dirt and soot, poked his head above what seemed to be a trap door leading underground.

"Hurry up you bastard, or they'll find us!" the man implored as Henry jumped across the room and down through the trap door, into total darkness. All that he could see was a faint light at the end of what looked like a never-ending tunnel. The pair sat in total silence, Henry trying to control his rasping breath, as he overheard the door above him being smashed in.

"Find him!" screamed one of the guards, as the footsteps battered the floorboards that lay above Henry and the mysterious man. The noise of barrels being thrown and stands being dismantled left Henry on edge, but after a short while, a new voice was heard.

"He's not here", the voice claimed.

"Fuck!" shouted the original voice. "Keep looking out the front and make sure if you see him, you shoot to kill!"

With that, the footsteps slowly left the room, until Henry was sure the room was empty. He lifted the trap door nervously and peered over the edge.

"I dropped my pen knife as I jumped over here, I'll just go and get it", exclaimed Henry, but before he could put his head above the parapet, he was dragged down by the mysterious man.

"Don't be an idiot, it's only a pen knife! We have to go!", and with that, he threw Henry to the floor of the tunnel and shut the trapdoor behind him. "You've escaped already, don't risk being recaptured. These thugs have the ears of a bat. Come on!"

The man walked off towards the faint light at the end of the tunnel, and Henry followed him.

"Thanks very much, sir", said Henry calmly, still breathing heavily from the chase.

"My pleasure. You're a British spy, correct?" asked the man looking towards Henry as he struck a match to gain some light.

"Yes sir", said Henry, already suspecting that this man already knew all about him. "Henry Irthing, sir". Henry held out his hand to shake the man's, who returned the favour.

"Dietmarr", the man replied. "Dietmarr Schultz."

The flame of Dietmarr's torch occasionally lit up his face. It was covered in dirt but Henry sensed an evergreen glow to him, his eyes lighting up the route more than the torch ever could. The tunnel stank more than the rooms above, but Henry was distracted, following Dietmarr along the bumpy track in complete silence. The occasional shout from up above caused them both to pause, and then smile to each other in relief.

Henry had come face to face with the enemy but had not laid a finger on the target. He sensed his saviour that night could help him…

3.

The pair continued walking along the tunnel, avoiding the sewage water and the rats that scurried through. The smell was getting worse as Henry suspected they were walking through Berlin's sewer system. Dietmarr, unshaven and dirty from head to toe, was limping slightly as he too dodged the rats and the water.

"Dietmarr Schultz... I know that name..." said Henry slowly as he gazed over towards the limping Dietmarr, who winced slightly on every other step.

"Wouldn't surprise me. I used to work for the Abwehr." Dietmarr looked solemnly towards Henry. "We should be enemies." He turned to continue looking forwards. "I reckon that light is a few miles away. Could be a long walk. We can't risk going up any more trapdoors".

"Wait, so... Why are you helping me?" enquired Henry, stopping in his tracks, his hand hovering over the blazer pocket that used to house his pen knife. It was a default movement that Henry had picked up over his years of espionage.

"What are you going to stab me with? Your fingernails?" said Dietmarr with a smile on his face. "Relax. I was betrayed. I have no interest in the Abwehr anymore. They're still trying to eliminate me". Dietmarr lifted his trousers to show a deep gash along his calf. His black trousers were dripping with blood.

"What happened?" asked Henry, as he offered a handkerchief to Dietmarr to hold against the wound.

"I was set up. The Abwehr has a rogue, a wrong'un. I was observing a Spag in Africa who was getting weaponry for the uprising mafia. The rogue, a fake German by the name of Brankhurst was always one step ahead of me. Told the prick to go to the places I wasn't, so I ended up losing him. Von Hindenburg dragged me through a tribunal where I was found guilty of 'unprofessional behaviour'".

Dietmarr put on a fake voice to signal his hatred for the phrase. The pair were almost in complete darkness now, with only a dim fire inside a lantern guiding their route.

"I've been on the run ever since. Von Hindenburg has ordered a select few agents, including one who was after my job, to take me out."

"Shit." stated Henry calmly. "Tough break".

"Hmph, that's one way of putting it said Dietmarr, stumbling slightly over a small crevice in the ground. "I've escaped three assassination attempts. First one was in Altona. Eighteen people were killed, but not me. Second one in Belgium, where I was enjoying a joint and some bastard jumped me. The third one was yesterday when they did this", said Dietmarr, pointing to his leg in pain.

"That's been bleeding like that for a day? Shouldn't you get it checked out?" implored Henry.

"I could do, but chances are I'd be busted in a hospital somewhere. Much less risky to just tend to it myself. I have things in my hideout to help with it. I'll live, I'm a tough one."

The pair continued to walk along the tunnels, with the noises of the German public noticeable above them. Every now and then Dietmarr would let out an audible gasp in pain as he walked over an unexpected dip in the ground. Henry still wasn't completely convinced by Dietmarr and his stories, but chose to go along with them. Dietmarr had helped him out of certain death after all.

"How did you know I was in that particular pub?" asked Henry about ten minutes later.

"I've got to do something with my time", replied Dietmarr in haste. "I noticed you sitting in the cafe this morning. Your German is atrocious, the accent is easily detectable to a trained ear. Be careful!" Dietmarr pointed to Henry like a school headmaster telling off his pupil. "I saw you walking in to the Reichskanzler through the renovation and knew you were up to something."

Henry was listening intently, keen to pick up any information that Dietmarr may have about impending German plans.

"Not many intruders get into the place and come out alive. I took your seat outside the cafe and watched. As you ran out, I saw you sprint into an alleyway, so I worked my way underground to try and find where you'd gone. Luckily, I found you just in time."

"Why were you bothered about my fate? I'm just another British spy", claimed Henry, speeding up his walk slightly.

"Come on Henry, keep up. Germany has abandoned me. I offered my life, my skills and my expertise for Germany and she gave up on me. I don't like being given up on." Dietmarr's voice got lower and shakier as he continued to limp through the tunnels.

They continued to walk for what felt like hours, getting closer and closer to the light at the end of the tunnel. Many trapdoors emerged along the way, but Dietmarr merely shook his head at any suggestion of going up them.

"We can't risk being seen now. We're both wanted men and the police will probably be on high alert", Dietmarr stated, swearing as he tripped over a loose pipe. He looked at his lantern, where the fire was growing dimmer by the minute.

"I think we're going to have to hurry up. This is the last of the light and walking along here without any is dangerous", said Dietmarr, looking at Henry for ideas.

"Come here", said Henry resolutely. Dietmarr's look in return was one of confusion.

"Come on, hurry up. Like you say, we don't have much time", stated Henry as Dietmarr limped over to Henry.

"Get on my back".

"Are you serious?" remarked Dietmarr, a look of shock spread across his face.

"Get on with it! And hold on tight, I'm not going to hang around", declared Henry as Dietmarr climbed on to his back and wrapped his arms around Henry's neck, holding one arm out in front of him with the lantern.

"Secure?"

"As I'll ever be", responded Dietmarr, as Henry broke out into a light jog, guided by the hand of his accomplice. His training with Lieutenant Pooley included running many miles with a bag of bricks on his back. He knew it would come in handy at some point, as the sewers began to incline drastically.

After half an hour of jogging uphill with Dietmarr on his back, Henry came to a swift stop as the fire in the lantern gave its last before going out. The light in the distance was much brighter, about a few hundred yards away, so they both slowly walked towards it, staring intently at the ground to avoid going into the sewers.

Upon reaching the light, they looked upwards and noticed an unguarded manhole, with a rusty ladder leading up to the entrance.

"You first", said Dietmarr as he shoved Henry towards the ladder. "I think this manhole is outside Berlin, so we should be okay", he added, as Henry started climbing. At the top, he clambered up on to the soil above, the low sun blinding his eyes as he looked up. It took a little longer for the injured Dietmarr to climb, but they had ended up in a deserted industrial estate, overlooking the city of Berlin, so they were very safe.

"Yeah, I thought so", said Dietmarr to himself as he ruggedly got to his feet. "We're safe from here. My humble abode is this way", as he pointed Henry towards a dirt track that led back towards the town where he had started very early this morning.

After two more hours of walking, the pair turned a corner to reveal a terribly small yet covered gazebo, that included a variety of blankets, a basket that was half-full of discoloured food, a collection of wood that Henry presumed was last night's fire, and a shaggy looking dog, tied to a wooden post.

"Beautiful isn't she", said Dietmarr calmly, noticing Henry staring at the dog. "Wilma she's called. Has kept me company this past year, haven't you Wilma!" expressed Dietmarr, limping over to the dog to give her a shake and a stroke.

"I'm not a huge dog fan", declared Henry, turning away to sit himself down on the damp floor by the extinguished fire.

"Nonsense, she's completely harmless aren't you, you sexy thing you!" said Dietmarr excitedly, still ruffling the fur of the German shepherd. "Now, where's my first aid box?" asked Dietmarr, scrabbling around in the concoction of blankets strewn all over the compound.

"Is this it?" asked Henry, producing a small blue box down by his feet.

"That's the one", stated Dietmarr as he opened the box and produced a small bottle of green-coloured liquid. He took a pipette and squeezed the liquid on to the wound on his leg, wincing in pain as he did so.

"Ahhh, that feels SO DAMN GOOD!" Dietmarr shouted. "I needed that", he said as he grabbed all the bandages from the box and began to wrap it tightly around the gash. Henry sat and stared onwards, still considering if Dietmarr was who he said he was. He could still return to Potsdam, as von Manstein hadn't actually seen him, but Henry was eager to try and drain as much information out of Dietmarr as he could before doing so.

"What do you know about the German government then?" asked Henry, after a small pause to allow Dietmarr to complete his remedial work.

"A slippery, cowardly lot", remarked Dietmarr coldly. "Sure von Hindenburg is the leader on paper, but Adolf Hitler is starting to call the shots. Hindenburg hasn't got any balls", said Dietmarr snidely, looking up at Henry. "Why, is he your target?"

"I'm sorry, I can't discuss my mission with anyone, Dietmarr", said Henry plainly.

"Oh fuck off you stubborn Brit!" pronounced Dietmarr. "I want the same thing you do, trust me. Von Hindenburg is a bastard. I want his cold, black heart on a silver platter. And Hitler's for that matter. Anyone associated with either of them would be a bonus." Dietmarr's eyes narrowed at the idea of murdering the people who betrayed him, but Henry was still suspicious.

"Sorry mate, I've only just met you. I need to establish you're the real deal. You could be anyone", Henry gesticulated, but Dietmarr jumped in and interrupted.

"I'm not anyone. Look in that bag, the black one with the white handles." Dietmarr pointed to the left of Henry and to a bag that had a lone file in it.

"Read it. That'll tell you everything you need to know."

Henry took the file out of the bag and opened it up. Inside were countless newspaper cuttings, purportedly reporting the hearing at which Dietmarr had been accused. Looking at the pictures, Dietmarr was there, albeit looking much younger and clean shaven. Reading the reports, the words condemned the "unnamed agent" for letting his country down. All of the other cut outs held similar sentiments. There was also a collection of papers, covered in a brown paper bag, that had Dietmarr's files from the Abwehr and a summary of all of his missions on active duty.

"There are some proper stinkers in that lot", affirmed Dietmarr as he attempted to start a fire. The sun was just beginning to go down, signalling that it was mid-afternoon, and the snow began to fall again. Henry sat on a battered tree trunk near the edge of the gazebo, letting the snow litter his shoulder as he read through Dietmarr's files. He had been all over the world for the Abwehr. To the Americas and to Asia and indeed to Britain. His file looked pristine and faultless.

"I was the best damn agent they ever had and they screwed me over", said Dietmarr sentimentally as he looked over Henry's shoulder. "I still don't know why they wanted me gone. Maybe I was doing my job too well", he added scornfully, walking over to a nearby pile of wood to add to the fire.

The file included final notes from a man called Kurt Van Easting, who lambasted Dietmarr for his 'failures as an agent and as a human being'. They also included a passage from President von Hindenburg, whose words were full of equal disdain.

After a short while, Dietmarr managed to get a small fire lit in the middle of the compound as Henry put Dietmarr's file back in its original black bag.

"That's fucked", stated Henry simply, before turning towards Dietmarr. "Okay, I trust you", he said plainly. "You've been through a lot so why endanger yourself and live like this?" Henry gesticulated around him, pointing specifically at the pile of blankets that he presumed were Dietmarr's bed for the nights.

"Because I want revenge. It's as simple as that", said Dietmarr coldly. "I won't stand for being ruined by a group of jumped up little shits like that lot", he pointed towards the city, that shadowed the hill top that was home to Dietmarr.

"I understand. So, can you help me?" asked Henry, hoping that the answer was going to be a solid yes.

"Help you? Of course I'll bloody well help you, why do you think I'm doing all this?!" stated Dietmarr with a surprised look on his face. "Jesus, you're slow for an agent aren't you!" he said jokingly, punching Henry on the arm.

"Haha, I'm glad to hear it", said Henry, slightly relieved, as he held a dirty piece of red meat over the fire. "We can make a good team", he added jovially.

"We can." said Dietmarr simply.

For the next couple of hours, the pair talked as the sun set. About their lives, their upbringings and how they ended up as agents. Their missions to different places on the planet and the most dangerous situations they faced. They laughed and chatted like old school friends, and Henry got the impression that this was the first time in a long time that Dietmarr had even laughed.

"So", said Dietmarr in a hushed tone. "Who are you after?" Dietmarr looked intently at Henry who looked up from gazing into the fire to address him.

"von Manstein", he replied.

"I see", noted Dietmarr inquisitively. "And why do you want

him?" Dietmarr stared intently at Henry, almost as if he was trying to hypnotise him.

"Without von Manstein, Hitler would be useless. Our intelligence suggests all of Hitler's actions are the brain child of von Manstein. My superiors claimed going straight for Hitler would be too dangerous.

"Yeah, they got that right", conceded Dietmarr. "That bastard has men who would jump in front of bullets for him." Dietmarr set the uneaten bones of his meat down by the side of the fire and walked over to his bundle of blankets. From within its midst, he pulled out a rucksack and opened it, dragging out more clothes.

"Here", he said, throwing a pair of jumpers at Henry. "Get changed into something dry, the nights are cold out here."

Henry was confused.

"Dietmarr, during all of that, von Manstein didn't see me. I can go back to Potsdam and not be detected. I was just about to go. You can come with me if you like?"

"Risky, but it's your call. I'm most certainly not going there. Von Manstein and I go way back, he'll recognise me in a heartbeat if he sees me. You go." Dietmarr turned his back on Henry as he stripped off his old, beaten clothes.

"We can pick this up tomorrow", said Dietmarr as he turned around to reveal deep cuts to his chest and abdomen. "I can show you the ins and outs of the German hierarchy!"

Henry could not help but notice Dietmarr's muscly body.

"Dietmarr, you need to get those seen to", but before he could finish, Dietmarr's hand shot up to silence him.

"You don't need to worry about me. I can survive. Walk about five minutes that way", Dietmarr pointed to the left of the gazebo, "and you will come across a track that will lead all the way back to Potsdam. I'll see you tomorrow."

Dietmarr was final in his words and seemed upset that Henry was not staying with him. However Henry, wishing him goodbye, grabbed his coat.

"I'll be here at 7am tomorrow morning", he said as he walked off into the increasing darkness.

"Fine by me!" shouted Dietmarr in response.

The walk home was long and cold. He had already made half the journey with Dietmarr, but without a bike, it took Henry another three hours to make his weary way back to Brock's motel. He needed to pen another letter to headquarters, updating them on the presence of Dietmarr and that they would be working together, but upon walking in through the front door, he collapsed into Brock's comfortable leather chair and fell asleep.

...

Henry awoke in the middle of the night, juddering awake at the sound of a smashing window. It had come from upstairs and he could hear Brock's American accent shouting at what seemed like an intruder. With the stealth of a ninja, Henry went via the kitchen to grab the nearest knife and worked his way up the winding staircase as quietly as he could. About halfway up, he heard the piercing screams of Brock flooding the night. Stopping near the top of the stairs, he noticed a shadow coming from the master bedroom.

"Find the spy", said a voice, in a thick German accent.

"Yes boss", was the response, as an armoured man made his way into the hallway, covered head to foot in splatters of blood, which Henry presumed was Brock's. He was crouched down on the staircase, not wanting to draw attention to himself by way of a suspicious shadow.

Another man appeared in the hallway, instantly recognisable to Henry. It was Erich von Manstein. His accomplice was busy, flying from room to room in search of Henry, who was still crouched at the top of the stairway, knife in hand.

"He's not here", stated the accomplice gruffly, waltzing out of the bathroom.

"Clean yourself up, we don't want to look suspicious", prompted von Manstein. Henry quickly made his way back down the staircase, but as he did so, trod on a silver object that was sitting idly on one of the steps. The crash of the object, an innocent tea spoon, alarmed von Manstein and his accomplice.

"Downstairs!" shouted von Manstein, as Henry sprinted from the bottom of the staircase to the drawing room, closing the door in the process.

"He's definitely down here somewhere", stated von Manstein. "If you find him, kill him!" He was unrelenting in his tone, as the footsteps crashed down the staircase and straight into the room where Henry was hiding, crouched once again behind the leather chair he had earlier fallen asleep in. The pair stormed into the room, as the accomplice, dressed in black security gear and matching woolly hat, set about trashing the room in search of his target. Von Manstein stood by the doorway, a menacing smile spread across his ageing face. He could smell blood.

The accomplice was getting nearer, as he worked his way across the room, throwing everything in his path on to the marble floor. Glasses smashed against the wall, china cutlery was broken into a thousand pieces as the accomplice shoved them off shelves, hungry. He was getting ever closer.

"Guten Morgen Henry Irthing."

Von Manstein had crept up behind Henry and grabbed him by the arm, a glistening silver knife held against his throat.

"Did you have fun following me yesterday?", von Manstein breathed sarcastically as Henry struggled against the surprisingly strong grip of the strategist.

"Get off me you monster!", shouted Henry as he attempted to throw von Manstein from his grasp. It was impossible as his arm was wrapped around his neck as if he was being bound.

"Our mutual friend, Adolf, wants you dead. Tell me why I shouldn't just kill you right now?" said von Manstein menacingly. The accomplice was stood opposite Henry, knife drawn, ready to do the deed.

"Let me go, and I'll go back to London and leave you alone!" Henry pleaded as he continued to fight against the chokehold.

"Ha! Yeah right. Do you think I was born yesterday? You swine!" spat von Manstein as he strengthened his grip against the struggling British spy.

"Just lock me up, throw away the key if you have to, just don't kill me!" begged Henry, trying everything he could to release himself.

"I'm not convinced..." stated von Manstein chillingly." Are you convinced Angel?" he looked up to the accomplice.

"I'm not convinced either..." copied the accomplice, who walked towards Henry, knife outstretched in front of him.

"I would have expected a better answer from a British agent..." whispered von Manstein intensely. "If this is the best that his Majesty can throw at us, I think the rest of Europe will simply roll over..."

Von Manstein continued to whisper threateningly in Henry's ear as he tried to wrestle his way free.

"Me or you, sir?" asked the accomplice simply, clearly growing impatient at the lack of action.

"Anything else Mr. Irthing?" questioned von Manstein as Henry continued to splutter at the strength of the chokehold.

"No. Don't", struggled Henry as von Manstein let out a deplorable laugh.

"After you Angel..." stated von Manstein as the accomplice walked nearer. Henry could feel his rasping breath against his face as he stood before him.

"No! Please! Von Manstein, please have mercy!" Henry implored.

"Goodbye Mr. Irthing. It was a pleasure meeting you", von Manstein nodded towards the accomplice who drew his hand back and plunged the knife deep into Henry's neck. The surge of red blood spread across the air as Henry let out an ear-splitting cry. The chilling laugh of von Manstein tore through the air...

...

Henry felt a strange falling sensation as he quickly opened his eyes, to find himself lying on the floor at the feet of the leather chair.

"Are you okay kid hey?" Brock was stood over him, holding a candlelit lantern. Henry could feel beads of sweat running from his forehead on to his cold, clammy face.

"Erm, yeah, just a bad dream Brock, thanks", said Henry embarrassingly as he climbed to his feet in haste.

"What's the time?" he added, looking around the room for the presence of a clock.

"Five thirty in the morning", responded Brock, turning round to go back upstairs.

"Shit!" replied Henry, quickly gathering his belongings and stuffing them into his rucksack. "I'm so late! Brock, forget breakfast, I'll see you this evening!" Henry ran out the front door and sprinted in the direction of the von Manstein cottage and out towards the woods.

"I wasn't going to make you any anyway..." replied Brock

dejectedly as he began his climb up the winding staircase.

Being careful not to slip on the ice that had again formed overnight, Henry jogged through the town of Potsdam, wishing Derick the Greengrocer a good morning as he unloaded the day's delivery. The loaded rucksack smacked against his back as he ran through the streets and into the wooded area that protected the town.

Two hours later, with the rising of the sun, Henry reached a small enclosure, which led to Dietmarr's gazebo. Breathing heavily, Henry dumped his rucksack at the side of the tent and sat down on the same tree trunk he had warmed the night before. Dietmarr was nowhere to be seen, so Henry waited.

This gave him time to contemplate the episode at the motel. His nights had always been blighted by nightmares, a problem he had failed to address since childhood. As a result, he was always sleep deprived.

"Where the fuck have you been? You're late!" shouted Dietmarr as he emerged from a dense wooded area behind the gazebo, carrying a pile of wood.

"Sorry Dietmarr, I overslept", said Henry truthfully.

"What kind of secret agent oversleeps? Are you still a teenager?" joked Dietmarr, as he set the wood down next to the fire, which had again gone out from the night before.

"Sorry", repeated Henry. "But I'm here now, so what's next?" Henry was eager not to go into too much detail over his late arrival, and waved an arm towards Dietmarr to urge him to continue.

"Right, well, let me eat first and then we'll get going. We can talk about our next steps then", said Dietmarr as he reached into the food basket and produced two eggs, covered in soil. Henry looked at them disapprovingly.

"You can take that look off your face, I have no choice. I steal them from a farm on the other side of the city, so I earned them!" said Dietmarr sternly, as he threw them into a small metal pan and began to work on getting a fire started.

For the next hour, Henry merely sat and watched as Dietmarr struck a match and lit the fire, piling wood on to it laboriously. Occasionally, Dietmarr would throw Henry a dirty look, as if he was still angry at Henry's time keeping. Meanwhile, Henry sifted through the same file he read last night, looking to find out more information on the Weimar Republic. All of a sudden, his eyes drifted across a particular passage that interested him.

"Hey Dietmarr", said Henry, breaking into the silence. "It says here you worked with von Manstein a few years ago? What were you doing?"

Dietmarr stopped his fire-making to look over at Henry. His eyes were full of hatred as he chose his words carefully.

"We were friends", he said quietly. "Colleagues and friends." He went back to attempting to start a fire, but Henry dug deeper.

"Friends?" he asked. "Why were you friends with von Manstein?" Henry stared at Dietmarr, not sure whether he was wanting to hear the answer or not.

"You don't want to know", responded Dietmarr coldly as he continued his work.

"Yes I do", stated Henry plainly. "If I'm going to work with you, we need to be honest to each other." The tension rose as Dietmarr laid down the wood and strolled over to where Henry was sat. He pulled up the selection of blankets that lay next to Henry and sat on the floor.

"Erich von Manstein is my cousin". Henry looked at him in shock. "His father, the one that waits outside their cottage for him every night, is my mother's brother. The whole family have a history of working for the government or the Army and when I was posted on a mission with von Manstein as my contact, I was excited." Dietmarr stared intently, past Henry and into the distance, where the Sun was creeping above the line of the trees.

"We found ourselves in a compromising position in China", continued Dietmarr as if he was reading from a manuscript. "Some Chink, can't even remember his name, had us locked up in a dirty prison cell in the middle of Shanghai. We were after a Russian code-breaker, but the whole place was full of them because of the revolution. He was well hidden but we got captured."

Henry listened carefully, taking in every detail. Dietmarr shot back up to his feet and strolled back over to the fire, producing his box of matches to try and restart it.

"And?" questioned Henry. "You were captured, why was that von Manstein's fault?" Henry looked at Dietmarr, mistrust increasing by the moment.

"It turns out von Manstein had sold us down the river", said Dietmarr after a brief pause. "Twenty-four hours later, the guards simply let him go and left me to rot. Von Manstein's laugh as he left the cell gives me nightmares".

"Bastard. How did you escape?" asked Henry as he put the file back in its bag.

"I was in jail for eight months. They then sent me to a labour camp indefinitely, but I managed to break out of my cell after seducing the guard." A smile broke out across Dietmarr's face as he recalled the process.

"Erm?" said Henry, confused.

"I know", replied Dietmarr, laughing slightly. "I'd found out one night that the guard situated outside my door day and night was... That way inclined". Dietmarr mimicked a sexual act as he laughed at the very idea. "One evening, I caught him fondling himself looking at another guard. I worked on his insecurity for hours before I lured him into my cell. He obviously doesn't get much action..." Dietmarr laughed once more.

"So, what happened?" asked Henry curiously, a confused smile strewn across his own face.

"I promised I'd suck him off if he came into my cell. He refused at first, but his temptations got the better of him once night fell. He opened the cell, and I told him to take his shirt off, which he did. Just as he was doing it, I kicked him in the bollocks, knocked him unconscious and walked out. I managed to escape through the back door. No pun intended!", he added, as Henry laughed at the euphemism.

It seems Dietmarr had been betrayed more than once, not only by his colleagues but also his own family. His resentment for the establishment was starting to become clear, as he rigorously battered the pieces of wood together. A spark suddenly appeared, causing Dietmarr to jump slightly as he threw the wood on to the bigger pile and stood back, allowing the flames to gather pace. The sun was now up, casting a shadow across the woods as the outline of the city became visible through the snow.

"So, what do you want to know?" Dietmarr had taken a seat next to the fire, holding his hands over the flames to warm them up.

"Tell me everything", said Henry enthusiastically as he too dragged the chopped tree trunk and sat down next to the fire.

"Screw that, we'll be here until the 50s!" laughed Dietmarr. "We'll start with the basics." Dietmarr cracked open one of the eggs and let the yolk slide on to the pan. As he did the same with the other egg, slightly brown from the dirt, he began to tell Henry about the German establishment.

"Von Hindenburg. President", started Dietmarr holding up a single finger. He's about to pop his clogs. He's been ill for some time. How he was voted in is beyond me, but there you go." He shrugged slightly as he continued. "The Chancellor at the moment is a chap called Kurt von Schleicher who is about as powerless as a doll in a playhouse. He'll vanish as soon as the main man is in office."

Dietmarr's voice lowered once more as he gestured towards Henry to continue.

"The main man?" asked Henry tentatively.

"Hitler you fucking idiot!" shouted Dietmarr. "Were MI6 drunk when they hired you? Fuck me." Dietmarr continued to gesticulate wildly as Henry sighed and dipped his stale bread into the egg that had just finished cooking.

"Hitler is nailed on to be the next President", Dietmarr continued, as he too tucked into the stale bread from the basket. "Even when I was still at the Abwehr, there was talk that he would be Chancellor by now", he added as Henry nodded along.

"Then you've got my dear cousin, von Manstein. Granted, he is an extremely intelligent man but put him in a ring with a lightweight and he'd be down before the bell." Dietmarr mimed punching a couple of jabs and an uppercut, a glint in his eye that suggested he would love the opportunity to do it himself.

"Von Manstein is the man I've been instructed to eliminate", choked Henry as he took a large bite out of the remaining slice of bread. "I need to find out as much information about Hitler's plans as possible first though", he added after receiving a sceptical look from Dietmarr.

"After your crazy effort yesterday, they'll know Britain are on to him. He'll be protected now, von Manstein. He didn't cycle past here this morning anyway", Dietmarr said, as he pointed towards the dirt track, hiding behind the trees a couple of hundred yards away.

"He cycles past you every morning?" asked Henry in shock. "Why don't you take him out?"

Dietmarr looked at him in surprise. "Come on lad, really? I'm safe here. Once Hitler finds out von Manstein was killed en route, he'll have the whole Republic out looking for the culprit. I'm in enough trouble as it is thanks!", he laughed as he finished his bread and set his bowl down by the fire that now burned brightly lighting up the shadowed gazebo.

"I suppose", sighed Henry as he placed his bowl on top of Dietmarr's. "So, how should we go about it?" he added, looking to the former German agent for help.

"We could kidnap him..." said Dietmarr quietly, contemplating the very notion. "As soon as he leaves the Reichskanzler this evening, that's when he'll be at his most vulnerable..."

Dietmarr cleared a pile of burnt wood from the floor, grabbed a stick and started to dig into the ground, drawing out a map of some sort. Henry looked on, astonished yet slightly amused at Dietmarr's bizarre method.

"Don't you have a pen and paper?" he asked sarcastically.

"Unless we rip it up into tiny pieces, someone could find it. This is easier and safer", replied Dietmarr. "Here, we can just stamp it out as if it never existed." Dietmarr continued to scrape into the soil, planning out what started to look like the map of a building.

"If his schedule is still the same as it was last year, von Manstein leaves the building at about eighteen hundred hours", stated Dietmarr with an edge to his voice. "The bike sheds are round the back of the building and because of the renovations, he'll leave out the back way. That's good for us."

Henry was listening intently, scribbling down notes on a scrawny piece of paper with a dull lead pencil.

"We can wait around the back of the building without much hassle", Dietmarr said as he drew a large cross at the edge of the map. "Our only issue is finding a vehicle large enough to house us both and a hostage." Dietmarr tapped the ground with the stick, in deep thought.

"How about..." Henry started but Dietmarr raised a dirty hand to shut him up before he could get going.

"Thinking", Dietmarr said rudely, as Henry fell quiet. "Come on Schultz, think think think..." Dietmarr rapped the ground harder with the stick, his eyes flickering around as he tossed ideas back and forth across his brain.

"Got it!" he said alarmingly. "We steal a van. They're building an airport near Brandenburg, there must be some sort of industrial vehicle there!" affirmed Dietmarr, scraping another smaller map next to the existing one. "Okay, so this is the plan."

Dietmarr scraped a third area, and labelled it 'HQ'.

"We leave here at sixteen hundred hours. Walking to Brandenburg, and the site of the airport. There HAS to be some sort of large vehicle we can steal. It is Hitler's idea after all, he'd have the top kit there." Dietmarr scraped an arrow from 'HQ' to the second map, labelled 'Airport', while Henry scribbled as quickly as he could on to his own pad.

"From there, we drive to the back of the Reichskanzler building, and wait. The size of the vehicle should allow us to drive off-road, so we can go undetected." Dietmarr's voice got faster with excitement as he drew an 'X' into the soil denoting their stopping point. Henry continued to scribble.

"At eighteen hundred hours, von Manstein appears, completely unaware. We paralyse him with this", Dietmarr produced the green bottle that he had used to douse his wound with, "and we bundle him into the vehicle, before taking the same route back to headquarters." Dietmarr completed the route with a swish of his stick on the third map signifying the end of the operation.

"Wait, sorry", interrupted Henry. "I thought you said you didn't want Hitler knowing von Manstein had been killed?"

"That's because we're not going to kill him", added Dietmarr resolutely. "Once we get back here, we'll tie him up, threaten him a little and use a few torture techniques you know!" Dietmarr winked in Henry's direction who allowed himself a brief smile before continuing his questioning.

"What sort of torture techniques?" asked Henry cautiously.

"Don't you worry about that, you can leave that bit to me. I'll take great pleasure from it..." Dietmarr laughed evilly as he grabbed a large rope from his rucksack and lay it on the floor.

"We get him to tell us about all of Hitler's plans, however long it takes and then release him. You know where his family live. We can say that we'll kill his family if he blabs. That should shut him up. He always was a Daddy's boy..." Dietmarr's eyes carried a squint in them as he recounted his childhood memories.

"Are you sure that's wise? I've been instructed to eliminate him!" said Henry sternly.

"Look mate. I'm the German here, I know how the Republic

think. If you kill one of their own, they will use all of their resources to hunt you down and brutally murder you. If you want that, go ahead, stab my cousin in the heart. If you don't, I suggest we do it my way." Dietmarr once again sounded final in his words.

"Fine", agreed Henry. "Plan A it is." He settled his notes on the damp grass in front of him.

"You can get rid of that lot as well", Dietmarr added. "What did I say about paper? It's all up here", Dietmarr said pointing to his temple nonchalantly. He grabbed the papers and threw them on to the fire.

"Fuck sake Dietmarr, you could have at least let me read them first!" Henry said as he groped at the flames, all to no avail.

"Don't worry so much kid. It's a simple kidnap operation, no sweat", as he leant back and took a sip of water from his army bottle.

"Sixteen hundred hours", he added putting his bottle down. "I'd get some kip, you look knackered", Dietmarr added pointing towards the pile of blankets, untouched from the night before.

"Yeah good idea", agreed Henry, walking over to the blankets and wrapping himself in them. In a few hours, he would need to be on top of his game.

4.

It was three hours later that Henry stirred from his sleep. Curled in countless blankets, he opened his eyes wide to wake himself up.

"Coffee?" enquired Dietmarr, holding out a small metal cup.

"Thanks", responded Henry, taking the cup and taking a sip, wincing slightly at the heat burning his mouth. "How long have we got?"

"Half an hour. I was just about to wake you. Seems your timing isn't half bad after all", smiled Dietmarr, pouring himself a cup of hot coffee. "So", he added. "The walk to Brandenburg should take about an hour. We'll have about thirty minutes to manoeuvre ourselves into a position where we can steal something. I'll need you to keep a strong lookout while I kick start it". Dietmarr was once more carving into the ground with a stick, drawing a series of X's and squares, outlining the plan.

"Then we drive along these series of rough roads to the Reichskanzler, wait by the back entrance and give him a dose of this bad boy." Dietmarr held up a bigger bottle of the green liquid, wrapped in a white handkerchief. "Smuggle him in to the vehicle, tie him up. Job done." Dietmarr clapped his hands as he reached the end of his plan.

"Sorted!" stated Henry holding up his cup to salute Dietmarr's work.

Half an hour later, their bags were packed and the pair set off into the snowy morning. Instead of turning left like Henry was used to, they continued in a straight line, into the woods.

"It would be slightly quicker to go round, but there's more chance of being noticed". Dietmarr had noticed the look on Henry's face as they trampled through the twigs and shrivelled leaves that littered the ground. "Von Manstein didn't cycle past again this morning", Dietmarr added as he jumped over a fallen tree. "That suggests he is still being monitored."

Henry was half listening, concentrating on the ground below him.

"Right", he replied swiftly, skipping over the same tree trunk that lay solemnly on the ground, covered in patches of snow. The low sun crept through the thick branches of the trees as the pair walked deeper into the woods. The calls of birds were the only sounds along with the snapping of twigs as Henry and Dietmarr battled their way through the thick forestry.

The undergrowth got denser as they tripped and stumbled their way through, getting damper as the snow fell thicker. It was an hour later that the terrain got easier to manage and they appeared on the other side of the woods to a vast area of concrete.

"Welcome to what will be Brandenburg Airport", announced Dietmarr successfully, as he guided Henry round the side of the concreted area, sticking close to the woods.

"Stay close to me, there may be guards", warned Dietmarr as the pair stealthily but quickly walked towards a large hut that was situated on the corner of the estate. About two hundred yards later, without warning, Dietmarr quickly grabbed Henry and shoved him back into the woods. Henry, startled, fell over and lay on the ground as Dietmarr jumped next to him.

"There's a group of three guards hiding behind that bulldozer there", whispered Dietmarr carefully. "We need to take the next bit of the journey in here, as quietly as we can, okay?"

Henry lay on the ground staring into Dietmarr's deep blue eyes, which were wide in anticipation of an answer from Henry.

"Okay?!" whispered Dietmarr again. Henry nodded quickly and got to his feet as quietly as he could, helping Dietmarr up.

"This way", Dietmarr suggested as he guided Henry slightly deeper into the woods. The guards materialised on the other side of the bulldozer, dressed in full army gear. Henry noticed silver pistols fastened to their waists, as they were speaking very loudly in confusing German accents. All three of them had their backs turned, drinking a hot drink and leaning against the vast bulldozer that sat idly, unused. Henry and Dietmarr took each step carefully, avoiding similar twigs that they had trampled through just minutes earlier.

Just as they were past the vision of the guards, Henry stifled a sneeze that he just managed to grab hold of. Dietmarr turned around in shock, as the pair froze in their positions. One of the guards turned around briefly and looked vaguely in the direction of both Henry and Dietmarr, who were standing as motionless as possible. The guard, who had not spotted anything, turned back round to talk to his colleagues. Henry let out a brief sigh.

"Come on!" seethed Dietmarr as they both continued slowly making progress towards the hut.

Ten minutes later, both Dietmarr and Henry were stationed directly outside the main door to the hut, a thin building stretching about half a kilometre across the runway.

"Slight change of plan", announced Dietmarr, taking a fluorescent jacket out of his large rucksack. "I'm going to run straight in there and announce there's been an accident on the other side of the complex". Dietmarr was once more flailing his hands around, guiding Henry through the process.

"Fingers crossed, the guys sat in that office there", Dietmarr pointed through a window, where two gentlemen were sat talking, "They will jump up to follow me. Its then up to you to get in there and take the keys to the door of that 4x4 there. That particular model is one of the only ones that lets you lock your doors. It shouldn't be difficult to find", said Dietmarr looking towards Henry for affirmation.

"It's one of those new Mercedes Benz beasts, the logo looks a bit like a compass", continued Dietmarr before Henry interrupted.

"I'm not that thick!" he said, "I know what it looks like don't worry!" Henry added, gearing himself up.

"Okay", said Dietmarr, putting on the fluorescent coat in haste. "Once you get the car started, drive in the direction I run off in. It should just be a start button. You'll see a large group of people by that collection of bulldozers over there", he said, pointing in the direction of five bulldozers, all of which were in action digging through piles of bricks.

"I'll be in that group and as soon as I see you approaching, I'll run and get in." Dietmarr nodded to Henry.

"Ready?" he asked.

"As I'll ever be", responded Henry, as Dietmarr walked out on to the grey concrete and began to sprint round the side of the cabin. Henry watched on, curious as to the route his ally was taking, but it all became clear as Dietmarr emerged on the other side. Henry could see Dietmarr running into the office with a panic-stricken look on his face, followed swiftly by the men in the room jumping to their feet and following him out the door.

Dietmarr emerged from the cabin, running off into the distance, followed by the two men who were sat in the office and a few others, all in hot pursuit of Dietmarr, who ran at the speed of an Olympic sprinter.

As soon as the coast was clear, Henry jumped from the wooded area to the concrete and ran towards the cabin. The door had been left open as the workers left in a hurry as Henry ran through it and into the office. The first thing Henry noticed was the name on the desk.

'Frederick von Manstein', it read.

Unperturbed, he began his search for the keys. Henry opened every drawer in the room that were mostly filled with files and accounts. There was also a metal cabinet that Henry tore his way through, but he could not find the keys. Running through the office, he threw more files on to the floor in a smaller attached room, before stumbling across a set of keys hung up on the other side of the door. Each key was labelled with a letter and a number, with a heading above with 'Industrial Vehicles' written in scrawny black ink. Time was running out, as the workers would soon notice Dietmarr was not one of theirs, so Henry took all the keys and stuffed them into his coat pocket.

Running out of the office, first making sure the coast was clear, Henry looked around the gigantic airfield. He noticed a large shelter opposite him, housing what seemed to be a collection of yellow vehicles, ranging from small buggies to huge bulldozers and even a crane. Sprinting over to the shelter as quickly as he could, Henry took out a key from his pocket and looked at the number on it. 'H4' was scruffily written on the back, in the same handwriting as the heading indoors.

Two minutes later, he reached the enclosure and set about finding out which vehicle was 'H4'. All the vehicles were organised in size order, with the H's lined up towards the end of the selection. They were small two-seater trucks. Finding the fourth in line, Henry unlocked the door with the key and climbed inside. Pressing the starter button, he lurched forwards, crashing into the similar truck in front.

"Fuck sake!" swore Henry as he quickly turned the steering wheel to the right, finding his way out of the queue, and bolted out of the enclosure and towards the site of the bulldozers.

The top speed of the truck was not very fast, but Henry didn't have far to travel as he could see a lone man sprinting towards him, pursued by a number of others. His arms were waving erratically as Henry noticed it was Dietmarr. Putting his foot down, he sped across the airfield towards him. He could hear the shouting of his pursuers, who must have realised that Dietmarr was an intruder and there was no accident.

Lurching to a halt, Henry opened the passenger door as Dietmarr climbed inside.

"Fucking drive!" shouted Dietmarr, as Henry did a full turn and drove off, narrowly avoiding the pursuers who were very close to jumping on the back of the truck.

"What the hell is this?!" screamed Dietmarr, breathing heavily and gesturing towards the truck's dashboard.

"I couldn't find the keys to the Mercedes Benz!" shouted Henry in reply. "All I could find were these keys!" he said, emptying his pockets to release tens of sets of keys on to the floor of the truck.

"Watch out!" shouted Dietmarr, as Henry swerved wildly to prevent crashing into a similar truck that was heading straight for him. Looking in the rear view mirror, he could see three vehicles in hot pursuit of the pair, with angry looking executives at the wheel. Henry had his foot flat to the floor as they made their way towards the entrance to the site, which lay wide open, leading to a main road.

"That way!" shouted Dietmarr fervently.

"I can see you twat!" shouted Henry, as he drove full pelt towards the gate. There were now only two vehicles following as the bulldozer could not keep up with the pace of the three identical trucks ahead of it.

Flowing through the gate and out on to the main road caused another car to swerve and smash into the wall of the airfield. The truck squealed round the corner and set off down the road, still being followed by two trucks that avoided the pile up that was left in its wake. Reaching into his bag once more, Dietmarr took out a gun, recognised by Henry immediately as an Enfield pistol, and worked his way towards the back of the truck.

Henry, keeping his eyes on the road in front of him as much as possible, turned round to see where he was going. Opening a door leading to the truck's storage space, Dietmarr climbed out and crawled to the edge. Laying on the bed of the truck, he poked his head above the parapet and shot towards the pursuing trucks. Henry could only hear three shots being fired as he looked in his rear view mirror once more. He could see the trucks swerving all over the road, before the first one collided with a tree and burst into flames.

The second truck, swerving to avoid the fireball, crashed head on into a car travelling in the opposite direction and halted in its tracks before it too exploded in a flash of flames.

Dietmarr emerged into the cab of the truck, slotting the Enfield pistol back into his bag.

"You chose the right vehicle", he said simply as he settled down into the passenger seat. Henry smiled and held out his hand to shake Dietmarr's, who shook it and smiled.

"Stage one complete", he said triumphantly. "Now, stage two. To Berlin!" he announced with a flourish.

"Yes sir!" Henry replied, turning off the main road and into the countryside. Henry could see the outline of the city on the horizon as the sun began to set on another day in the German capital.

"Just out of curiosity", added Henry, as the truck bounced along the bumpy hilltops that Dietmarr had directed him across. "How did you come across a British Enfield?" Henry pointed towards the bag, which held the gun that Dietmarr had used.

"Sydney 1929", said Dietmarr simply. I was after a guy called Jim Devine, a right thug." Dietmarr smiled as he recalled the events.

"I remember reading about the Devines", said Henry as he nodded along to Dietmarr's story.

"Just so happened his wife, Mary, had that", he said, pointing once more to the bag. "So I stole it. I thought it would be useful one day!" he laughed, leaning back in his chair and sighing.

"Those were the days..." he added remorsefully as Henry gave him a pat on the back.

"Chin up my friend, you're back in the game!" he said cheerfully as Dietmarr smiled in response.

The sun had set by the time they had reached the capital, driving around the back roads to avoid prying city eyes. It was 5:30 in the evening as they came to settle outside the back entrance to the Reichskanzler.

"Half an hour wait I reckon, until he appears", noted Dietmarr as he took out the bottle of green liquid, that Henry had worked out was chloroform.

"About ten minutes before he's due to come out, I'll get out and hide behind that bin there", Dietmarr said, nodding towards an industrial bin that was full of wood. "From there, I'll walk up behind him and give him a good dose of this", he said, shaking the white handkerchief in the air. "Because you were a fucking idiot, we'll have to squeeze him in here", added Dietmarr as he took hold of some idle boxes that were sitting in the cab and threw them into the back of the truck.

"So, what have I got to do?" asked Henry quietly.

"Drive", retorted Dietmarr simply. "Leave all the work to me, I've knocked out hundreds of people in my time. I'd never think I'd get the chance to do it to my cousin though!" he said joyously, kicking the boxes further into the midst of the truck.

"Okay", stated Henry, sitting back in his seat. "Easy enough!"

A short time later, Dietmarr got out of the truck and took his position behind the industrial bin. Right on cue, a small bespectacled man appeared from the building works and began to make his way to the bicycle he used to get to and from the Reichskanzler. Looking out from the comfort of the cabin, Henry noticed Dietmarr stealthily crouching behind the unsuspecting strategist. Just as von Manstein turned round, Dietmarr pounced, tackling him to the ground and stifling von Manstein's face with the handkerchief. The strategist writhed around, attempting to escape, but Dietmarr was far too strong. After a short time, the writhing of the German strategist got weaker before he became motionless altogether. Picking him up in a fireman's lift, Dietmarr trudged back to the truck and dumped von Manstein's limp frame between Henry and Dietmarr, who climbed back into the passenger seat.

"Evening cousin!" said Dietmarr, laughing as Henry reversed back up the bank and drove off across the grass. Von Manstein's body lurched about as the truck bounced its way over the rough terrain.

"Maybe it would be better if we dumped him at the back?" suggested Henry, but Dietmarr was quick to stamp on the idea.

"And what if he wakes up? He'll just jump off and run!" said Dietmarr emphatically.

"But, this looks suspicious. People can see him through the window!" stated Henry cautiously.

"Fine, he can swap with me. He'll just look asleep if he's sat upright." Dietmarr climbed over von Manstein's lifeless body and switched places with him, hoisting the body up on the seat, strapping him tightly against it. Dietmarr was now positioned above the gear stick, crouching slightly and wincing at each bump.

It was a long, slow journey back to the compound. They took the back roads, just as they had on the way to the Reichskanzler, but it was tougher to navigate in the pitch black of Germany's early evening. Henry kept throwing nervous looks at von Manstein, who was still unconscious in the passenger seat.

"What if he wakes up in here?" Henry asked.

"I'm prepared", replied Dietmarr, holding up the white handkerchief, making sure he didn't hold it to close to his own mouth.

Von Manstein did not wake up, as the truck laboured up the final hill and rested outside the gazebo. The fire had gone out again as Henry locked the truck and helped Dietmarr position the still inanimate body of von Manstein over to a tree. Dietmarr grabbed a large amount of rope and bound him to the tree overlooking the gazebo. Making sure he had tied it properly, he then walked over to collect more wood to start the evening's fire.

"It'll be a while before he wakes up, I'm sure", declared Dietmarr as he settled down next to the burnt out fire and began to rub the collected wood together, a now nightly ritual.

After an hour, the fire had been lit and burnt brightly as muffled noises could be heard from von Manstein's tree.

"Here we go..." said Henry as he gestured over to the tree where von Manstein was stirring.

"Let's do this!" declared Dietmarr, as he jumped to his feet and strolled over to the tree where von Manstein was tied.

Von Manstein grunted and slurred, getting over the effects of the chloroform.

"Here, let me wake you up!" shouted Dietmarr, slapping him hard across the face.

"Fuck! What the? Where the hell am I?" shouted von Manstein, as he wriggled to try and get free from the rope's tight grip.

"Evening cousin..." repeated Dietmarr as von Manstein's eyes widened in shock at the picture in front of him.

"Dietmarr..." he said quietly. "What are you doing, why am I tied to a tree?!" Von Manstein looked confused and dazed as he questioned his cousin.

"My friend and I", started Dietmarr, pointing towards Henry, "need to have a little chat...", as Dietmarr slapped the startled strategist once more.

"Why the fuck are you hitting me, you idiot!" shouted von Manstein, but Dietmarr's eyes raged, as if he had waited years for this opportunity.

"Why am I hitting you? WHY AM I HITTING YOU?!" screamed Dietmarr, as he aimed a kick at the midriff of von Manstein, making him scream in pain and wheeze heavily. Dietmarr kicked him again, in the exact same place, as von Manstein cried out again. Dietmarr repeatedly kicked him in the stomach and you could hear the ribs of von Manstein crack with each one.

"You fucking bastard! You treacherous, low life, cowardly BASTARD!" bellowed Dietmarr as he continued to kick von Manstein, switching between his head and his stomach. Blood surged from the head of the strategist as he implored Dietmarr to stop the assault.

After a few more kicks to the stomach, Dietmarr resented, leaving Erich von Manstein to sway from side to side, clearly disorientated from the attack.

Dietmarr walked over to his food basket and took out a small bottle, filled to the brim with a brown liquid. Henry looked on passively, surprised at the brutality of Dietmarr's assault towards his own cousin.

Dietmarr, bottle in hand, waltzed back over to von Manstein, whose blood covered his face completely.

"Now. We've done the pleasantries", whispered Dietmarr in his cousin's ear. "Now for the reason you're here. You're going to tell us all about your little friend's plans. Hitler. What is he doing?" demanded Dietmarr as he opened the bottle and poured some of the contents over the wounded von Manstein.

Von Manstein screamed in pain. "I don't know what you're talking about!" he implored as Dietmarr poured more of the brown liquid, that smelt strongly of vinegar, over the cuts that covered von Manstein's forehead.

"We can do this the easy way or the hard way", mentioned Dietmarr as he aimed at another kick to the body of von Manstein, who reeled in pure pain.

"Why are you doing this Dietmarr?!" whined von Manstein, as Dietmarr, halfway through executing another kick, stopped in mid-air.

"Why am I doing this?" he asked, with a hint of amazement in his voice. "Why... Am I doing this?" Dietmarr poured the remainder of the bottle over the face of von Manstein who recoiled in pain and let out another piercing howl.

"How about, being completely betrayed by my own country?" started Dietmarr, who completed his kick to the face of his victim. "How about, every single one of my colleagues lying to get me struck off?" Dietmarr kicked again, snapping another one of von Manstein's ribs, whose tears began to trickle through the mixture of blood and snot that had invaded his face. "How about, being left to die in a prison cell in China?" Dietmarr threw a punch at von Manstein, his nose crumbling under the force of the onslaught. "Is that good enough for you?!" he shouted, throwing countless punches to von Manstein's face, which was totally and completely ruined by the viciousness of Dietmarr's attacks.

Henry, looking on in horror, held Dietmarr back to calm him down.

"Remember why we are doing this", he said simply, as Dietmarr sat down on the snowy grass, tears running down his own cheeks.

"Manstein." Henry walked slowly over to the tree that was plastered with the blood of Hitler's strategist. "Make this easy. Tell us what Hitler is planning." Henry was calm in his approach as he sat opposite von Manstein, both of his eyes closed and bruised.

Von Manstein sat silently, breathing heavily, blinking blood out of his eyes. He stared directly into the eyes of Henry, who sat patiently waiting. Dietmarr sat a short distance away, wiping tears from his eyes but staring evilly towards the battered body of his cousin.

"Why the fuck would I tell a British rat...?", seethed von Manstein, spitting blood in to the face of Henry, who threw his head back in surprise.

"Wrong answer", said Henry, as he began to lay into the head of von Manstein. He threw three punches to his head, drawing more blood and more shouts of derision from von Manstein.

"I'll ask you again", said Henry calmly. "What are Hitler's plans?" Henry sat down once more, opposite von Manstein whose head began to drop, dazed from the barrage of hits he had taken.

"Fuck off", said von Manstein shakily.

"Fair enough. Your choice. Hey Dietmarr, shall we up this a notch?" Henry looked menacingly over to Dietmarr who merely nodded and grabbed a metal pole, holding up a small section of the gazebo. He walked over to the fire and held the pole above its roaring flames before cockily strolling over to von Manstein.

"Last chance..." whispered Dietmarr as von Manstein shook his head in defiance.

The shrieks cracked through the night sky as Dietmarr pushed the burning metal pole against the head of von Manstein.

"It doesn't have to be this way, dear cousin..." added Dietmarr coldly as he removed the thick pole and thrust it once more into the bloody face of von Manstein, who let out another wail in pure pain.

"Stop this! Please!" pleaded von Manstein.

"Tell us Hitler's plans and we will", said Dietmarr as he drew the pole back for a third time and pushed the pole deep into the face of the strategist, who was growing weaker with each assault.

"Please. Dietmarr. Please don't do this", he continued to plead as Dietmarr punched him in the face once more.

"You do know this is going to go on and on until you tell us?" asked Henry cheekily as he too aimed a kick at the side of von Manstein, who let out another cry in pain. Von Manstein was weeping heavily now, the effects of the attack taking hold of his punished body.

Dietmarr had walked back over to the fire to re-heat the pole as Henry continued to punch Dietmarr all over his body. Von Manstein let out a high-pitched bark at the impact of each of them. Dietmarr sauntered over to him, hot metal pole in hand and unbuckled the belt of Von Manstein.

"Trust me cousin, this doesn't get any prettier. We can end this now if you spill the beans?" asked Dietmarr, but von Manstein continued to shake his head in boldness.

"I will never give in!" shouted von Manstein, as Dietmarr plunged the searing pole down von Manstein's trousers, leaving the German schemer to scream so loudly that the ground beneath them shook.

Henry winced as he witnessed the latest torture tactic from Dietmarr.

"That has got to hurt...", he whispered to himself as Dietmarr shoved the pole down his sufferer's trousers once more, causing von Manstein to cry out again.

"Henry. Grab the horseshoes that are tying the gazebo down.

Let's cause some proper pain for this stubborn son of a bitch". Henry obeyed the order, pulling the horseshoes out of the ground, causing the gazebo to collapse slightly.

"Bring them here", ordered Dietmarr, holding out the flailing legs of von Manstein, who was cursing and spitting with every breath. "Secure him", he said, pointing towards von Manstein's ankles. Henry obliged, digging the horseshoes into the frozen ground, holding von Manstein's legs into place. Meanwhile, Dietmarr had made his way to the truck and started the engine.

"I don't have to do this you bastard!" shouted Dietmarr over the roar of the engine. "Tell us now, and we'll stop!" he added, reversing into position.

"NEVER!" screamed von Manstein, as Dietmarr drove towards the outstretched legs of von Manstein and proceeded to drive straight over them. The snapping of bones perforated the darkness as von Manstein screamed in utter distress. Dietmarr laughed as he put the truck into reverse and drove back over the legs of Erich who yelled in pure agony.

"I can do it again if you like?" questioned Dietmarr, as he revved the engine in earnest.

"No! Please!" von Manstein beseeched, as Dietmarr, hell bent on causing as much suffering as possible, drove over his legs once more and laughed boorishly as von Manstein screamed again. Meanwhile, Henry, who was standing back when the truck drove over von Manstein, jumped in at opportune intervals to dish out more punishment in the way of kicks to von Manstein's already pummelled body. Dietmarr was revving the engine loudly once more.

"Please, stop this!" implored von Manstein, roaring again as Dietmarr reversed over the legs that were already hanging in precarious positions. Henry continued to assault the strategist until he could take no more.

"Okay!" screamed von Manstein. "I'll tell you, just stop, STOP!" He bawled as Henry stopped himself planting the latest punch into his skull.

"What was that?" asked Dietmarr, as he walked up closely to von Manstein. "I didn't quite hear you?" Dietmarr placed an open palm to his ear, imploring von Manstein to speak louder.

"I'll tell you everything. Just, please... No more..." said von

Manstein weakly as Dietmarr jumped back.

"FINALLY!" shouted Dietmarr happily. "You lasted longer than your Father anyway, he lasted about ten minutes!" he joked as von Manstein painfully thrust his head up at the mention of his Father.

"I'm only kidding my dear cousin! We haven't touched him... Yet..." Dietmarr roamed over to the barely standing gazebo, grabbed the tree trunk and dragged it opposite von Manstein.

"Oi, Henry. Now's a good time to grab your precious pen and paper" said the former Abwehr agent sarcastically, as Henry floated over to his bag and took out a pad and his silver coated pen.

"Okay. In your own time..." said Dietmarr quietly looking directly into the eyes of von Manstein, whose head hung limply, still bleeding profusely on to a puddle of blood on his lap.

"Hitler is planning to invade Europe", stated von Manstein eagerly. He sounded as if he wanted to rush through giving his knowledge so he could escape as quickly as he could.

"Hitler wants the whole of Europe to be his own. No Jews. No Slavs. No one but pure blooded Germans." von Manstein was grimacing with every word, unable to hold his broken ribs as he was still tied strongly to the tree.

He continued.

"Von Hindenburg is gravely ill. He's been given a year to live. He can't run the country, so Hitler is doing it for him."

"Why has Hindenburg told Hitler to do it?" interrupted Dietmarr quickly. "What happened to von Schleicher?"

"He's useless, we all know it!" spat von Manstein as Dietmarr nodded in agreement.

"So, Hitler is running the country? Why isn't he Chancellor yet?" Dietmarr asked crudely.

"He will be within the next couple of weeks", gasped von Manstein. "We then have two months to wait before the federal elections, when von Hindenburg will step down and Adolf Hitler will become Germany's sole ruler! Until then, we can work on getting troops so we can attack the ports of Poland. From there, we will massacre central Europe and run it under Nazi rule!" Von Manstein's voice gained a modicum of fight as he spat more blood out of his mouth.

"And the Treaty of Versailles?" questioned Dietmarr again.

"Fuck the Treaty of Versailles", spat von Manstein. "Japan have already broken it. Italy are going to invade Ethiopia. If they can break it, so can we!", shouted von Manstein in defiance. "We will re-arm the Rhineland and bulldoze through Europe!" Von Manstein's confidence had returned, smiling through copious amounts of blood at the concerned look on Dietmarr's face. Henry was scribbling intently, occasionally looking up to see his accomplice's reactions.

"And what if the German people don't vote in Hitler? Then what? You'll massacre Germany too?" Dietmarr slapped von Manstein hard across the face, but von Manstein just laughed in response.

"The people LOVE Hitler!" he responded gleefully. "If by some chance he doesn't get a majority, we have an act of parliament ready to decree that will make Hitler Fuhrer! We will rid Germany of all other pointless political parties and lead the greatest Dictatorship to ever exist in the modern world!"

Dietmarr's face held an angry frown as von Manstein laughed deliriously at the plans he had divulged.

"And you really think you're going to get away with this now we know?" asked Dietmarr, raising his eyebrows in suspicion.

"As soon as I escape this rat-infested shit hole", von Manstein looked over towards Henry who was still scribbling in his notepad, "I will tell the future Fuhrer everything and we will hunt you down with a pack of dogs!" deplored von Manstein as he spat into the face of Dietmarr again, causing him to flinch.

"What makes you think you're leaving?" responded Dietmarr simply, reaching towards his pocket and producing the Enfield pistol. Without any warning, he pulled the trigger, sending a single bullet into the temple of Erich von Manstein.

The echoes of the gunshot reverberated around the woods as Henry stood in shock at the shaking hand of his partner.

"WHAT THE FUCK DIETMARR?!" screamed Henry. "I thought we weren't going to kill him?!" Henry grabbed the pistol out of Dietmarr's shaking hand as he stared straight ahead at the limp body of von Manstein, blood squirting out of the gunshot wound with extreme velocity.

"I had a change of heart", answered Dietmarr chillingly, as he unlatched von Manstein's ankles from the horseshoes and drifted back to the gazebo. Henry stood motionless, staring into the still open eyes of the dead strategist. It looked as if he was staring right back.

Dietmarr set about repairing the gazebo, as he fastened the metal poles to the horseshoes and dug them into the turf. There were still tears running down his cheeks. Henry knew that, however much bad blood there was between the two, shooting dead your own cousin could have an effect on Dietmarr. Wiping away his tears, he continued to gather up wood and throw them on to the fire, in a determined effort to keep busy.

After a short while, Henry was throwing dirt on to the dead body of Erich von Manstein, who slowly vanished from view. Levelling out the turf so that the grave was not easily noticed, Henry gazed over at Dietmarr who was still collecting large swathes of wood and throwing them on to the fire, which had reached a great height.

"Come on mate, time to stop", said Henry caringly as he walked over to Dietmarr and guided him towards the tree trunk that had been put back in its original position.

Dietmarr looked at Henry, tears flooding his eyes. This was the first time Henry had seen his partner in crime look vulnerable.

"I hated the guy. I really, really, really hated the guy", mumbled Dietmarr, wiping away more tears. "But my Mother would have hated me doing that", he pointed over to the tree which still had a large amount of von Manstein's blood dripping down its surface.

"I think we did the right thing in the end", said Henry, attempting to console Dietmarr. "He would only have gone back and told Hitler everything, and then our job would have been ten times harder." Dietmarr shook his head in disagreement.

"He's going to notice he's missing isn't he", noted Dietmarr, but Henry was quick to jump in with a response.

"Better missing than on crutches with two broken legs and a mangled face!" said Henry, realising he was smiling.

"Hmm...", mumbled Dietmarr as he let out a heavy sigh. "Maybe you're right", he added resolutely, wiping away the remainder of the tears from his face. "Plus, Hitler's now one man down. That'll stop him." Dietmarr's voice had regained its swagger as he lay back on to the pile of blankets. Henry pulled up his rucksack and lay his head against it as he lay next to Dietmarr.

"Let's leave the debrief till the morning?" asked Dietmarr desperately. "It's been too much action for one day." Henry nodded in agreement.

"Tell me more about yourself", asked Dietmarr as Henry turned to face him.

"What do you want to know?" he replied, as he wrestled with the blankets to make himself comfortable.

"I don't know. Childhood. School. Girlfriends. Anything." Dietmarr's tone had become softer as he contemplated an eventful day.

"Well, I was educated at Harrow and Cambridge. I suppose I was a bit of a loner." Henry's mind went back to his early days at Harrow as a fag for the most brutal of senior boys. He still had the scar across his cheek that was the result of his master throwing a knife at him. Each junior went through a stage of being a "fag" to one of the seniors, becoming their personal servants for the school year.

"I was bullied a bit because I was a swat", added Henry as Dietmarr nodded intently. "It eased when I got to Cambridge but I still received comments here and there." Henry sighed as his memories flooded back to being hung by his trousers on trees and pushed over constantly.

"I'm presuming none of that stopped you from graduating?" asked Dietmarr with a friendly shove towards Henry, who smiled in return.

"Top grades", he responded shyly. "I suppose all the trouble was worth it. I went into politics straight from university but it was so boring. I needed more action. More danger. Which is when MI5 came knocking."

"Ahh, domestic stuff hey", said Dietmarr, sounding impressed.

"Yeah. But even that wasn't amazing. So I transferred to international a couple of years later and here I am", Henry gestured to his surroundings, wrapping himself tighter into his blankets.

"It's all very well talking about school and work and work and school", said Dietmarr inquisitively, but tell me more about the real you..."

Henry's mind went back to the briefing in London, where Michael Langley had encouraged Henry to talk about the "real Germany".

"What do you mean?" asked Henry innocently looking towards Dietmarr.

"Come on..." he responded with a cheeky smile across his face.

"A good-looking chap like you, you must have had girls crawling all over you!" Dietmarr gave Henry another nudge as Henry smiled nervously.

"Hardly", Henry said, feeling slightly embarrassed. "No, all the girls were after the sportsmen, and I was never very good at rugby or fives."

Dietmarr laughed. "Yeah right!" he added, giving Henry a third nudge in the ribcage.

"What about you?" asked Henry, eager to take the subject off his own troubled teenage years.

"Well, I went to Waldorf boarding school in Hannover for 12 years. My parents worked abroad. My Father worked as German Ambassador to America and lived in Boston. My Mother was a private tutor and regularly travelled all over Europe. I originally trained to be a doctor, but accepted an invitation to trial for the Abwehr and never looked back. At least until last year..."

Dietmarr's eyes filled with sadness as his mind took him back to the events of the hearing in Munich.

"I am a firm believer that everything happens for a reason", added Dietmarr resolutely. "We meet people because we are meant to. We kill people because sometimes, it is necessary." His gaze turned towards the bloody tree once more and the slight bump in the ground that housed the corpse of von Manstein.

"No wife? Kids?" asked Henry, almost knowing what the answer was going to be.

"God no", said Dietmarr expectedly. "My parents never showed any love to me. I don't know if I've ever learnt how to love someone", he murmured as he continued to look at the grave.

About an hour passed, with both Henry and Dietmarr staring at the ceiling of the gazebo, which had a small tear in it. Henry could see a few stars lighting up the night sky through the gap and his mind wandered towards them.

"Have you ever been in love?" Dietmarr broke the silence, looking over at Henry who was still staring up at the sky.

"I don't think so", lied Henry. His thoughts returned once more to his Cambridge days and the person who sat ahead of him in most lectures. A feeling of lust burst through his heart, but it was quickly replaced with pain as he remembered flattening his feelings for his classmate.

"Me neither", responded Dietmarr as he turned back towards the stars. "I'm jealous of the people who can simply love without regret or risk." Dietmarr's voice was shaking slightly as Henry turned over on to his side to face him.

"What do you mean?" enquired Henry, a shaky element noticeable in his voice too. Henry and Dietmarr were facing each other again.

"You see people all the time. Walking through the streets, hand in hand, without a care in the world. They all look happy. I'm jealous of that happiness." Dietmarr continued to look into Henry's eyes as Henry nodded.

"Me too." Henry could feel his heart bursting from his chest as Dietmarr's stare pierced him. His eyes were at their deepest blue, loving and caressing.

"Can I ask you a question?" Henry asked, his voice still shaking.

"Of course", whispered Dietmarr, still staring deep into Henry's eyes.

"Why have you never been in love?"

Dietmarr lay silent for a moment. A smile spread slowly across his face as he pondered his response.

"The right person has never shown their face". Dietmarr continued to smile.

"I see..." replied Henry. His heart was pumping at a mile a minute.

"Can I ask you a question?" asked Dietmarr, quietly. The atmosphere was deathly silent, as if the whole world sat and watched them.

"Erm... Yes..." mumbled Henry, shifting his body weight slightly closer to Dietmarr.

"Why have you never been in love?" Henry felt a feeling of fear and excitement as he looked deeper into Dietmarr's eyes.

"The right person has never shown their face".

Dietmarr moved closer to Henry, their faces within millimetres of each other. Henry could hear the beating of Dietmarr's heart, which was going as fast as Henry's.

Dietmarr opened his mouth.

"I do however... Think that might change..."

Dietmarr placed his hand on the side of Henry's face and kissed him sensitively. The energy that ran through Henry's body felt delightful. He felt as free as a bird, as Dietmarr released Henry and looked at him, as if expecting to be pushed away. However, he merely smiled in response and kissed Dietmarr once more as he rolled over on top of him. His hands ran all over Dietmarr's body entrancingly as the two men continued to lock lips. Henry's heart was beating faster than it ever had, as Dietmarr took off his layers of clothing and threw them on to the sodden grass. Henry felt the chill of the night air against his body with Dietmarr's tongue cajoling his chest as he felt a rush unlike no other.

As Henry let go, he collapsed on to the pile of blankets next to Dietmarr, who laid his head against his shoulder.

"Wow", stated Henry, still breathing heavily after the episode. "I've never felt like that before." Dietmarr smiled and kissed his shoulder.

"I'm so glad you feel the same way. I saw it in your eyes as soon as I saved you from the cellar." Dietmarr turned Henry's head towards his own. "Back to business tomorrow though. We've got some major investigative work to do", he said as he kissed Henry once more on the lips and rolled over, pulling the assortment of blankets over him. Henry smiled, putting his layers of clothing back on, including his underwear and his trousers. Dietmarr followed suit, as he rolled over and pulled Henry towards the Earth. He placed an arm over Henry's body.

"Good night lover boy!" said Dietmarr cheekily, with a smile still torn across his face.

"Good night Dietmarr", replied Henry as he kissed Dietmarr on the forehead and let his head rest against his shoulder. However, before he allowed his own head to lay back against his makeshift pillow, he felt a familiar falling sensation...

...

Henry awoke, looking up at the ceiling of his bedroom. Sweat was dripping from his face on to the bed sheets and he felt clammy and feverish. Turning towards his bedside table, he grabbed his watch and looked at its face, squinting into the darkness. It was 4am. The snow continued to fall outside, covering the only window in the room. The street light directly outside Henry's window was flashing, almost as if it was warning Henry to wake up.

Henry fell back on to his pillow, wiping his forehead once more.

"Concentrate Irthing", he whispered to himself, placing his watch back on the table. He would grant himself a couple more hours of sleep.

5.

The sun was rising by the time Henry awoke for a second time, climbing out of bed to change out of his sodden night clothes. He could already hear Brock downstairs, preparing a hearty breakfast and the hustle and bustle of Potsdam's early risers outside his bedroom window. The snow had been replaced by pure blue skies and a viciously low sun that pierced Henry's bedroom like a sword.

Henry looked outside the window, taking a glance at a small group of people huddled around a small boy. He was lying on the ground, his bicycle lying motionless a few feet away from him and newspapers whirling around in the air. Sighing slightly, Henry took the pen out of his waistcoat pocket and tore a small piece of paper from his pad. He began to write in squalid italics. Neat writing had never been his forte.

"Agent Snake to Control. Have joined forces with ex-Ab D.S. We have gained info from primary target, now deceased. Will stay on to hunt queen bee. Update soon. H."

Henry was unsure his superiors in London would understand a single word of the scrawled note, as his mission had taken an unexpected twist. He had told them Erich von Manstein was dead, as Henry began to come to terms with last night's vicious ordeal. Sealing the note in a brown envelope, he put on his black boots and walked down the winding staircase, greeted with the smell of bacon from the kitchen.

"Morning lad!" shouted Brock from amongst the steam, as Henry took a seat at the dining table, grabbing the local newspaper in the process. He was instantly struck by the face on the front cover. The headline across the top was striking.

"SON OF LOCAL MAYOR MISSING!"

Henry looked at the picture. A small, bespectacled man stared straight back at him, arm in arm with his Mother and Father standing outside a battered looking cottage, and the hills in the distance. Henry recognised the face immediately. It was Erich von Manstein. He continued to read, as Brock dumped a plate full of bacon sandwiches in the middle of the table.

"I'm amazed the bastard's shouting didn't wake you up last night, hey!" said Brock boldly. "4am it was and he was screaming down the street! No consideration for anyone else!"

Henry nodded, half-listening to Brock's protestations as he began to read the article.

"There was panic in Potsdam last night after Mayor von Manstein ran through the streets demanding the town wake up and look for his son. Erich, who has allegedly not returned from his day at work, is small in stature, about 5 foot 7 inches tall. He wears steel-rimmed glasses and has a small bald patch in the back of his head. It is thought he was wearing an all-black suit as he left for work on his bicycle early yesterday morning. If anyone has any information regarding the disappearance of Erich von Manstein, please get in contact with police immediately."

"Good riddance if you ask me", added Brock, who was now sat opposite Henry shovelling down copious amounts of bacon and sausage whilst reading the same paper.

"The guy was so up himself it was unreal!" continued Brock. "Just because he's the Mayor's son, he thought he was our ruler. Complete prick!"

"Do you mind if I take this?" questioned Henry, ignoring Brock's rant and holding up the newspaper.

"Of course lad, why do you think I got two! I knew a mysterious story would grasp your attention!"

Henry nodded once more and looked down at the photograph on the front of the newspaper. Erich von Manstein was smiling, his arm around his similarly small Father and his Mother, who was wearing a pinny and holding a basket. He looked happy. Henry's mind went back to the events of last night, throwing mud on to the limp body of the missing man. His eyes staring blankly ahead...

"I've got to go", said Henry quickly, leaving the vast majority of the sandwiches Brock had made.

"Take a couple with you!" Brock demanded, pushing the sandwiches into a paper bag and handing them to Henry.

"Thanks Brock", replied Henry, gladly accepting the bag. "I may not be back for a day or two, so don't wait up for me." Henry picked up the paper and shoved it under his arm along with the sealed brown envelope and put it in his pocket.

"Stay safe kid!" said Brock brashly as Henry sidled his way out of the door. The child who had fallen off his bicycle was sat up against the wall of the Greengrocer's, holding his shoulder and crying. A woman, presumably his Mother, was sat next to him cradling his head and feeding him tissues.

"Is everything okay?" asked Henry courteously, walking past the young boy.

"Nothing too serious", responded the woman. "Think it's a dislocated shoulder..."

"Ouch!" responded Henry enthusiastically, wishing the boy well as he walked up the now familiar route towards the city.

Walking past the von Manstein cottage, Henry noticed a pair of people through the window, sitting at the table with their heads in their hands. Henry felt a huge pang of guilt as he quickly strolled past the cottage and towards the hills of the countryside.

The walk took longer than usual, with Henry mulling over the events of last night and his dream. His ill-judged feelings towards Dietmarr were wrong, he knew that, but it was difficult to suppress them. He knew he was different ever since he was a young teenager, but feared being locked up if he showed them. There was no way he could have been a British spy had he admitted his homosexual tendencies. Besides, there was no way the manly and boisterous Dietmarr shared his feelings. It was better for everyone if he remained silent.

A few hours later, with the bright sun poking through the branches of the trees, Henry turned the corner and noticed the gazebo. The fire was already burning brightly. The raised lump of Earth, now white from the snowfall, sat next to the tree von Manstein had been strapped to, his blood now dried against its trunk. Henry stood still, staring at it for a while. He could still hear the ear-splitting cries of the strategist in his ears. The sound of the gunshot emanating from Dietmarr's pistol. The blood spurting out from the wound...

"Morning!"

Dietmarr had emerged from the woods, carrying a small pile of wood that he threw on to the raging fire.

"Just in time for some breakfast if you want some?" enquired

Dietmarr. "I've been into the city already, broke into the butchers and stole some frankfurters!" He successfully held up his basket, showing off a vast array of sausages.

"I'm okay thanks, I've got some already", replied Henry, holding up the paper bag Brock had given him.

"Suit yourself", said Dietmarr, throwing the raw sausage into a pan and holding it above the flames.

"Have you seen this?" said Henry, handing the newspaper to Dietmarr. He grabbed it with unexpected force and unfurled it. His eyes scanned the front page before he threw it on to the fire.

"Who cares?" he stated coldly. "The bastard's dead, nothing we can do about it. As long as you keep silent..." Dietmarr stared up at Henry who scoffed at the very idea of him blabbing.

"Of course I will, who do you take me for?" Henry said, taking his seat on the lone piece of tree trunk. "His parents looked pretty upset this morning. His Father was running through the streets screaming at 4am apparently".

"Doesn't surprise me", Dietmarr replied in equal disdain. "He always was an overprotective faggot!" Henry looked briefly at the floor as Dietmarr tossed the sausage meat about in his silver pan. Henry dug out his now cold bacon sandwiches and ate in silence, with the hiss of the flames the only sound in the cold morning air. Every now and then, Henry threw a glance over to the noticeable bump in the ground that kept the dead body.

"Do you think we should have killed him?" asked Henry, turning round to look at Dietmarr.

"Of course we should you soft git!" retorted Dietmarr. "He'd have only gone and blabbed to his His Hitlerness otherwise! He's better off a dead man, trust me."

"Hmm", replied Henry, not convinced. His mind wandered back to the cottage and his parents, crying.

"Forget about it!" said Dietmarr, chucking a piece of bread at Henry who's attention was brought back to the present.

"Next step, we need to find where Hitler is. They'd have moved him after your shit attempts at infiltration." Dietmarr had grabbed his stick again and was carving into the Earth.

"He could be anywhere in the world?" asked Henry confusingly before Dietmarr held a hand up to stop him talking.

"Don't be nonsensical Irthing, he's definitely in Germany. We know he's about to be made Chancellor right? They could still house Hitler at the Reichskanzler with heavy security but I doubt it." Dietmarr was hitting the ground with his stick as he was in deep thought.

"They might hold meetings in the Reichstag..." hinted Dietmarr who drew a large circle into the ground. About ten miles from the Reichskanzler, the Reichstag was the German parliament building, where all new appointments were ratified by the German government.

"That would be heavily guarded as well", said Dietmarr who was drawing crosses into the circular shape.

"Wherever Hitler is, he's going to have guards", said Henry after a small period of silence.

"Thanks for that detective", replied Dietmarr sarcastically as Henry rolled his eyes in dissatisfaction. Dietmarr began to rap the side of his head, attempting to persuade an idea out of the inner most workings of his brain.

"What can we do...? What can we do...?" he said quietly, continuing to batter his temple into submission.

"What about a disguise?" suggested Henry as Dietmarr looked up at him inquisitively.

"Like what?" he said slowly. "It has to be a bloody good disguise for the establishment to not notice me!"

"True", admitted Henry as the pair fell silent once more.

"I could be the one in disguise?" suggested Henry but that was also shot down by Dietmarr.

"Your German accent is terrible, you'll blow your cover in about five minutes!" He laughed, but Henry looked at him disapprovingly.

The hours dragged by, with Dietmarr stamping out any suggestions from Henry and labelling them as "idiotic" or similar.

"We need to know his schedule..." said Dietmarr after a considerable pause. "We need to know what he is doing, where he is doing it and when he is doing it..."

"How are we going to do that?" asked Henry.

"I don't know do I you fucking idiot! Otherwise I'd have come up with something already!" Dietmarr was growing frustrated at the lack of progress the pair were making as the hours ticked by.

"We can get him when he's made Chancellor?" suggested Henry, expecting to be shot down once more, but Dietmarr looked up at him, interested.

"How do you mean?" he asked.

"I've heard Hitler likes his big, grand speeches. Maybe he'll hold some sort of rally when he's made Chancellor, or maybe there will be an initiation ceremony or something?" Henry's voice got slower and slower as Dietmarr cut a disapproving look.

"It has potential... The last two Chancellors have both had rallies to welcome them to office. Knowing Hitler and his ego, he'd want one too."

Dietmarr continued to rap the ground with his stick. Henry, noticing that Dietmarr may finally be impressed, continued to talk Dietmarr through his idea.

"We can go back to London. They'll have intelligence on when Hitler is to become Chancellor and we can get back here to take him out."

"What are we going to kill him with?" asked Dietmarr, throwing a shady look at Henry.

"MI6 will have something suitable", said Henry unconvincingly.

"Worth a shot. We have nothing else", admitted Dietmarr as he scrubbed out his diagrams from the earth. "How are we going to get to London?" he added.

"We can ring them and ask for a plane to be sent over. We have to make our way back to the motel." Henry went to pick up his bag.

"Fine", said Dietmarr as he started packing away his things.

Starting the long walk along the now familiar route to the motel, the pair discussed how they would go about killing Adolf Hitler and fantasised about what they would do to him given the chance.

It was three hours later that the sight of the von Manstein cottage greeted the pair to the town of Potsdam once more.

"This way", gestured Henry as he guided Dietmarr to a side path that led round the side of the town. "I don't think I can walk past his house yet." Dietmarr nodded in agreement, as he avoided large boulders of ice that had formed.

A short time later, the pair walked in through the front door of the motel, greeted by a cautious looking Brock. Henry was quick to introduce Dietmarr before anything drastic took place.

"Brock, this is Dietmarr Schultz. He's been helping me on my mission". Brock took a deep breath in relief and held out his hand to greet Dietmarr who nodded in response and shook the outstretched hand.

"Listen, can I borrow your telephone? And have you got the code so I can ring London?" Henry had not waited for the answer, picking up the telephone and holding it to his ear.

"Sure kid, give me a sec!" replied Brock enthusiastically, walking up the staircase. A few seconds later, he came walking down with a large pad and opened it towards the back.

"S... T.... United Kingdom!" he said proudly, entering the phone number for Henry who nodded and held the phone tightly to his ear. It was a long pause to wait for the phone to ring, causing Henry to look nervously up at Brock, but before he could double check he had entered the right number, a brief ring was halted by a British voice.

"Pursey", was the response.

"Commander, its Agent Snake", replied Henry nervously.

"Snake, how are you lad?" responded Commander Pursey cheerfully. "I got your first note, thanks very much for letting us know you landed with Brock safe! How's things?"

"Good sir thank you", said Henry, attempting to cut to the chase. "I have sent a further note outlining a partnership with a former Abwehr agent. I am with him now", he looked across at Dietmarr who merely smiled in response.

"Is it Dietmarr Schultz by any chance?" asked Commander Pursey, curiously.

"Yes it is, how do you know him?" Henry was surprised his accomplice was known by MI6.

"We heard of his hearing a while back. Between you and me, the Governor isn't going to be happy about this..." responded Commander Pursey nervously.

"Oh", said Henry, not knowing how to respond to his Commander's reservations. "Listen Commander, we need to get back to HQ, can you send a plane over to land in Loftheim Woods, just outside of Potsdam?"

"Of course, consider it done. It will be with you in a few hours", responded Commander Pursey. "Is there anything else? Just this line..."

With that, the phone went dead. It mattered not, as the plane had been confirmed.

"ETA three hours" said Henry simply, as he took his boots off and walked into the drawing room, followed by Dietmarr who had been waved in by Brock. They both sat down as Brock walked into the kitchen to make tea. The cosy feeling of sitting as a group brought back rare memories of family times for Henry, sitting down for dinner in their finite house in the Home Counties. Those days felt so long ago. Dietmarr was also staring into space, with Henry suspecting he was thinking similar thoughts.

"There you go", said Brock calmly, causing Henry to jump slightly as he was brought out of his stupor.

"So, what are you guys planning?" Brock was insistent on trying to find out what Henry was up to, but he merely smiled in response.

"Oh I know, I know! You can't tell me and all that, I get it lad!" said Brock cheerfully as Dietmarr stared out of the window.

"So what do you do Dietmarr?" asked Brock, causing Dietmarr to bring his attention back to the room.

"I'm an ex-Abwehr agent", said Dietmarr. "But I was betrayed by my own colleagues last year. Hindenburg's troops have been searching for me ever since." Dietmarr took a sip of tea, ignoring Brock's raised eyebrows.

"What if they hunt you down and find you here? You're not destroying my motel just because you're washed up!" Henry threw a dirty look at Brock who just shrugged.

"What?! It's true!" stated Brock as Dietmarr amazingly nodded in agreement.

"Yeah you're right. I shouldn't be here."

With that, he got to his feet and made his way to the door.

"Wait, where are you going? The plane will be here soon! Where are you going to go?" Henry had jumped to his feet, attempting to stop Dietmarr from walking out.

"Back to the compound", said Dietmarr. "You're not to follow me, I'm a dangerous man to be around at the moment." He picked up his bag and walked towards the door, but Henry jumped in his way, covering the door with his arms.

"Don't be ridiculous Dietmarr, I need you! Who's going to teach me how to speak with a proper German accent hey? Come on!" Henry was attempting to crack a few jokes to ease the tension that had appeared out of nowhere.

"Get out of my way Irthing", said Dietmarr quietly.

"No", said Henry resolutely.

"Sit down kid, I was only joking. I like a joke, don't I Henry?"

"Yes mate", responded Henry as Dietmarr looked at him, tears welling up in his eyes.

After a short pause, Dietmarr relented and slouched back to his chair and sat down, dumping his bag in the process.

The three sat in near silence for the remaining time, waiting patiently for the plane that would take them back to London.

"I need to use the bathroom", announced Dietmarr nervously after a short while.

"Up the stairs, first on the right", guided Brock waving Dietmarr towards the door leading to the winding staircase. Waiting for him to leave the room, he turned back towards Henry.

"Is he alright? He seems a bit... Unstable..." asked Brock. Henry sighed in response. Something was wrong with Dietmarr. He was usually so confident, so brash yet he had spent the best part of three hours in complete silence staring out of the motel window, refusing any food or drink, despite not eating for days.

Dietmarr reappeared from the bathroom, water dripping from his face.

"Can I have a drink?" asked Dietmarr extremely politely, at which Brock jumped to his feet, relieved that his new guest was to accept his offers.

"Of course lad, sit down. What do you want? Water? Coffee?"

"Have you got anything stronger?" suggested Dietmarr, looking longingly at the cabinet that was full with spirits and small glasses.

"Of course!" said Brock happily. "Whiskey okay?" Dietmarr nodded, as did Henry, as Brock took out two glasses and poured a generous serving of whiskey into each.

"Are you not having one?" asked Henry politely.

"No lad, I make a habit of not drinking before dusk. I'd never stop otherwise!", joked Brock as he punched Henry on the arm playfully and handing him the glass. He then handed the second glass to Dietmarr, who grabbed it and downed it in one and held the glass out before Brock had made it back to his seat.

"May I have another?" he asked, extremely politely.

"Yes. Yes of course!" said Brock obligingly, taking the bottle of the whiskey out of the cabinet and placing it on to the table in the middle of the room. "Help yourself!"

"Thank you sir", said Dietmarr as he filled his glass with whiskey and once again downed it in one. Henry was looking at him, eyes squinted, trying to take in what was wrong with his accomplice.

"Are you okay mate?" Henry asked once more, only to be greeted with a nod from Dietmarr who had filled his glass once more and downed it.

"I'd go easy on that my friend, its strong stuff!" said Brock cautiously, but Dietmarr merely ignored him as he downed a further glass before leaning back into his chair and sighing loudly.

"Cheers...", said Henry slightly sarcastically, taking a sip from his own glass. "How long have we got until this plane arrives?" he asked Brock, nodding to the clock on the wall.

"About twenty minutes is my guess!" replied Brock. "Would you like me to ruffle up something to eat before you set off?" Brock was looking mainly at Dietmarr who shook his head slowly.

"I think we'll be fine", added Henry.

Not long after, the breeze outside had picked up and the noise of an aeroplane could be heard not far away.

"I reckon that's us!" said Henry successfully, gathering his things and shoving them back into his bag. "I can't imagine we'll be long Brock, maybe a couple of days, so I'll be back then." Henry shook Brock's hand, who wished him farewell.

"Oh! Before I forget!" said Brock, rushing into the kitchen. He emerged a few seconds later with an envelope. "Pass this on to your Commander for me. It's an invoice. I'm not letting you stay here for free you know!"

"Righto!" said Henry, imploring Dietmarr to come as he had stumbled slightly to his feet. Henry feared the quick dosage of whiskey had gone to his head.

"Take care Brock, thanks for the whiskey", said Dietmarr politely, shaking Brock's hand.

"You're very welcome Dietmarr! Don't be a stranger!" said Brock boldly, waving them out of the door. Henry could see the wings of the plane in the near distance and the force of the engine, causing the trees to swing from side to side.

A short walk later, and the pair clambered on to the plane. Dietmarr paused slightly before climbing the steps. He took a deep breath as he stepped on to the plane, while Henry made himself comfortable in his seat. Dietmarr sat opposite him, looking extremely pale and sick.

"Are you sure you're okay? You don't look very well?" repeated

Henry, only to be waved down by Dietmarr, who went for his bag and revealed the huge bottle of whiskey that he had helped himself too in Brock's motel.

"You stole it?! You bastard, he was being good to us!" said Henry as Dietmarr opened the bottle and took a huge swig from it.

"I need it", he said quietly, wincing as he swallowed before taking another big gulp.

"Why? Are you scared of aeroplanes or something?" quipped Henry, while Dietmarr looked at him with fear in his eyes. He took another mouthful of whiskey and stared out of the window, looking jealously at the ground below him.

"You're scared of flying?!" said Henry with amazement. "How the fuck have you travelled all over the world when you're scared of flying?!" He laughed before being kicked hard by Dietmarr in the shins, strapping himself tightly to his seat.

"With difficulty", responded Dietmarr who also nervously strapped himself in tightly.

"Good afternoon gents, I am Second Lieutenant Marsh, you're pilot for this short flight back to HQ in London. The flight should take no more than two hours. Please feel free to ask our specialist on-board maid if you require any assistance. Happy flying!"

The high, cheery voice of the pilot made Dietmarr flinch slightly as he downed another huge helping of whiskey.

"God help me", he whispered as the engines fired up and the plane began to move.

"You'll be fine!" said Henry jokingly. "Our air force is the best in the world, the chances of crashing are minute!"

"Fuck off", replied Dietmarr to more laughs from Henry as the engine roared and began to pick up speed.

"I think I'm going to be sick", said Dietmarr quiveringly as Henry waved to the maid who was already rushing over with a brown bag. As the plane lifted itself off the tarmac below, Dietmarr wretched loudly. Henry laughed at his friend's misfortune.

"Attractive! The maid loves you already!", said Henry jokingly.

"I'm guessing she's not your type?" replied Dietmarr coldly, looking up from inside the brown bag as Henry quickly looked out of the window. They were level with the low-flying clouds.

"Nope", said Henry as casually as possible.

Dietmarr emerged from the bag, opening the bottle of whiskey once more and taking another generous dose.

"Are you sure that's wise, we are in the air now?" asked Henry cautiously, but Dietmarr merely cursed in return and continued to drink. Henry merely shook his head in response.

"Well don't be drunk for our meeting! We're meeting my Commander straight off the plane remember!" Henry held out a hand, asking for the whiskey but Dietmarr held it away from him.

"Whatever. I've heard about you lot, you appreciate a drink or two!" he said as he took another gulp of the whiskey, and then another.

Half an hour passed as Dietmarr continued to take a friendly helping from the bottle at regular intervals. Henry continued to look at him, sitting well back in his seat as the plane went through turbulence, much to the discomfort of Dietmarr who was sweating profusely.

"Don't show me up Dietmarr! Stop drinking!" Henry was getting rather desperate with his pleas now as Dietmarr continued to knock back the alcohol.

"I need it to combat my fear!" said Dietmarr defensively, taking larger helpings from the bottle. Henry could see that nearly half the bottle had been downed.

"You've had half a bottle in about an hour! That's enough!" shouted Henry imploringly, as the maid looked over with a concerned look on her face. Dietmarr was now downing the contents of the bottle with alarming ease, before Henry jumped up from his seat, despite the plane shaking, and snatched the bottle from his hand, passing it to the maid.

"Lock that up", he said as the maid nodded and held it in her hands.

"Spoil sport", slurred Dietmarr as he slouched into his seat.

"You need to sober up, we've got less than an hour until we land!" hissed Henry angrily. "Maid, can I have some water over here please?"

The maid, looking nervous in her own seat looked reluctant to help as she gestured towards the shaking cabin.

"I would highly recommend that you sit down sir, we are going through some damaging turbulence." The maid looked as scared as Dietmarr, who was shaking as he looked out of the window. Night had fallen as the rain battered the windows. The plane shook and took occasional drops, causing Dietmarr to squeal like a hurt dog. After a short while, Dietmarr seemed to find the turbulence funny as the huge amount of whiskey began to take effect.

"Apologies for the lengthy turbulence there." The cheery yet slightly shaky voice of the pilot could be heard on the speakers once more. "We should arrive in London in about twenty minutes."

Henry looked at Dietmarr who was giggling at the maid who was trying to persuade him to drink some water.

"You have a cracking pair of tits if I may say so myself Ma'am!" said Dietmarr with a terrible slur as the maid jumped up alarmed and went to sit back in her seat looking unimpressed.

Henry had his head in his hands as the plane began to descend.

"Arghhh we're crashing!" shouted Dietmarr, as he pulled at the chord below his seat, releasing a small rucksack on to the floor. Dietmarr attempted to jump to his feet but the maid came over and sat on his lap, causing Dietmarr to lean back with a drunken smile on his face.

"Oh hello there..." he said cheekily as the maid perched herself on his knee, looking bashful." Are you going to suck me off as we die?" The maid looked in disgust as Henry attempted to persuade Dietmarr to behave.

"I'm so, so sorry", said Henry apologetically as the plane landed bumpily on to English soil and ground to a halt. Dietmarr, looking unhappy as the maid quickly got off his lap, got to his feet and immediately fell forwards into Henry's lap, his head coming to rest on Henry's groin.

"Woah!" said Dietmarr, falling backwards. "Bet you'd have loved your cock in my mouth wouldn't you! Haha!" Henry, embarrassed, helped Dietmarr to his feet and put his arm round his neck. He could see Commander Pursey on the tarmac outside, side by side with Governor Michael Langley, all dressed up with countless badges on their chests.

As they both reached the doorway to leave the plane, Dietmarr proceeded to vomit all over Henry's arm. Disgusted, Henry looked up to see the faces of his superiors, both of whom looked astonished at the sight that had greeted them. Stumbling slightly down the steps, Henry and Dietmarr stepped out on to the tarmac. Henry let go of Dietmarr, who promptly fell to the floor, before getting back up swiftly and placing a hand to his forehead.

"SARGEANT!" he roared, saluting the Governor who stared back at him with daggers in his eyes. Henry had closed his eyes, dreading his Governor's response.

"Please tell me your name isn't Dietmarr Schultz and Irthing here has just picked a rat up off the street?" asked Langley strenuously.

"Dietmarr Schultz, reporting for duty Sarg!" slurred Dietmarr again, placing an open palm against his forehead once more.

"I am not a fucking Sergeant, I am a GENERAL!" bellowed Langley, slapping Dietmarr round the face, who fell on to the tarmac with a crack.

"What the fuck is this Irthing?!" demanded Langley, pointing at the groaning Dietmarr. Henry looked at him blankly.

"I have no idea Sir. He said he was scared of flying so downed most of a bottle of whiskey before we left. He carried on drinking on the plane, I could barely stop the guy." Henry spoke quickly, trying to exonerate himself of any blame as Commander Pursey merely stood tight-lipped.

"What a fucking disgrace. Private!" Langley shouted into thin air but a Private appeared at his side and saluted.

"Yes Sir!" shouted the private cordially.

"Take this waste of space and put him in a prison cell. Feed him nothing but water until he sobers up." Langley continued to stare at Henry, who was looking shiftily at the floor while Dietmarr had fallen asleep on the tarmac.

"Yes Sir!" shouted the private again, hoisting Dietmarr to his feet as he woke up and began to mumble inaudibly.

"This hasn't gone well so far has it..." said Commander Pursey in a disappointing tone.

"No Commander. It hasn't", said Henry regrettably as he began to follow Langley who had stormed off towards the building on the other side of the airfield, which housed MI6 operations. The three of them walked in complete silence to the building, with the sounds of Dietmarr being dragged to a separate room by the small private, who was struggling to contain him.

As the trio reached the building, Langley ushered both Commander Pursey and Henry inside to his office. Henry and Commander Pursey both sat in silence as Governor Langley was heard talking to another officer. Henry was dreading the dressing down he was about to receive from his Governor, looking across to Commander Pursey who simply looked back at him and shrugged. The door slammed as Langley strolled in.

"Start talking." Governor Langley stared at Henry disapprovingly who looked up tentatively from the floor.

"I didn't know anything about his problem with flying or the drinking until it was too late Governor, I'm sorry". Henry fell silent, with Governor Langley staring at him intently.

"Let me tell you something Irthing", began Governor Langley menacingly. "We know what Adolf Hitler is doing. He has the potential to blow Europe apart. YOU are our man in Germany. We trust you to do your job properly. NOT MAKE FRIENDS WITH FUCKING DRUNKS!"

Langley picked up a china plate sitting in front of him and threw it in the direction of Henry who ducked just in time, letting the plate smash into the wall behind him and break into hundreds of pieces.

"DO YOU HAVE ANY IDEA HOW UNPREDICTABLE THIS MAN IS?!" Langley voice boomed, causing the walls to shudder as if they were as scared as Henry.

"Yes sir, massively sir. I won't have anything more to do with him sir." Henry talked quickly and precisely, looking down to his feet, trying to avoid the ferocious glare of his Governor.

"Too fucking right you won't!" shouted Langley as he took his seat behind his desk. Commander Pursey sat in complete silence next to Henry, who continued to look at his perfectly polished black shoes.

"Why the hell are you befriending Germans in the first place?!" asked Langley, sounding more and more exasperated as the exchange went on.

"He had… Information", responded Henry, finally looking up to meet the gaze of Governor Langley. "He was telling me how much he hated the German establishment for betraying him last year and how much he wanted his cousin dead." Henry stopped to allow those final words to reach the ears of the baying Governor.

"His cousin?" asked Langley, turning to Commander Pursey who shrugged in response.

Henry took a deep breath.

"Dietmarr Schultz is Erich von Manstein's cousin. Von Manstein is dead. Schultz and I tortured him for information on the movements of Hitler before Dietmarr shot him in the head. He is buried in woodland just outside Berlin."

Langley sat mesmerised, his head bowed slightly at Henry's revelations. Commander Pursey looked confused.

"You mean to say this drunken lout shot dead his own cousin?" Commander Pursey questioned Henry, who simply nodded in response.

"That is correct", he said quietly.

Langley laughed slightly at the confirmation and folded his arms leaning back into his chair.

"The perfect person to work with. A man who tortures and kills his own relatives." Langley got up and walked over to a filing cabinet and produced a small file. On the front, the deep red letters of 'Strictly Private' stood out as Langley opened the folder.

"Dietmarr Schultz", he began, perusing the first page. "Estranged member of the Abwehr, found guilty of unprofessional behaviour in an official military trial and struck off indefinitely. Under no account is he to be accepted on to any mission due to unpredictable personality." Langley looked up at Henry, holding the piece of paper aloft.

"Didn't it cross your mind to check with us who Schultz was?"

Commander Pursey looked across at Henry. The pair had always got on, but the Commander could provide no defence as the Governor grilled Henry about his judgement.

"No sir", said Henry quietly as Langley threw his fist against the table.

"WHY NOT?!" he screamed, getting to his feet once more. "This is pure basics Irthing, PURE BASICS!"

"I trusted him", responded Henry defiantly but the Governor scoffed at the suggestion once more.

"Trusted him! Ha! For fuck sake Henry's he's a fucking Fritz! The enemy! How the fuck can you trust the enemy?!" Langley's face had become red in pure anger.

"I don't know", said Henry ashamedly, going back to staring at his boots.

Langley retook his seat once more, holding his hands as if he was in prayer.

"This is bullshit!" said Langley after a short pause. "I simply can't get my head around how a trained MI6 agent can trust a

German after a few days without any suspicion at all?"

"He spoke with great sincerity and I read his file", replied Henry softly but Langley laughed again.

"Oh that's alright then, he spoke well, he MUST BE FINE!" Langley strolled over to the drinks globe and opened a bottle of whiskey. Throwing the liquid into a glass, he downed it and sighed heavily. Henry remained rooted to his seat.

"You're a fucking idiot Irthing. He could go back and feed every little bit of intelligence we have on Hitler and blow our whole operation!" Langley poured himself another drink as Henry clenched his teeth.

"He won't", he stated quickly but Langley's temper once again caused him to shout in raised volumes.

"HOW DO YOU KNOW THAT?!" Langley screamed. "The guy just got off a plane, knowing he was meeting me completely rat-arsed and you say he can be trusted! Can you believe this Alfred?!" Langley threw his glass down on the table as the Commander merely nodded in approval, before throwing an apologetic look towards Henry.

"He's been through a lot Sir, I firmly believe he is now against Germany. He can be a great advantage to us!" Henry was growing impatient at Langley's insulting tirades but the Governor was not going to concede the argument.

"We are a hair's breadth away from another Great War and you want to throw our whole operation into the hands of a potential enemy? Are you completely deluded?!" Langley looked at Henry aghast.

"He is not the enemy! He is a good guy!" Henry got to his feet, growing in confidence and stature as the minutes ticked away.

"HE'S A FUCKING GERMAN!" yelled Langley. "HOW THE FUCK IS HE NOT THE ENEMY?!" Langley was becoming incredibly irate as the pair faced each other in the middle of the office. Commander Pursey merely sat completely silent, opting not to move at all.

"Dietmarr Schultz can be a great asset to our mission." Henry tried to remain calm, but his voice shook and his heart raced rapidly. "He knows things we don't. He knows the inner most workings of the German government and how to get around them. He can stop Adolf Hitler!"

Langley froze in the middle of the room.

"He can stop Adolf Hitler? Kid, you've just handed him Europe on a silver platter." Langley resumed his seat and grabbed his telephone, winding the numbers quickly whilst Henry remained standing, nearly out of breath as if he had gone fifteen rounds of a boxing bout.

"Smith, instruct Pooley to terrorise our drunk guest. Lock him up indefinitely. He's dangerous." With that, he threw the phone down and stared menacingly at Henry, who reacted angrily to Langley's words.

"You can't lock him up! He got drunk, so what! Everyone makes mistakes!" Henry pleaded with Langley to change his mind but Langley was having none of it.

"MI6 is NOT everyone", he said. "MI6 do NOT make mistakes." Langley walked back across to the filing cabinet, aiming to throw Dietmarr's file on top of it, but Henry strolled over to it and grabbed it out of his hand.

"This man!" Henry stated, pointing to the sombre looking photograph of a clean-shaven Dietmarr, "Can stop Adolf Hitler!" Langley turned his back on Henry and walked back to his desk. "This man can kill that beast and without him, the job will be ten times harder! THIS MAN will save Europe!" Henry slapped the file back on to Langley's desk who simply laughed.

"I think you've lost your mind, Irthing", said Langley quietly as Commander Pursey looked on intently. "I cannot understand how you can trust a man who, just over a decade ago, probably fought against us in the Great War. What the hell is going through your mind?"

"He's changed! He's been betrayed and betrayal hurts Governor!" implored Henry, who remained standing and shaking. "Do you have any idea what it's like to be betrayed by your own family?!"

Langley froze once more, staring down at the file on his desk.

"Don't you DARE emotionally blackmail me, Irthing. I was in the trenches on the Western Front for nearly TWO DAMNED YEARS fighting the very people you want to invite back into our country! I will not allow it!" Langley was shaking with rage as his fists clenched on his desk.

"Swallow your pride and do what is best for this country Sir", said Henry calmly but Langley's rage was uncontrollable.

"HOW DARE YOU TELL ME TO SWALLOW MY PRIDE!" Langley tore off the medals on his chest and threw them at Henry who ducked out of the way. "That's my pride! Those medals! I EARNT THOSE MEDALS!" Langley got up and flew across the room to recover his pride and glory but Henry continued to goad him.

"Your blatant nationalistic ways have blinded you to the best option, sir." Henry knew coercing his boss would surely lose him his job, but he had gone too far this time.

"You piece of scum... You FUCKING TRAITOR!" shouted Langley. "Why are you so obsessed with this German low life you shit?!"

"BECAUSE I'M IN LOVE WITH HIM!"

Time froze. Henry was glued to the spot, attempting to summarise the effects of what he had just said, but his brain was blank, frozen with the room. Governor Langley was standing, staring at Henry with shock in his eyes, his mouth hanging open slightly. Commander Pursey had turned slowly in his chair to confront Henry, whose breathing was uncontrollably fast. The silence was deafening. It was Commander Pursey who broke it.

"Excuse me?" he queried, raising his eyebrow. Langley looked perilously at Henry, who shuffled slightly on the spot.

"Henry?"

Henry stood with his arms behind his back, shuffling on the spot and staring at the floor. He could feel the glare of Governor Langley's eyes burning into his skull. Henry slowly raised his head, and looked straight at his boss.

"I'm so obsessed with him... Because I'm in love with him..." Henry repeated, a tear falling on to his cheek. He turned around and walked out of the room, leaving Governor Langley and Commander Pursey standing in shocked silence.

He walked through the entrance hall and out into the cold air, allowing more tears to run down his cheeks. Henry's career as an agent was over.

Henry could not walk very far before he sank to the floor in floods of tears. His homosexuality had played on his mind ever since he could remember. The Cambridge days were full of hiding and lying. The amount of times he had to fend off questions from his doting Mother about potential girlfriends left Henry feeling physically sick. He had not told a single soul about his ways. Henry had worked so hard on his studies and his career to quash these feelings, but in the end, they were to be his downfall.

Wiping away the tears from his face, he followed the directions to the prison quarter. Maybe he could continue the mission to eliminate Hitler without official guidance. His anger for Dietmarr's behaviour was cancelled out by how much he cared for the ex-German agent. The walk to the prison quarters allowed Henry to gather his thoughts as he considered a strategy to release his friend.

Walking in through the metal gates, he sidled up to the reception where a suited gentlemen sat, looking thoroughly bored and reading a newspaper.

"Yes?" the man said, without looking up.

"I'm looking for the manager. I've been sent from Governor Langley." Henry said as cordially as his wobbling voice would allow.

"Through the doors, his office is on the left", the receptionist said, continuing to peruse his newspaper.

"Thank you", said Henry politely, as he took the key from the receptionist's hand and opened the main doors before throwing the keys back behind the desk. Henry was greeted with a long, snaking corridor with huge metal doors leading to individual prison cells. Each one had a name on them, as Henry walked slowly down the corridor, looking at each label closely. About half way down, he noticed the name 'Shultz', spelt incorrectly. Walking back down the corridor, he knocked three times on the main office door.

"What?" A huge beast of a man opened the door, slapping a baton against the palm of his hand, looking with eyebrows raised at a slightly cowering Henry. "What do you want?" he asked again, in a low booming voice.

"I have a message from Governor Langley. I am Henry Irthing, MI6. He wants to speak to a Dietmarr Schultz?" Henry attempted to play dumb, pretending not to know who Dietmarr was.

"Fine", replied the prison manager, snatching a gigantic set of keys from off his desk and barging past Henry as he strode through the corridor. Henry skipped behind him, as if he was a small boy following his Father.

"Schultz!" shouted the manager in his brash voice. "You've been summoned!"

Dietmarr emerged from the cell, looking extremely rough. Henry put his finger to his lips, imploring Dietmarr to remain silent. The prison manager, looking round to Henry, guided Dietmarr out of his cell.

"You're not out of the woods!" he boomed again. "You're to follow this MI6 agent to the Governor!" He shoved Dietmarr in the direction of Henry who quickly turned around and marched towards the door, with Dietmarr in toe.

"What the fuck are you doing?" hissed Dietmarr as he jogged to keep up with Henry who was walking with the speed of a power walker.

"Shut up for a minute", whispered Henry back as the stomping of the prison manager rescinded as he walked back into his office.

"I'm getting you out. As soon as we get outside, we're to turn left and run. Got it?" Henry looked at Dietmarr who was holding his forehead and blinking constantly to try and clear his fuzzy head.

"Got it", he replied.

Ignoring the receptionist, who was still engrossed in his newspaper, Henry and Dietmarr skipped out of the building, turned left and ran. The landscape of the city lay on the horizon, as both Henry and Dietmarr sprinted away from the isolated buildings of MI6. Ahead of them lay a main road which led straight into the heart of London.

"Should take about an hour to reach civilisation", sighed Henry as they both ground to a halt as soon as they were out of sight of MI6. They set off along the side of the road, with cars flying past at breakneck speed to keep them company. The pair walked in silence before Dietmarr put a hand on Henry's shoulder.

"I'm so, so sorry", he said genuinely. His eyes were full of sorrow as Henry looked into them and smiled.

"We all make mistakes", he replied continuing to step along the bumpy footpath. "Maybe this is for the best." He continued to walk, trying to hold back the tears as the realisation of what had just happened hit him. Despite being upset that his career was over, there was also a slight tinge of relief. He had opened up about his deepest secret. For the first time ever, he had not lied about himself. His career in official espionage was finished yet he felt a pang of pride at how he had finished it.

"Did you get into much trouble?" asked Dietmarr, oblivious to the events that had taken place in Langley's office.

"He was furious", replied Henry continuing to focus ahead on the journey. "He was furious that you disrespected him, furious that you were drunk and furious at me for working with the enemy." Dietmarr's face painted a picture of sorrow and disappointment as he apologised profusely again.

"Stop apologising, it was my own fault. We got into an argument and... Things were said." Henry stopped short of revealing the real reason why he had walked out, but Dietmarr kept plying the questions.

"You've been sacked?" Dietmarr stopped in his tracks.

"I suppose so..." Henry had merely presumed he would be fired as it was against the law to be a homosexual. MI6 could not be seen to be working with homosexuals. He did not let Dietmarr know this fact however, as Dietmarr started to apologise again.

"It's all my fault. If I hadn't of gotten so fucking smashed, none of this would have happened."

"Don't worry about it, it was on the cards anyway", lied Henry as the pair continued to make slow progress along the pathway. "We look to the future, always".

It took them nearly two hours to navigate the tricky pathways and routes towards the city, but as they walked along the river bank, it dawned on Henry that they didn't have a plan.

"What are we going to do?" Dietmarr asked, taking the words out of Henry's mouth. It was true, they had nowhere to go and with no tools to use from MI6, they were stranded.

"Let's sit down somewhere and just take stock of things", suggested Henry as they took a seat next to the River Thames. The city looked so large and grand, with the Tower of London dwarfing the houses of Parliament. The river wound its way into the distance, with boats drifting up and down.

"London is a beautiful city", said Dietmarr quietly, staring into the distance. They both sat in silence, taking in the city skyline. Henry was determined to keep the mission alive, albeit without the help of MI6 and was thinking of ways they could get back to Berlin with a chance of defeating Hitler. Staring into the murky waters of the river, Henry's mind went back to the days he used to spend with his Grandfather, touring the countrysides of Surrey, shooting pheasant.

"I've got it!" shouted Henry triumphantly, causing Dietmarr to jump out of his daydream.

"I used to go shooting with my Grandfather around these parts. He lives in the city now. I wonder if he still has his long-range sniper rifle..." Henry cracked a smile as he remembered the skill at which his Granddad Joe shot birds out of the sky from a great distance. "Come on!"

He helped Dietmarr to his feet as Henry ran along the edge of the river and up on to the bridge. He sprinted along it, to the surprise of Dietmarr who kept shouting for Henry to slow down. A wave of excitement had spread over Henry. He had not seen his Grandfather in years, as he was always too busy with work to spend some quality time with him. He still knew the exact house at which he resided though. A steep mansion house, bang in the middle of the city. Granddad Joe had always preferred the hustle and bustle of city life since he had moved from the calm and collected world of the countryside.

Henry continued to run through the streets of London, avoiding the calls of market traders to stop and take a look at their goods. Dietmarr ran behind him, breathing heavily and holding a stitch on the left side of his stomach. After a short while, Henry stopped, staring up at a grand looking house on the outskirts of Westminster. Waiting for Dietmarr to turn the corner on to the street, completely out of breath, seemed to take an eternity as Henry's excitement to reunite with his Grandfather reached fever pitch.

"Come on, hurry up man!" shouted Henry as Dietmarr slouched to a stop, doubled over in pain and holding his stitch.

"What was the rush?" breathed Dietmarr as Henry walked up the steps to the front door of the great house. A golden door knocker sat in the middle of the large black door, that had engravings dug into its wood. Taking a deep breath, he knocked three times on the door.

Henry could still hear the deep panting of Dietmarr, stood slightly behind him as he waited for the door to open. He was about to knock again before the door slowly opened ajar. An elderly man, walking stick in hand and his spectacles hanging from a chain around his neck stood before him. He looked extremely tired and ill, crouched over his stick, almost as if he would fall flat on his face without it. His medals, gained during countless years of active service, sat proudly on his breast and a black bowler hat cast his ageing face into shadow.

Henry stood proudly before him.
"Hello Grandad."

6.

Joe Irthing stood in shock before his grandson. He had not clapped eyes on him for nearly twenty years, as his career and Henry's education did not allow them to meet at all. Taking his spectacles and placing them on his nose, a tear slowly trickled down his cheek.

"Henry?" he asked, almost pleading for confirmation before Henry embraced him, wiping away a tear of his own.

"It's so good to see you Grandad!" said Henry excitedly, as Dietmarr merely stood behind them looking slightly sheepish.

"Come in son, come in!" Joe pushed Henry indoors, followed swiftly by Dietmarr who nodded to Joe, who simply nodded back in response. "Oh, what a day this is!" said Joe in great delight as he embraced his grandson once more, a beaming smile spread across his face.

"Grandad, this is Dietmarr. Dietmarr, meet my Grandad Joe!" Joe looked slightly bemused by the introduction, just as Brock had back at the motel in Berlin.

"You're German?" asked Joe reluctantly, but Dietmarr laughed at his insecurity.

"Don't worry sir, I'm an estranged German agent, working for Britain." Henry smiled at his partner's quick thinking.

"Ahh a double agent!" Joe waltzed towards the kitchen with the speed his years usually defied. "A very brave soul you are!" Dietmarr looked a little embarrassed at the welcome but thanked Joe for his words. Henry shrugged happily as the pair settled down into the deep black chairs in Joe's living room.

A short while later, Joe walked back in holding a huge tray of tea and biscuits at which Dietmarr thrust himself lavishly, wolfing them down as quickly as his hands would let him. Joe looked at him confused but allowed Dietmarr to consume the majority of his offerings as he took a seat of his own.

"So lad! What have you been up to?"

Dietmarr looked up from the plate and stared at Henry, who took his time over his answer. He didn't want to tell his grandfather he'd been effectively sacked from his job after not seeing him for twenty years.

"I've been working for the secret services", said Henry as Dietmarr continued to scoff at the biscuits in front of him.

"Well I never!" exclaimed Joe in surprise. "And you've survived for this long!" He laughed at his own joke and Dietmarr joined him with a mouthful of biscuit spraying on to the floor as he did. Joe Irthing was always the clown of the family, cracking jokes at family occasions and playing tricks on his many children. He had picked up the nickname 'Joker Joe' during his times with the Forces and for good reason.

"Whereabouts have you been then?" Joe was genuinely interested in his grandson's career, as he leaned forwards to listen to the answer. Henry smiled at the eagerness of his grandfather's questions.

"Oh, all over", he replied happily. "America, Asia, Southern Europe, the Caribbean, China. I started off in domestic security but I started working for MI6 about five years ago."

"Good lad! Doing your bit to keep this country safe! And what about you Dietmann? Why are you now British?"

Dietmarr looked up surprisingly, but Henry was quick to interject.

"It's Dietmarr, Grandad", he said, slightly embarrassed but Joe was quick to brush off his error.

"Oh whatever, close enough!" Joe said, as Henry threw an embarrassed look at Dietmarr who was laughing along with Joe.

"I've been called worse!" retorted Dietmarr cheerfully. "I used to work for the Abwehr but was made a scapegoat by them and they betrayed me, so fuck them."

There was a brief silence as Henry considered the use of bad language under his grandfather's roof. He had distinct memories of his grandmother severely objecting to the use of bad language in their house, but again, Joe shrugged it off.

"You've joined the better side!" exclaimed Joe without any hint of sarcasm. The trio sat in silence considering the event, as Dietmarr continued to help himself to the pile of biscuits in front of him. Joe continued to quiz Henry.

"So, tell me about what you're up to at the moment!" He leaned forwards expectedly but Henry sighed.

"I can't tell you Grandad, sorry". He felt slightly guilty at not telling his own family his business, but it was a strict rule he had maintained for the entirety of his career.

"Oh come on son! Not even to your old Grandad!" Henry shook

his head, as Joe laughed again, but slightly disappointingly. "Ahh well, one day I'll find out". Henry nodded. Dietmarr was polishing off the last of the biscuits, despite Henry and Joe not having a single one.

"But Grandad... there is a reason we are here". Henry was keen not to hang around for too long. "I... we... need your help". He nodded across to Dietmarr who simply smiled along.

"What can I do for you son?" Joe seemed eager to help in any way he could.

"You remember those country days, shooting pheasant from the skies of Dorset?" asked Henry enthusiastically.

"Ahh yes", began Joe, his eyes rising to the sky as he recalled his country upbringing. "We had some cracking days out in the fields didn't we son!" Henry nodded again.

"Do you still have that rifle?" Henry questioned curiously as Joe looked at him bewilderingly.

"Yes, yes I do. Up in the attic. It hasn't been used in about thirty years though lad!"

Henry looked on, hoping his grandfather would merely get up and go and get it, but he didn't move.

"Does it still work?" asked Henry.

"I should think so yes. Why?" Joe looked confused. Henry realised he would have to tell his grandfather about the events of the day.

"Granddad, I no longer work for MI6. I got released of my duties." Henry looked over to Dietmarr, who was staring at the floor in guilt. "I got released today."

There was another silence. Joe looked onwards, still confused by what his grandson was asking from him. Henry continued to look expectedly, hoping for a positive answer.

"You want me to give you the gun?" asked Joe quietly.

"I still wish to complete the mission we were given", said Henry.

Another silence washed over the living room as the tension rose. Henry realised what he was asking. After twenty years of nothing, he had suddenly converged on his grandfather to ask for a gun. He could not of course, ask for one from MI6.

"I will give you the gun on one condition", said Joe after a lengthy pause. "You tell me what you are doing with it."

Henry had suspected he would be asked that question. He had no choice but to let his grandfather in on the mission.

"Our mission is to eliminate Adolf Hitler." Dietmarr said simply before Henry could get a word in, causing Joe to raise his eyebrows once more.

"What's he done?" Joe was obviously unaware of the impending German plans to invade Europe.

Dietmarr once again was quick to respond.

"Adolf Hitler is planning to become the President of Germany and then use his popularity to invade Europe. Our intelligence suggest he has a whole army of weaponry and personnel, hell bent on causing torture."

Dietmarr was ploughing ahead with the explanation, obviously eager to leave the house now that he had got some food. However, Joe's questioning had not ended.

"And you think you're going to take him out on your own? It sounds like a suicide mission to me..." Joe got up from his chair with the expected creak that his old age would suggest and wandered over to a glass cabinet that held a number of photographs and mementos. Opening the cabinet, allowing a huge cloud of dust into the room, he took out a wooden urn and placed it on to the coffee table in the middle of the room. There was an eerie silence as Joe retook his seat.

"These are the ashes of my best friend. Henry Bollinger. You're named after this man lad."

Henry stared at the urn, almost expecting Henry to burst out from it. But it lay there motionless as Joe continued his story.

"We were just kids. Called up to the British Army at 17, to fight Russia in one of the most pointless conflicts of all time. Fighting over a God that doesn't exist, my friend." Joe looked at Dietmarr who looked solemnly towards the urn.

"We were ordered by an idiot called Lord Raglan to help the French capture Sevastopol. Within days, we were fighting on pools of blood. My comrades fell all around me, but Henry and I continued to plough through it all. We were so close..."

A tear dropped from Joe's cheek on to the carpet as he continued to stare at the urn.

"We were probably two out of about fifty soldiers who were still alive. Camped up in a horrible cave as the Russian army advanced. Henry..." Joe stopped in his tracks, struggling to recreate the memories of the day his friend died.

"Henry ran out into the onslaught. He shouted at us. "I'm going for glory!" He ran from the cave and all we could hear was a huge bang. The Russians had these modern shells. All we could see was bits of Henry..."

Joe was crying now, as his grandson got up to console him. Dietmarr continued to stare into the depths of the urn that contained so much history. Wiping away the tears, Joe continued.

"My point lad. Don't throw your life away going for glory. We managed to escape into another cave that the Russians simply walked past. Henry would still have been with us... I told your Father all about him and he decided you were worthy of his name."

Henry looked at the urn once more, with a sense of pride. The man he was named after sounded as if he resembled him. Proud, brave and up for a fight.

"Grandad, we have to do this. We have to stop Adolf Hitler."

Henry hugged his grandad as he went to put Henry's urn back into the glass cabinet.

"There is no one else who is in a better position than us two." Henry held his arm out to Dietmarr who nodded. Joe was still wiping tears away from his face.

"You do what you have to do son". Joe stood with his hand still holding the brass handle to the cabinet. After another pause, he turned round, not looking at either Henry or Dietmarr as he disappeared into the room next door. Henry stared into the dusty cabinet, watching the wooden urn, imagining the man inside.

It was a whole ten minutes until Joe re-emerged holding a long, thin weapon. The lights bounced off its glistening frame and the bayonet attached to the front looked menacing and deathly sharp. Joe was also holding a silver box that he placed on to the table next to the rifle. He opened the box to reveal a shining stripper clip of bullets, shaped like missiles. Also in the box was a telescopic sight, looking lonely and forlorn as if it belonged in Joe's dusty cabinet. Joe went to fit the sight on to the gun, but Dietmarr had jumped to his feet as he inspected the gun.

"This is a Gewehr 98!" he implored excitedly, picking up the gun and pointing it towards a fake target. "Where on Earth did you get this?"

"The Great War", responded Joe as he snatched the gun back

from Dietmarr's nose. "Our army gained lots of them throughout the years as German blood spilled." Dietmarr consoled himself slightly, wincing at the thought. The tension between Joe and Dietmarr was palpable as Henry attempted to cool the situation.

"It's an extraordinary piece of kit, Grandad. May I?"

"Of course son", replied Joe, finally getting round to fixing the telescopic sight on to the top of the rifle. Henry took it from his firm grasp and pointed it towards Dietmarr's forehead, playfully making the sound of gunfire as if he was shooting at his friend.

"This is perfect", whispered Henry menacingly, adjusting the sight. "Don't you think Dietmarr?"

Dietmarr was still staring at Joe, clearly annoyed at the old man's joy of killing his native people.

"Yes Henry... It is..." he said, not taking his eyes off Joe whose face had a slight smile on it, as if he was taking great pleasure from intimidating a German in his living room. Henry had become oblivious to the tension as he set the gun back down on the table. Dietmarr instantly picked it up and copied Henry in playing with the sight, stroking his fingers along the thin barrel.

"Thank you very much Grandad", said Henry, giving him another loving hug. "However, I need to ask one more favour." Henry looked up into his grandfather's eyes, feeling slightly guilty at asking for more from his long lost relative.

"Anything my boy, anything." Joe sat down in his chair once more, lighting a thick cigar and taking a huge puff of it, exhaling a monumental cloud of smoke into the air.

"We have no way of getting back to Germany. Can I borrow a car?" Henry's voice cracked slightly as his guilt plagued him.

"No problem son, take my Nash. I don't drive it anyway, I don't even know why I bought it!" laughed Joe, as he got to his feet once more. He picked up the rifle with its accompanying box, walked over to the doorway and gestured for the pair to follow him. He opened the large front door to reveal the street outside.

On the road sat a lavish bright red car, with a beautifully sculpted bodywork and gigantic wheels propping it up. The curves flowed exquisitely along the body of the vehicle, as the sunshine bounced off its sleek paint. The sheer size of the machine dominated the scene with people walking past slowly to steal a look inside at the elegant interior. The dashboard had an alluringly varnished wooden texture, with the black leather seats filling most of the inside. Henry and Dietmarr stood in awe as Joe walked to open the door.

"I understand you have a job to do", he said as he guided Henry to the driver's seat. "If I can help you in any way, then my job as a grandfather will be done." He opened the back door and placed the rifle and the box inside.

"Thank you Grandad", said Henry, climbing into the driver's seat. "You're a life saver!" Dietmarr got in beside him, as Joe patted his grandson on the back and walked round the back of the Nash to start it up. Cranking the handle as hard as he could, almost breaking his brittle bones in the process, the engine roared into action, with Henry revving the engine with an almighty rumble.

Pulling out into the middle of the empty road, Henry waved goodbye to his grandfather, who waved them both into the distance. It would be the last time Henry would ever see him.

...

It was a long drive to Germany. The car rumbled along the bumpy roads of the English countryside as the pair headed to the south coast, largely in silence as Henry took stock of the day's events. Dietmarr had fallen asleep next to him, his loud snoring taking an annoying pattern leading Henry to jolt him awake countless times. The rifle in the back lay motionless, as Henry continued to throw a few nervous glances at it. If they could kill Hitler, without the help of MI6, they would be saving the whole of Europe. Henry was extremely sure of it, despite his ex-boss' reservations.

The mid afternoon sun shone low as the car drifted along the south coast towards the ferry port. Dietmarr was still asleep, still suffering from the alcohol he had consumed on the flight. Henry felt exhausted from the long day but continued onwards, shielding his eyes from the descending sun.

It was dusk as they reached the ferry port and Henry shook Dietmarr awake once more. Dietmarr muttered something inaudible as he came round, looking slightly shocked at the descending darkness in front of him. The car jumped over the hurdles as it boarded the ferry, with Henry parking it in the largely vacant hold deep below the ship's deck.

"Come on, we've only got ten minutes before the ferry leaves!" Henry quickly snatched his bag and the rifle as Dietmarr slowly gathered himself and followed suit. They ran upstairs, straight past the guard who was fast asleep and into the main section of the ferry. They had made it.

Henry and Dietmarr found themselves in the hub of the ferry, surrounded by hundreds of busy looking people. Businessmen with top hats and ladies with flowing dresses were being pampered by the snobbish looking waiters who were carrying delicate glasses of wine on silver platters.

"Come on, over here", said Henry, directing his friend to the corner of the room. "We could do with keeping a low profile."

They both sunk into the cosy seats provided, as Henry placed the rifle under the chair and stared out of the window. The ferry was just disembarking, causing it to sway from side to side, the engine roaring as it did so.

"Champagne?"

A waiter, dressed in a gold waistcoat and striped trousers was holding out a silver platter. Henry politely declined, but Dietmarr was quick to pounce and took two glasses, downing both of them in quick succession. He let out a sigh of relief.

"Don't have anymore!" said Henry coldly, as Dietmarr began to get to his feet. "You've caused enough trouble with your dirty habits as it is."

Dietmarr paused slightly, but relented and sat back down.

"Sorry", he said quietly, as if he had been told off by his father. The pair sat in silence as the ferry gathered momentum, with the coastline drifting out of view...

"Can I tell you something?" Dietmarr's eyes were glistening and teary as he looked at Henry, hoping for a positive response.

"Of course you can", replied Henry, sitting up in his seat and listening intently.

"This is really, really hard for me to say so please hear me out." Dietmarr's voice shook as he began his confession. "You know how people get married and have kids and they settle into that family life? I'm jealous of them..."

Henry's eyes narrowed, eliminating possible meanings for this conversation.

"Why so?" he asked intently.

"I don't know whether I should say...", said Dietmarr, wiping tears from his cheeks.

"Go on. I won't judge you, whatever it is...", said Henry, leaning forwards.

"I'm jealous of them because I will never be in that position", said Dietmarr, who was sobbing so loudly that he was drawing attention from nearby passengers.

"Why?" asked Henry, shaking a little himself as he anticipated the answer.

"Because I'm queer."

Henry's heart was racing as Dietmarr continued to cry. He wasn't the only one. The man he loved was just like him. Henry was trying to keep his broad smile concealed but was failing badly as he jumped up and kissed his friend.

...

"Oi! Henry! Wake up!"

Dietmarr was shaking Henry awake, with the sounds of footsteps clambering towards the deck all around him. The ferry had docked at its destination, as the clear night sky showed off countless constellations.

"Come on, we've got to go!" implored Dietmarr as Henry rubbed his eyes and got to his feet. The pair joined the back of the queues, attempting not to draw attention to the gun. Dietmarr grabbed a final glass of champagne and drank it quickly, much to the disgust of Henry who cast him a fiery look.

As soon as they had escaped the long snake of people clambering to get off the ferry, the pair found their bright red car and drove off on to the French roads. Another long drive was to greet the pair as they made their way back to Berlin.

Just half an hour into the journey, Dietmarr delved into his backpack with a longing smile on his face, producing two bottles of fine French wine from its depths.

"What the fuck?!" shouted Henry irately. "You stole wine?!"

Dietmarr laughed at his friend's anger.

"Come on! Haven't you stolen anything from a hotel in your life! It's gotta be done!" He dived back into his bag and produced a wooden corkscrew and set to work on opening the first bottle. It didn't take him long, as the top of the bottle flew against the windscreen before Dietmarr took a large gulp of the liquid.

"You're not gonna spend the whole of this journey pissed off your nut!" shouted Henry, snatching the bottle from Dietmarr's grasp. He opened the window and proceeded to throw the bottle out of it, much to Dietmarr's despair.

"WHY THE FUCK DID YOU DO THAT?!" shouted Dietmarr, punching Henry repeatedly on the arm.

"Because you've already lost me my job by being drunk today! Don't you think you owe me some peace and quiet?" Henry's anger was plain to see as Dietmarr sat back in his chair and looked forlornly out of the window.

"Sorry mate", whispered Dietmarr.

"It's alright, just don't piss me off anymore", replied Henry.

They drove in silence through France as the sun came up on another day. Henry was unbelievably tired but wanted to make it to the motel in good time. Dietmarr had fallen asleep once more.

It was only once they had crossed the border into Germany when Dietmarr stirred from his latest sleep.

"You look knackered..." he said as Henry battled to stay awake. "I can drive if you want?" offered Dietmarr but Henry was quick to knock him back.

"I don't trust you with my Granddad's car", said Henry quickly. Dietmarr opened his mouth to retort but chose against it as he turned his head towards the window once more.

It was a full five hours later that the town of Potsdam came into view. The pair had spent the majority of that time forging a plan for the execution of Hitler that would happen to take place the next day. Dietmarr had discovered that he was due to talk at the Alexanderplatz, in the heart of Berlin. They agreed on a suitable building to climb, opting to shoot from the rooftop, before escaping. It was a simple plan, but they both shared their nerves for the event with each other.

As Potsdam emerged on the horizon, Henry noticed the von Manstein cottage, looking lonely and battered yet dominating the scene below it. Pulling up outside the motel, Henry clambered out of the car and stretched his arms high into the air.

"Bye then."

Dietmarr had got out of the car and started to wander off.

"Where are you going?" asked Henry, oblivious to the fact that Dietmarr wasn't staying at the motel.

"To the compound, where else?" said Dietmarr, continuing to walk into the distance.

"Oh, come on, I'm sure Brock has a room for you in the motel!" implored Henry, but Dietmarr was having none of it.

"I'm okay, I want to be on my own. See you tomorrow." With that, he turned around and strolled off at a sprightly pace. Seizing the gun and the silver box out of the back seat, Henry sauntered up to the motel door, only for Brock to open the door for him.

"Henry!" he said enthusiastically. "How have you been son?" He welcomed him inside as he galloped to the kitchen to put the kettle on.

"Well, Brock, well, but if you don't mind I'll skip on the tea. I'm exhausted, I just need my bed." Henry yawned profusely.

"Of course, of course, your room has been untouched since you left!" added Brock, looking mystifyingly at the gun in Henry's hand.

"Don't worry, just MI6 stuff", added Henry, noticing the concerned look on Brock's face. He dragged himself up the winding staircase holding the gun tightly and collapsed on to his bed without undressing. He fell asleep almost instantly.

The sun was rising once more as Henry awoke, still clutching the rifle in his hands. The sun glistened off the top of the silver box, casting a blinding ray of light across the room. Henry took a few moments to reflect on the past few days before his mind jumped to Dietmarr, who was cold and alone in his compound outside Berlin. His reluctance to stay in the motel concerned Henry, but he still had complete confidence in his friend's ability to help in the mission. He looked down towards the rifle. The day of the operation had arrived.

"Morning lad!" said Brock jovially as Henry descended into the living room. "Good night's rest?" Brock walked in holding a tray of tea and toast which Henry began to devour. He had not eaten since he was sitting in his granddad's house in London.

"Yes thanks", spluttered Henry as he worked his way through his breakfast.

"Good lad", replied Brock, settling down to eat his own stack of toast.

The pair sat in silence, the sounds of the birds and the people outside walking to work the only noises in the air. Henry felt slightly nervous of what lay ahead, but he knew it had to be done. He had a solid plan in his head and knew the Nazi ideas for the day, with the help of Dietmarr's immaculate knowledge of German operations. Before long, it was time to go and Henry picked up his heavy backpack along with the gun inside its long, oak case.

"I may be a while again Brock", said Henry, his hand on the door knob. "If I'm not back inside a week, presume I'm dead." Henry said it without any sense of sarcasm as Brock's eyebrows raised in shock at the statement.

"Sounds ominous lad! Take care!" said Brock, in his unnaturally cheery tone, as he shook Henry's hand and waved him on his way. "It's been a pleasure meeting you!"

"Yeah alright, don't act like I'm dead already!" responded Henry, laughing. "Bye Brock. Thank you for your hospitality." With that, he took off down the road, towards the von Manstein cottage in the distance and on into the woods.

Whistling along as he walked, hoisting his hefty backpack higher on to his shoulders, he cast an eerie glance towards the cottage. It was still boarded up and looked as battered as ever. There was no sign of any human life inside.

Henry waltzed into the woods and on towards the compound. The birdsong accompanied him the majority of the way as he stumbled and strolled his way through the forest. As usual, it took a few hours to reach the now familiar turning to the compound, as the smoke drifting in the cold air signalled he was close.

"Henry!"

The voice sounded cheerful and slurred. Just as the compound came into view, an enthusiastic Dietmarr came bounding towards him, embracing him in a huge bear hug.   "Good morning sir! And how are we on this beautiful morning?!"

Henry pushed Dietmarr off him, watching him drop to the floor as he did so.

"Don't you dare tell me you've been drinking on today of all days..." warned Henry, but Dietmarr, climbing gingerly back on his feet merely scoffed at his suggestion.

"No, don't be silly Henry! I'm not drunk!" Dietmarr walked back to the gazebo, losing balance as he wobbled over stray branches.

"Yes you are!" shouted Henry, dumping his rucksack and the gun case on the floor next to his usual decapitated tree trunk. "You promised me you wouldn't drink anymore!" he shouted but Dietmarr was quick to rebuff the suggestion.

"No I didn't! You were just being a party pooper!" slurred Dietmarr, as he picked up a bottle of wine and took a huge swig from it.

"I can't believe this... Do you know what day it is today?!" said Henry angrily, but Dietmarr merely laughed.

"Tuesday?" he joked, but Henry, seething with anger, slapped him hard round the face, causing Dietmarr to fall over once again.

"OW!" screamed Dietmarr, holding his cheek dramatically, but Henry was busy scouring through the compound, trying to fish out alcohol. He found two empty vodka bottles but nothing else, as Dietmarr regained his footing once more and laughed at him.

"You won't find anything else! It's all gone! Haha!" Dietmarr sounded triumphant as Henry shook his head in disappointment.

"Right... Well, you're going to sober up before we leave for the city, but we need to get there for 11am!" Henry continued his search for full bottles, throwing the two empty ones into the trees. Ten minutes later, he discovered a third, full bottle and turned around in disgust.

"What the fuck is this?!" he shouted, but as he turned around he realised he was alone. "Dietmarr?" Henry looked around frantically for his friend, but he was quick to realise he was not there.

"DIETMARR?!" shouted Henry once more, but there was no response apart from the birds that fled from the branches in fright. Henry ran to the edge of the clearing, looking left and right for any signs of life, but he was completely alone in the woods. Dietmarr had vanished.

Running quickly back to the compound, he picked up the third empty vodka bottle and threw it with the other two into the forest. After a short while, he gave up looking for Dietmarr, deciding to complete the mission alone. He would probably find it easier without having to deal with his friend's drunken antics. Henry walked over to his tree trunk to pick up his rucksack and the gun case, before realising the case was gone. It didn't take long for Henry to realise where it was.

"No...", whispered Henry, slinging his bag on to his back and running as fast as he could in the direction of the city. It was extremely hard work, but he had to stop Dietmarr.

Sprinting through the forest, occasionally tripping over thick, loose branches, Henry continued to shout after Dietmarr, but with no response.

It took Henry an hour and a half to find himself overlooking the city, but there was still no sign of Dietmarr. Henry looked around frantically, hoping to see him close by, but there was no trace. He continued to run, towards the building that they had both agreed would be the location for the shooting. Henry careered through the streets, out of breath but barging the locals out of the way, desperately searching for any signs of his friend. He followed the increasing noise of crowds until, turning off the main road, he ran straight into the centre of the Alexanderplatz. Metal barriers had been erected and a huge crowd was assembled before a gigantic stage and a podium slap bang in the middle of it. Thousands of German flags were flying high and the deafening music burst through the air, with people cheering and belting out the national anthem. The massive clock on the tower overlooking the square said there were five minutes to go before Adolf Hitler would appear. Henry continued to barge through the crowds, to repeated cursing from the assembled people.

As he reached the edge of the hub of onlookers, Henry noticed Dietmarr, sprinting towards the building, holding the oak gun case. Continuing to barge the rest of the people out of the way, Henry ran after him, shouting his name to try and grab his attention, but to no avail.

"DIETMARR! STOP!" Henry shouted, beginning the long ascent up the building's staircase, but Dietmarr was not listening. A searing pain shot up Henry's spine, the result of hours of running with a weight on his back. He winced, but continued to climb, imploring Dietmarr to stop. Bursting through the door at the top of the building, Henry was greeted with Dietmarr, gun assembled and pointing towards the crowds below. They were cheering and applauding loudly, as Adolf Hitler appeared at the podium, urging the excitable crowds to calm down.

"Don't shoot, Dietmarr..." Henry urged, walking slowly towards him with his hand outstretched.

"Why not?" asked Dietmarr without turning round, his gaze fixed into the telescopic sights.

"Because you're drunk!" seethed Henry. "You can't fire a gun accurately when you're drunk!"

"You underestimate me, dear friend..." said Dietmarr carefully, the gun swaying slightly from side to side. Dietmarr's index finger hovered shakily over the trigger.

"You're shaking..." said Henry, getting nearer to Dietmarr who was still attempting to focus on his target.

"We have to kill this bastard, and I want to be the one to do it!" said Dietmarr angrily. "This country betrayed me and I want payback..." The gun continued to wobble as Henry reached Dietmarr and placed a hand on his shoulder.

"Come on mate, this is silly. You're in no state to fire this gun..." Henry's hand was also shaking as he tried to persuade Dietmarr to surrender the gun to him.

"Fuck off!" shouted Dietmarr, violently throwing Henry's hand off his shoulder. "I can do this!"

Adolf Hitler's voice was booming across the city, as he spoke about the pride of Germany and his dedication to the country. The crowds continued to cheer and applaud his every word. Dietmarr was back staring down the barrel of the gun, continuing to shake as he did so.

"Dietmarr..." said Henry cautiously, approaching him slowly once more. "You can't do this..." Henry placed his hand on Dietmarr's shoulder again, but Dietmarr screamed in anger.

"GET THE FUCK OFF ME!" he bellowed, attempting to throw Henry away once more. As he did so, he overbalanced and fell to the floor, letting the gun collapse to the ground. Both Henry and Dietmarr were sprawled on the concrete, equidistant from the gun that lay motionless. They both jumped up and dived for the weapon, both of whom getting a hand to it.

"Dietmarr! Don't be a prick! Get off!" shouted Henry, attempting to get Dietmarr to release his grip on the gun, but Dietmarr was not budging.

"Fuck off! I need to do this! I need to kill the bastard!" Dietmarr pulled the gun, dragging Henry towards him, as the pair grappled over the rifle. They were both knocked to the ground as they aggressively fought for possession. Henry punched Dietmarr in the chin, only for Dietmarr to retaliate with a kick to the groin. They both yelped in pain, but still had a hand each on the gun, fighting to coax the other to release their strong grips.

Adolf Hitler's voice still clapped through the air to increased cheering and hollering from the thousands in the crowd, completely unaware that two men were fighting over a gun on the rooftops above them. Henry got Dietmarr in a headlock, but Dietmarr was stubborn and refused to let go. Using all of his strength, Henry swung Dietmarr round by the neck and threw him across the rooftop, but as he did so, a huge bang swept across the morning sky.

Both Henry and Dietmarr stared at each other in shock, staring at a crater in the brickwork, caused by the rifle going off. A moment of brief silence that seemed to last an eternity was broken by screams and shouts from the crowds below. Henry looked over the top of the building to see thousands of faces looking up at him, pointing and screaming. Looking towards the now empty podium, Hitler had disappeared from view, hustled into the back of a car and driven off.

"Shit!" shouted Henry in desperation, as Dietmarr cradled his arm that had been broken from Henry's throw. "What the fuck are we going to do?!"

Henry stared at Dietmarr who merely shrugged as he winced in pain. As far as Henry could tell, they had two options. They could wait to be arrested or jump from the building. Looking over the edge once more, he looked down to the floor. There was no way he could survive a fall of that magnitude.

"WHAT THE FUCK WERE YOU THINKING?!" screamed Henry as Dietmarr got to his feet. "WHAT IS YOUR PROBLEM?!"

"My problem?!" roared Dietmarr in response. "You're a fucking animal! Why did you throw me across a rooftop?! I had a good shot!"

"YOU'RE FUCKING DRUNK!" screamed Henry as he jumped at Dietmarr again, but before he could do anything, the door to the rooftop tore open to reveal a whole host of police with guns pointing directly at them.

"Hands in the air!" said one of the policemen, as Henry raised his arms. Dietmarr followed suit, although he shrieked in pain as he raised his broken right arm.

"So, you think you could shoot our new Chancellor hey?" asked the policeman sarcastically, goading Henry, who remained silent. "Boys, cuff 'em. You're going to be locked away for a very... long... time..." The policeman elongated his speech, a smile of pure glee spread across his face. Another policeman cantered over to Henry and handcuffed his hands behind his back and pushed him in the direction of the door. Another policeman walked behind him, a gun pointing to his spine. Henry could hear the pained whining of his friend behind him as he was handcuffed too.

Walking down the staircase, three guns aimed at him, Henry knew he had blown it. He would be locked away in prison for many years and without the backing of his former employers, his mission will have failed. His mind went back to his Grandad's voice back in London.

"Don't throw your life away going for glory". Henry's mother had always said to respect his elders. Now he knew why.

7.

The policeman's breath was rasping against Henry's neck as he was shoved towards the door. The gathering of armed police kicked him on to the staircase as Henry stumbled down the steps. The shrieks and shouts of Dietmarr were muffled by a pair of guards who were struggling to contain the intoxicated former agent, fighting with all his might against the falcon-like grip of the officers.

    The pair were flanked by the rest as they were pushed towards the exit of the building and bundled into the back of jet black vans. Dietmarr continued to struggle, before being kicked in the shins and punched. His screams flooded the air as the crowds below looked around at the heavens, aghast at the proceedings. Henry was pensive, not responding to the successful cheers of the German guard. He sat on the floor and stared at it. His career had not included a failure, let alone one as huge as this. He had been dragged in by the love for his companion, without noticing that he was a loose cannon and a danger.

    The van sped off at tremendous speed, throwing the unsteady Dietmarr to the floor, banging his head against the wall of the van as he fell.

    "Fuck sake!" he shouted as he attempted to regain his feet, falling once more as the van tore around a tight corner. Henry was transfixed by the floor, still considering his fate.

    After ten minutes or so, which felt like a lifetime, the van screeched to a halt. The pitch black of the van filled with light as the door was flung open. Before Henry could react, a guard grabbed him by his jacket and threw him out on to the road. Henry landed face first, unable to hold out his hands as defence. His nose cracked against the concrete and blood began to seep out of it. Dietmarr landed next to him shortly after, with another shout of pain.

    "Get up!" shouted one of the officers, aiming a kick to the gut of Henry, whose breath left his body in the swish of a boot. He gingerly got to his feet and was led inside a grey building. Smoke billowed out of two huge chimneys with boisterous metal gates surrounding the compound. Men in orange jumpsuits were lifting weights in the courtyard, looking menacingly toward the pair. Guns were still pointed at the shoulder blades of Henry as he was summoned inside.

"Why are you kicking me?!" shouted Dietmarr as he was shoved in behind Henry. "What is this place?" He looked confused and dazed as they both walked inside to be greeted by what looked like an incredibly dirty, run down prison. Rats scuttled along the ground, searching for their next meal, with dirt scouring the walls and the floors. The guards spoke in a thick German accent to the monstrous man behind the desk, who looked at Dietmarr as if he was mess on the sole of his shoe. The guards were laughing, but Henry continued to stare into space, while Dietmarr wobbled on his feet, still extremely dazed.

"Move!" shouted one of the guards suddenly, shoving Henry towards the nearest cell. Dietmarr was being dragged off to a different part of the building as the door creaked open and Henry was propelled into the cell. He fell to the floor once more, still handcuffed, as the door was slammed shut.

Henry had landed in a small box room, with a disgusting sink kept secured to the wall by a single nail. A pile of dirty blankets lay on the floor. There was no bed, no window and the only light came from the tiny square in the cell door. A moment later, a bowl was shoved through a cat flap at the bottom, containing what looked like extremely loose porridge. Henry left it where it landed.

His thoughts had strayed back to the brief time at his grandfather's house. His warnings were repeating in his mind, wishing beyond all that he had been wise enough to listen to them. There was no denying he had fallen in love with Dietmarr, but to let it distract him from his job was amateur. He had paid the ultimate price.

Hours passed with no word from anyone. Henry tried to rest on the collection of blankets, but sleeping was impossible. Inmates were screaming, pleading for their release with the laughing of the guards echoing off the hollow walls. With no indicator as to the time of day, Henry decided to sit up and take stock. He had fought out of capture before, although not from a place as guarded as this, and he began to work on an escape route.

As time passed, the footsteps and noise of fellow inmates emerging from their cells for breakfast grew louder. Henry had been sat in the same position, on the cold hard concrete floor for many hours, as he was gestured to his feet by a weary looking guard. Henry strolled out of his cell, with a renewed confidence, instantly spotting Dietmarr across the hall and taking the spare seat beside him. Dietmarr did not acknowledge his appearance until Henry gave him a shove on the shoulder.

"Hungover I'm guessing…?" suggested Henry, as Dietmarr threw him a dirty look. He looked incredibly tired, a huge bruise on the side of his face distracting from the redness in his eyes. He didn't say a word, as disgruntled chefs threw down two bowls of the same sloppy porridge that had been bestowed upon them the night before. Dietmarr picked up his spoon and twirled the porridge before dropping it again.

"I fucked up didn't I?" asked Dietmarr, putting his head in his hands.

"We both did", said Henry fortuitously as he ate half a spoonful of his porridge and grimaced at its bitter taste.

…

Three weeks passed, as the snow fell on the concrete floor outside, before melting and being replaced by a fresh coat. Both Henry and Dietmarr had lost a lot of weight; Dietmarr resembling a skeleton as he emerged from his cell on the morning of the first day in December. He sat down in his usual spot next to the main exit into the courtyard, dumping his bowl of porridge on to the table. Those close by shot him a dirty look, before turning slowly back to their own porridge, wincing at every spoonful. Nothing about the prison had changed. It was still the same dank, grey four walls that had welcomed Henry and Dietmarr on the night of their arrest. The same faces sat forlorn at the dining tables, absent from those around them, self-absorbed in their own troubles.

Dietmarr, staring deep into the confines of his own bowl, jumped as Henry sat down opposite him with an unusual smile across his face.

"I have a plan."

Dietmarr stared up intently. His eyes were full of pain and guilt, as if the events of the last two months had eaten him up.

"We're going to have to bide our time, but I think we can get one of these morons to aid us…" said Henry, gesturing around the hall. There were roughly fifty other inmates, all cramped over their own bowls of slushy porridge. Some were stick thin and gaunt, clearly drained from a long stint in the prison, while others wore huge biceps and tattoos that would scare the devil. One of the huge men looked up from his bowl, noticing that Dietmarr was blankly staring at him, and jumped to his feet. He rushed over, intent on creating a situation. He shouted something in German at Dietmarr, who merely held his hands up weakly and responded. The heated conversation continued as everyone else watched on, but Dietmarr simply was not interested in being his opinionated self. Whatever he said caused the burly man to back down as he bundled his way back to his table.

"What on Earth was that about?" questioned Henry as Dietmarr turned to him, eyebrows raised.

"Have you never been in a prison before? Simply looking at someone could leave you a dead man. What was this plan of yours?"

Hearing that caused Henry to have second thoughts, but he ploughed on with his idea anyway, leading Dietmarr over to a quiet corner of the room. A couple of the inmates followed them with deep black eyes, but they both went generally unnoticed.

"As I was saying", whispered Henry, as Dietmarr listened in. "I think we can get one of this lot to help us. One of them must be in here indefinitely, with nothing to lose! We can promise them release for helping us or something."

Dietmarr didn't look convinced.

"And how are you going to ask one of them to help? And how are they going to help? And how are we getting out? Have you thought about this at all?"

"Well, have you got any ideas?!" seethed Henry as he gave Dietmarr a slight push against his chest. "Give me today to come up with a plan and I'll update you again by dinner."

By this time, the pair had caught the attention of one of the guards who immediately brandished a baton and threatened the pair back to their seats. The huge men, all clambered against a small table, threw their spoons into their empty bowls as they rose from their tiny chairs. They spoke in deep German accents, as one of them led the crowd through the doors into the gym area where they would begin their first weightlifting session of the day. The rest of the inmates sat weakly in their chairs, continuing to sift through their lukewarm porridge, looking bereft of life entirely. Guards lined the walls, staring intently upon their prey, jumping on anyone who was acting suspiciously.

The days were long and fruitless for the pair, the majority of the hours spent alone and freezing in their miniscule and grubby cells. The only entertainment was brutally provided by the guards who aimed their clubs at unsuspecting inmates for no reason whatsoever. The temperatures dropped harshly at night, with the pair only seeing each other at meal times.

"Have you come up with anything?" asked Henry at dinner one evening.

"Nope", replied Dietmarr simply, his eyes looking blankly past Henry and into the distance.

"We really need to come up with something fast. We could be in here for years otherwise", responded Henry as Dietmarr merely threw him a cold, sarcastic look. Henry rapped his fingernails against the marble table, racking his brains for an idea. Any idea. Before, for the first time since they'd arrived, another man set next to them.

"Evening gentlemen." The man had a thick Eastern European accent and was dressed head to toe in thick black fur. He looked gaunt and battered, cuts under his eyes still bleeding down on to his dirty cheeks.

"Evening..." said Henry reluctantly, while Dietmarr just nodded in the direction of the random inmate. "Can we help?" added Henry.

"As a matter of fact, yes", said the man, speaking in a surprisingly posh manner. He looked side to side, keeping his head down low as to not draw attention to himself. He gestured the pair in closer.

"I hear you two are after the establishment?" He nodded inquisitively, while Dietmarr's eyes switched focus from his ropy dinner to the stranger.

"How the fuck do you know that?" asked Dietmarr, as Henry put a finger to his lips, suggesting that Dietmarr quieten down.

"You don't need to know", replied the man. "All that you do need to know is that I can get you out." Henry and Dietmarr looked at each other, puzzled but intrigued all the same.

"I don't even know who you are. Why the fuck would you want to get us out?" asked Dietmarr. It was a fair question, as Henry looked back at the man, interested to hear his reply.

"Again. You do not need to know all of this. Meet me in the courtyard at 8am tomorrow morning and I will show you the plan", and with that he got up and slouched back to his cell, closely followed by a huge security guard, who was wielding his baton menacingly. Henry watched him closely, pondering the conversation, before Dietmarr interrupted.

"Well?" he asked. "What are we going to do?" Henry sat stirring his cold coffee as he contemplated, but he quickly came to a decision.

"Listen to what he says", said Henry simply as he got up and strolled confidently back to his cell and settled down into his assorted range of dirty blankets. Tomorrow was going to be make or break.

As breakfast drew to a close, Henry and Dietmarr, who were sat on opposite sides of the room, gently nodded to each other before walking towards the courtyard. Henry went first, idly strolling past the troll-like guard next to the door and out into the cool morning air. Dietmarr waited ten minutes before doing the same, unwilling to attract attention. As he walked through the door, he immediately noticed Henry and the Eastern European man who approached them the day before, sat on a bench away from the mobile gym that was scattered across the floor.

"So, who are you?" questioned Dietmarr, as he sat opposite the stranger, Henry looking up at him desperately, silently pleading with him not to be rude or abrasive.

"What?" asked Dietmarr impolitely as the stranger smiled, grimacing as he did so, clutching his cheek with his dirty, battered hands.

"My name is Dmitri Ologvi. I am in here for life for an assassination attempt on President Hindenburg."

Dietmarr, gazing idly across the courtyard, snapped back into focus upon learning the identity of the man who sat opposite him. Henry merely sat in his spot, blissfully unaware of the presence of Dmitri.

"YOU'RE Dmitri Ologvi?!" whispered Dietmarr under his breath, trying not to gain attention from the collection of inmates who had joined them to begin their morning workout. "You're the man I was hunting for… I spent three years looking for you!"

"I'm honoured", said Dmitri sniggering slightly as Dietmarr sat amazed opposite him.

"You look nothing like you used to...?" questioned Dietmarr. The pair sat staring at each other inquisitively before Dmitri broke the brief silence.

"This place doesn't exactly help in aiding appearances", he said sarcastically.

"You can say that again..." exclaimed Dietmarr surprisingly, before Henry interrupted.

"I hate to break up the friendly reunion but we've got a job to do here. We need to get out of this place so we can carry on completing our mission". His tone was matter of fact and to the point, but Dietmarr was still reeling from the news from the man who was helping to save them.

"All in good time", said Dmitri calmly as Henry arose loudly from his seat, attracting the notice of the guards before Dietmarr dragged him back down. Dmitri wore a sly smile across his face, enjoying his moment of fame.

"Listen here, you imbecile!" seethed Henry under his breath. "We are trying to stop a mass invasion here and all you can do is sit here and play games!"

Dmitri was unmoved by Henry's anger, still smiling along as he slowly got to his feet.

"I guess you don't want my help then", as he went to shift his feet over the wooden bench, but Dietmarr, also quick on his feet, dragged Dmitri back down in the same manner he had with Henry moments ago.

"What's your plan?" asked Dietmarr politely, eager to get down to business. Dmitri paused for a moment, glancing over his shoulder at the guard who was still peering suspiciously in their direction before retaking his seat.

"Tell me what you're planning first. Then I will tell you a route out of here", whispered Dmitri, the smile from his face replaced by the look of a man who knew what he was doing. Henry looked at Dietmarr, contemplating their options. They didn't have much choice but to tell Dmitri everything, or else face continued imprisonment. Henry placed his hands on the table, with an open gesture and began to tell Dmitri.

"We are working on eliminating Adolf Hitler. We

understand he has arrangements to conquer Europe once he gets into power, and with Hindenburg on his last legs, it's only a matter of time before he is. We need to get rid of him before he does." Henry spoke quickly and quietly, barely at an audible volume in fear of being caught, but Dmitri nodded along with interest.

"And how exactly are you planning on doing that?" Dmitri asked, eyebrow raised suspiciously.

"Why do you need to know that?" interrupted Dietmarr, attempting to whisper, but instead raising his voice slightly, once again making the guard's ears prick up in anticipation. Henry nodded in agreement.

"Just curious…" admitted Dmitri leaning back nonchalantly. Henry continued to talk, adamant that the information they needed would not be given to them unless Dmitri knew the whole story.

"We have a man on the outside who is willing to work with Hitler and feed us information about his whereabouts. From there, we will choose the right time to assassinate him."

"Come off it!" scoffed Dmitri. "You think Hitler is going to let anyone and everyone be that close to him? He's going to have every single man, woman and child near him checked out before they're even allowed in the same room as him!" Henry was nodding along in agreement.

"We know, which is why the man we have is already in."

Dmitri's eyes narrowed as he mulled over what he had been told. The threesome sat in silence for a few moments, contemplating their next steps, with Dietmarr staring intently at Dmitri. After what felt like hours, Dmitri leant in closer to Henry and Dietmarr.

"Once a month, all of the guards and their bosses have a meeting in the offices upstairs", he gestured slightly to the upper floors of the building where a few lights were spotted around dirty looking office windows. "For ten minutes, once a month, this courtyard is left completely empty."

Henry looked around, disbelieving at first, but noticed the high-rising fence intersected with barbed wire scaling the perimeter.

"And how exactly do we get over that?" Henry pointed behind Dmitri, who merely smiled and shook his head.

"You don't. Well, not unless you want to get electrocuted." He laughed nervously at his own joke. "Behind you, by the pile of weights in the corner, DON'T LOOK!" he seethed, as Dietmarr turned around, but he was stopped just in time by Henry who realised it would look suspicious.

Dmitri continued. "Under those weights is a hollow piece of Earth, covered with a sewer drain. It's disguised as electrical cables, but out there is a route to the other side of the wall. No one but me and the people who work here know about it."

"Wait, wait, wait" interrupted Henry. "If it's an escape route, then why haven't you used it?" Dietmarr looked at Dmitri, expecting him to slip up.

Dmitri smiled. "My situation is unique. I can either sit here and be alive, or escape and be killed."

"That's the same for all of us", added Dietmarr. "They're not going to keep us alive if we escape." Henry nodded once more in agreement.

Dmitri interrupted. "Like I say, my situation is unique. I have been sentenced to death for the attempted assassination of Hindenburg. I'm going to die anyway."

There was a moment of silent contemplation. Deep down Henry knew this was their only escape route, and with time not on their side, they had to act first.

"And when does this so-called meeting take place?" asked Henry.

Dmitri took a dusty pocket watch from the inside of his coat, swiping away the dirt from the screen as he squinted at its face. As he did so, an alarm went off across the prison, stopping as soon as it started. No one else reacted to its sound, apart from the guards who all strolled towards the courtyard entrance and disappeared from view.

"Now", said Dmitri as he let out a rasping laugh. Henry and Dietmarr jumped up from their seats, shocked from Dmitri's revelation.

"You have got to be fucking kidding me?!" shouted Henry, aware that there were no guards to apprehend him, despite some interesting looks from fellow inmates.

"You want us to escape NOW?!" added Dietmarr, as he fell to the floor scrambling to get out of his seat.

"Well, I couldn't give a shit!" said Dmitri gleefully. "But if you want to escape, I suggest you do it sooner rather than later."

Henry had already left his seat, running over to the group of around two-hundred weights and began to shift them to one side. The weight of the metal slabs made it tough for him to move them, but Dietmarr soon joined him. All of the inmates in the courtyard had stopped what they were doing, transfixed on the scene in front of them.

"You only have ten minutes!" exclaimed Dmitri delightfully, as Henry and Dietmarr continued to work through the tens of weights, shoving them to one side. A huge vent began to show underneath them, a big handle with an inch of snow on top of it signaling the potential way out. Dmitri hadn't moved as he laughed at the manic situation in front of him.

"Six minutes left…" added Dmitri, looking once more at his pocket watch. The huge pile of weights were now split evenly in two, as Henry and Dietmarr continued to shove the weights to one side. Sweat was dripping from Henry as he mustered all of his strength to lift some of the heavier weights and move them. The rest of the courtyard was frozen in silence, watching the pair frantically move the weights a matter of meters.

The minutes passed at a rate of knots, as Dmitri counted down from five. With two minutes remaining, Dietmarr picked up the last remaining couple of weights and threw them into the large pile that had congregated a few meters away. Henry set to work on the handle, which was incredibly stiff and would not move an inch. His hands were frozen and hurting from the incredible effort taken to move the weights, as he put all of his effort into budging the handle. Dmitri was still counting down…

"Are you going to just stand there or give me a hand?!" screamed Henry as he gestured Dietmarr to come and help. However, just as Dietmarr grabbed the handle, a voice from above split the morning air.

"Escape Alert! Sound the alarm!" It was a guard from the offices upstairs, who then turned away from the window. Within seconds, a shrill alarm sounded, almost bursting the eardrums of Henry and Dietmarr, who continued to pull the handle with all their might.

"Pull harder!" shouted Henry as Dietmarr's screams caused Dmitri to laugh with derision. The footsteps of running guards could be heard in the near distance, as Dietmarr pulled the handle even harder, finally releasing it and flying backwards with the force of opening the hatch.

"YES!" shouted Henry, as he jumped into the black hole that had appeared in the ground, swiftly followed by Dietmarr who brushed himself off and jumped in after Henry. Dietmarr closed the hatch behind him, catching a brief glimpse of the running guards as he closed the lid to the escape tunnel. The stench of where they had landed was horrible; the noise of running water was all they could hear as they made their way through the sewers as quickly as they could. Just as Henry began to run however, he was dragged into a small opening in the walls of the sewers, as he felt Dietmarr's hand cover his own. Before Henry could react, a small chink of light appeared from where the pair had just come from, as the guards descended into the sewer and set off in the opposite direction. Dietmarr held Henry against the wall until the final guard was out of earshot.

"That's probably the smartest thing you've done in weeks", said Henry as Dietmarr pushed him with a guilty smile across his face.

The pair dusted themselves down, Henry shaking his hands from the effort it took to move the weights above ground. They began to walk off in the opposite direction to the guards, dodging in and out of flowing water and the occasional rat.

"That was almost too easy…" said Dietmarr thoughtfully, but Henry ignored him as he contemplated their next move. With no MI6 support and Grandad Joe's car lost, they were stranded in the heart of Germany.

"Wait…" whispered Dietmarr. The pair froze as they stopped to listen to the deep German accents approaching. It sounded like two voices, getting closer and closer. It was only when they turned the corner that Dietmarr realised they were security guards from the prison above. They were stranded.

The security guards, laughing brazenly from their chat, looked up and instantly drew their pistols at the sight of Henry and Dietmarr, who stood helpless opposite them. One of the guards gestured towards Dietmarr, who replied in his native tongue. Henry stood perplexed. A heated conversation only ended when Dietmarr turned to Henry.

"Yeah, we're screwed", he said as he turned back towards the guards and continued to speak in German. Henry had no idea what was going on, before the other guard began to speak in broken English.

"You!" he shouted in his thick German accent. "Get on the ground!"

It took a few seconds for Henry to realise the guard was speaking to him, as he slowly dropped to his knees, his hands behind his head. Dietmarr remained standing, a strained look across his face; the guards still pointing their pistols towards them. The first guard, smiling menacingly, continued to speak in German to Dietmarr, and supposedly told him to get down to as Dietmarr joined Henry on his knees.

"And how are we going to get out of this one?" whispered Henry as Dietmarr looked ahead blankly.

"Nice knowing you", he said as he closed his eyes and muttered something to himself. In that time, the guards had sidled up to them both and stood behind them, the click of their pistols ringing loudly in their ears and echoing around the walls of the sewers.

"Can I just say something before you shoot my brains out?" asked Dietmarr hopefully. He got no response from the guards, but continued to talk anyway.

"You'd really find more satisfaction in a career as an accountant. All this killing people and pointing guns in their direction, it really doesn't suit you."

Henry's eyes turned towards Dietmarr in shock, wondering what he was trying to do.

"Stop delaying it, I'd rather get this over and done with", whispered Henry as he turned back to face ahead of him, but Dietmarr continued to talk.

"You could always join us? Hunt down and kill a monster of society! It's much more fun than chasing petty criminals and shooting them in the head for no reason." Dietmarr continued to speak at pace, the guards behind them listening on.

"What do you say? I can see you've got the skills for detection and you clearly know how to handle yourself!" Henry was unsure how much of Dietmarr's monologue the guards could understand, but as soon as Dietmarr finished, the guards both pulled back the barrels of their pistols, and aimed for the back of their heads. Henry could feel the tip of the gun touching his skull, as he closed his eyes and waited for the inevitable.

"I guess that's a no then…" sighed Dietmarr as he too looked ahead. "But wait!" he shouted once more, the noise of his cracked voice echoing off the concrete of the underground.

"Don't you want to take us back up to the prison? You can shoot us there, in front of everyone else! Show you're not messing around!"

The guard standing behind Dietmarr replied in a harsh German accent almost instantly, hitting Dietmarr in the head with his pistol. The weight of the hit forced Dietmarr to face forward once more.

"I guess that's a no then…" repeated Henry, his eyes remaining closed. The deep voice of the guard behind Henry began to count down.

"Drei..." The guard waited between each number, the tension rising between each rasping breath that Henry knew were about to be his last.

"Zwei…" Both guards once more drew back their barrels and placed the pistols against the heads of their respective targets.

"Eins."

Henry held his breath; the next noise he heard was going to be his last. A huge bang exploded around the walls of the chamber, followed swiftly by a second. For a brief moment, Henry expected blackness, but a splatter of blood dropped down the front of his shirt followed by the weight of the guard as he fell on top of him. Henry quickly threw him off, as Dietmarr did the same. They looked at each other in disbelief for a brief moment before turning behind them to see the silhouette of a man, gun drawn, his face clouded by the smoke drifting off the barrel of his pistol.

From behind the gun, an American accent emanated.

"Hey I was told I'd have to bail you out at some point, Irthing." The smoke began to disseminate as a face emerged from the darkness. Dressed in a smart suit and bright orange tie, sunglasses still on despite the murky atmosphere, he continued to walk towards both Henry and Dietmarr, who stared at him in a mixture of awe and appreciation. It was only when he was a matter of yards away; it became clear who their saviour was.

"Brock?!" Henry held out a hand to greet him, but he quickly withdrew it and jumped on Brock with a huge bear hug.

"Easy there lad, you'll break me in two!" said Brock cheerily as he also shook the hand of Dietmarr.

"How the hell did you know we were down here?" asked Henry, still aghast at the last minute rescue.

"Your bosses knew you were imprisoned here so I came to get you out. Looks like you were way ahead of me, but managed to get in and follow you down here." Brock smiled as Henry gave him another hug.

"Not bad for a motel owner", added Dietmarr. Brock smiled in defiance.

"I'm not a motel owner you bimb!" exclaimed Brock. "My job was to look out for Henry and if that meant disguising as a motel owner, then so be it."

"You mean Alfred didn't trust me?" asked Henry quietly.

"Spot on hey!" responded Brock. "Come on; let's get out of this stink hole!" With that, he kicked one of the dead guards and strolled off down the sewer. Henry remained motionless, staring into the space that Brock had left. It was Dietmarr that broke the silence.

"We have more in common than we realised…" he said, as he followed Brock's path down the sewer.

Brock's fast pace didn't allow for much thinking, as Henry and Dietmarr struggled their way through the path of streams and flurry of rodents. Neither of them had any idea where Brock was taking them, as the tunnels winded underground like the largest of snakes. Henry was still reeling from Brock's revelation about being his guardian. He could not understand why MI6 didn't trust him, although after the last week, maybe he did.

After an hour of struggling through it, a chink of light appeared ahead.

"Bloody finally…" sighed Henry, as he followed Brock and Dietmarr up the metal ladder and out into the cold winter air. They all clambered out on to a run-down looking street, laden with battered looking warehouses and all sorts of waste filling the snow-covered ground.

"Lovely…" sighed Henry once more, as Brock punched him on the arm in annoyance.

"A thank you would be nice!" said Brock jovially as Henry smiled at his own negativity.

"True. This is far better than the other place!"

They had emerged into a dingy town, overlooking a huge city that was laid out in the distance. Brock's suit was covered in dust as he attempted to brush himself down, dark sunglasses still masking his face.

"That's Berlin", said Dietmarr simply, looking out over the distance towards the towering city that lay before them.

"Your geography better than your espionage I see", joked Brock as he laughed at his own joke. Dietmarr threw Henry a seething look as he laughed along. "Come on! There's something I need to show you!"

Brock once more took the lead, power walking along the grubby street as Henry and Dietmarr straggled behind. They were heading in the opposite direction to the city; deeper into the countryside that surrounded the landscape. It was only after an hour of walking that Henry realised where they were going. Henry and Dietmarr still lagged behind Brock's immense pace as Henry filled him in on where they were going.

"You know where we are, right?" asked Henry tentatively. He received nothing but a blank stare from Dietmarr. "He knows we killed von Manstein…"

"So?" responded Dietmarr. Henry remained silent.

A short walk later, the clearing in the forest presented itself. Nothing had changed from where they had left it, the mound that housed the body of Erich von Manstein still looming large by the oak tree. Dietmarr looked away nervously, but Henry was paralysed by it. He only snapped out of his daze as Brock walked into his line of sight.

"What… Is this?" asked Brock, finally taking off his sunglasses and pointing to the mound of mud. Henry looked nervously at Dietmarr who continued to stare at his feet. Brock looked at them both, like an angry father telling off his two young children. The silence was deafening.

"Alright, looks like I'll just have to dig it up myself!" and with that, he began to claw at the pile of snow-covered mud, throwing large clumps behind him. He had only managed a few handfuls when Dietmarr spoke up.

"It's the body of my cousin", he said quietly. Brock stopped and looked up from his task.

"Your cousin?" he asked inquisitively. "Your cousin is Erich von Manstein?"

Henry quickly looked aghast.

"Why the fuck were you going to dig him up when you already knew who he was?" he asked frantically.

"Why, why, why have you killed von Manstein?!" he asked, completely ignoring Henry's question. Henry looked to Dietmarr.

"It was me", said Dietmarr. "I killed him." Another silence fell across the enclosure as Brock walked slowly over to Dietmarr. He only stopped as he was a foot away from him, before giving him an almighty slap across the face.

"Idiot", said Brock simply. As Dietmarr recovered from the shock of being slapped, Brock walked back towards the mound and continued to dig, using his huge hands to grab large amounts of mud.

"What the hell are you doing?" said Henry as he ran to stop Brock, but that didn't stop the American agent as he continued to scythe at the mud, creating large holes in the mound.

"I think you've done enough damage don't you?" asked Brock simply, holding out a dirt covered hand to stop Henry approaching him any further. "Besides, I have a plan…"

Henry stopped in his tracks, while Dietmarr had made his way to the collection of blankets and lay down, eager to ignore the scene in front of him.

"And what plan is that?" asked Henry eagerly, but Brock merely ignored him as he continued to dig. After what seemed like a lifetime, patches of red had begun to emerge, mixed in with the mud as the body of Erich von Manstein closely came into view.

Not so long after, the battered body of Hitler's old friend was lying on the ground in front of them. Dietmarr had not moved from his position under the gazebo, as Henry and Brock stared at the corpse. The bullet hole in his head was as clear as daylight, his skin ghostly white. His clothes were brown from the mud, tinged with the red of his blood. Henry shivered while staring at the icy body that lay in front of him, but Brock smiled from ear to ear.

"What exactly is so funny?" said Henry as Brock let out a nervous laugh.

"Look at his face", he said simply. Henry couldn't not look as he glared at the lifeless eyes in front of him.

"What about it?" asked Henry nervously.

"It's perfect."

8.

The pair continued to stare down at the frozen body of von Manstein. A look of confusion was spread across the face of Henry as Brock's smile remained.

"What do you mean, it's perfect?" asked Henry. "Is there something you haven't told us about yourself, Brock?" He laughed nervously, as he looked over to Dietmarr who looked up with a brief smile on his face before returning to his pile of blankets.

"Don't be a bimb Irthing hey!" said Brock sternly. "I have an idea, but I'm saying now, it isn't nice."

"We need something Brock", implored Henry, looking intently at the American agent.

Brock looked intently at von Manstein before laying out his plan. Dietmarr was sat up, listening on.

"Last year, I met a man called Harold Gillies. I think he's a Sir actually and too right as well, he is a medical genius", added Brock before receiving a cold look from Dietmarr. Brock quickly got back on topic.

"Sir Harold Gillies is a plastic surgeon", Brock continued despite raised eyebrows from Henry. "He and a man called Archibald McIndoe were the first men to fix a broken face from The Great War. My idea..."

Brock stopped, contemplating the brutality of his thoughts, with both Dietmarr and Henry still looking on with a confused look on their faces.

"Please tell me if this is wrong but..." Brock stopped again, looking at Dietmarr.

"Spit it out come on!" said Dietmarr impatiently.

"We take out von Manstein's body and cut his head off."

Dietmarr shook his head in amazement but unperturbed, Brock continued.

"We cut his head off, store it in ice, and take it back to London. The two plastic surgeons I mentioned can cut his face clean off and transfer it... On to one of ours."

Dietmarr stared at Henry, his mouth open in pure shock. Brock continued, rushing to finish his idea.

"They can hopefully transfer his face on to one of ours and then we have free reign to stand side by side with Hitler and take him out when he's on his own."

Dietmarr continued to stare in amazement at Brock, his mouth hanging open slightly.

"You can't be serious? This is a joke right?" said Dietmarr, laughing nervously, as he wandered over to the pair who were still stood next to the dead body.

"Do you have a better idea hey?" said Brock, sounding extremely serious to try and deter Dietmarr's laughs.

"I... But... What?" Dietmarr was left reeled by the idea. "Surely they can't do a WHOLE face transfer? That's impossible!"

"If they can transfer and fix a whole cheek, why can't they transfer a whole face?" asked Henry, wishing he had not asked a stupid question.

"Even if by some sort of witchcraft they can do it, surely his face has been eaten by maggots by now? And why the fuck would you want to wear a dead man's face as a mask?"

"Look at it", said Brock. Dietmarr didn't seem keen on looking at his dead cousin, but did so anyway, remaining silent at the view that greeted him. Brock continued.

"The snow and ice must have kept it frozen enough so that the maggots didn't get to it…" Henry shivered at the thought. Dietmarr interrupted the shock silence.

"So who exactly is going to wear a dead guy's face?"

"I was rather hoping you were going to do it..." replied Brock quickly as Dietmarr spat his water out.

"Fuck off! I'm not wearing my dead cousin's face! Besides he has a fucking bullet hole in his head!" Dietmarr was squirming at the very idea.

"If these guys can transfer a whole face, they can fix a measly bullet wound", said Brock resolutely, attempting to persuade Dietmarr round to his way of thinking.

"That's the craziest idea I've ever heard..." said Dietmarr but before Brock could open his mouth to retort, Dietmarr had shrugged.

"But, we have nothing else." Henry smiled in response. "Do you realise what this means? You're going to have to BECOME Erich von Manstein. Not just at work. But at home, in the street, while asleep. His mannerisms, his accent. Twenty four seven."

Brock nodded in agreement.

"Why do I have to do it?!" asked Dietmarr desperately.

"Why can't Mr Motel Owner here do it, it's his idea!" Both Henry and Brock looked at each other.

"We're both too tall. You can't turn up at Hitler's office wearing his face having magically grown!" stated Brock defensively. Henry interrupted.

"Yeah, you're the same height as him, which is why you're best placed. Our accents are terrible as well…" added Henry quickly as Dietmarr punched the frame of the gazebo in frustration. Brock nodded in agreement.

"Oh for fuck sake!" shouted Dietmarr. "It's a shit idea, I'm not doing it!"

"I know it sounds horrendous, but how badly do you want Hitler dead? How badly do you want revenge for what they did to you?" Brock began but Dietmarr jumped in.

"Don't you dare emotionally blackmail me you fucking American *schizcoff*!" shouted Dietmarr. "You have no idea what you're asking me to do here!"

Dietmarr turned around and walked off to the other side of the gazebo. Walking towards his collection of belongings, he grabbed a bottle-shaped brown bag and opened the lid, before taking a huge swig of its contents. He shuddered as he took a second gulp and closed the lid.

"Don't you start drinking again!" shouted Henry angrily but Dietmarr did not look impressed.

"It's none of your fucking business what I drink", he retorted. "I'm not doing it. You're animals!" Dietmarr walked off into the woods.

"I'm going to get more wood", he added coldly, leaving Henry to sit idly on the tree trunk and assess what had just happened. Brock's idea, although gruesome, had the potential to work if the surgeons had the know-how to do it. He could understand Dietmarr's protestations, but the safety of a whole continent was riding on it.

Thirty minutes later, Dietmarr returned, carrying a small pile of wood that he chucked straight on to the flailing embers of the fire.

"Why are you still here?" he asked coldly, as Henry got to his feet.

"We need you to understand", Brock began but Dietmarr, anger still strewn across his face, interrupted once more.

"Understand? Understand what? That you want me to wear my

cousin's face as if it was a fancy dress mask?"

"You're the one who killed him!" protested Henry, instantly realising that his words may be a little insensitive.

"And I know I shouldn't have..." said Dietmarr quietly. "I've hardly slept recently. His face just haunts me... I've killed a family member, and I hate myself..." A tear rolled down Dietmarr's cheek as he picked up the brown bag, opened the lid of its contents and took another mouthful.

"You know what, just leave. Go home. I don't want anything more to do with either of you." Dietmarr lifted the bottle again and took an almighty swill, shaking as he forced the drink down into his stomach.

"Go on. GET OUT!" Dietmarr picked up a piece of wood and threw it in Henry's direction. Henry ducked, quickly grabbing his bag.

"Eliminating Hitler would be so much easier if there were three of us!" protested Henry, but Dietmarr didn't want to know.

"I'm not working with monsters like you! Get out!" He chucked the brown bag at Henry who ducked again. The contents, a small bottle of vodka, hit the tree next to the dead body and smashed over von Manstein's corpse.

Henry cast a small glance at the smashed shards of glass.

"Okay okay I'm leaving!" he stated, stumbling slightly as he walked back in the direction of the track leading to the gazebo. "Come on Brock, we won't be able to talk him round. Let's go."

"Good! I never want to see you again!" shouted Dietmarr, as Henry and Brock stumbled off across the track back towards Potsdam.

The walk back to the town went quickly as Henry paced along the countryside and down the snow-covered hills. He had always suspected Dietmarr had an angry streak in him, but Henry had been naive to think that the greater good would hold him back.

A couple of hours later, the small shadow of the von Manstein cottage came into view, looking over the busy town of Potsdam. Walking down the hill, Henry avoided the cottage by walking round the back of the town's main streets, through Mr. Schmidt's farm and across to the motel.

Henry walked through the front door and dumped his bag on the floor. Running upstairs, he found his notebook and tore out another small piece of paper. Using the same pen he had used that morning, he began to write his note.

"Agent Snake to Control. Further to previous correspondence, partnership has ceased with DS. Motel owner has blown cover. Over and out."

He read, and re-read it, thinking about whether he should let them know of his whereabouts at all. In the end, he decided to send it, signaling that it would be his last contact with base.

For the rest of the afternoon, Henry helped Brock out with the garden and other household chores. His mind flittered to and from the gazebo, where he wondered what Dietmarr would be doing without him.

As dusk descended over the town of Potsdam, Henry lit the fire in the drawing room and once again read the front cover of the morning's newspaper. Von Manstein's face looked back at him, smiling and happy. Henry was staring into his shining eyes, his mind going back to the blank, empty eyes that looked back at Henry as he was digging his grave.

Only a knock at the door brought Henry back to reality, as he dragged himself to the front hallway and answered it. A familiar looking face was on the other side.

"Hello sir, I am going door-to-door searching for information for Erich. Do you know anything?"

It was Mr von Manstein, similar in stature to Erich but without the glasses, he wore his Mayoral sash across his chest with defiant pride. He looked extremely tired, but was still pristinely dressed in a dark blue suit and overcoat. His black leather gloves looked menacing as he gesticulated.

"He hasn't been seen in months. He ALWAYS comes home after work. Always. This time, he did not. Do you know anything at all?" he asked fervently.

"Unfortunately, I don't know anything sir, I'm sorry", said Henry as innocently as he could.

Mr. von Manstein sighed in defeat.

"This is the last place I've asked and no one has heard a single peep from my boy!" he said frustratingly. "Thank you all the same."

With that, he promptly turned around and began the walk across town to his cottage. Henry remained stood leaning against the open door frame, watching von Manstein slouch his way across the icy streets. He was not to know that his son lay in a makeshift grave in the woods, a single bullet wound cut into his skull.

Henry closed the door, extinguished the fire and worked his way up the winding staircase to bed. It had been a long, tiring day and he needed a good night's rest.

...

There was another knock at the door, as Henry sat bolt upright in his bed. The moon shone brightly through his window as the silence of the night was broken. Another knock, knock at the door was proceeded by a shouting man, who began to bang at the wooden door with alarming anger.

"Okay I'm coming!" shouted Henry, forgetting that Brock was in the house too. He jumped to the bottom of the staircase and skipped across the floor to answer the calls. As soon as he opened the door, he was jumped upon by a small man, dressed in an all blue suit and dark overcoat. It was Mr. von Manstein.

"WHAT HAVE YOU DONE TO MY SON?!" he screamed as Henry fought to rid himself of the surprisingly strong grip of von Manstein senior.

"TELL ME!" screamed von Manstein, as Henry wriggled and squirmed on the cold marble floor of the motel.

"I don't know what you're talking about!" gasped Henry, as he managed to break free of von Manstein's grip. "I don't know where your son is!"

"Lies!" seethed von Manstein as he lurched towards him, fists clenched. Henry dodged the advance easily as von Manstein stumbled and fell with a crack on to the cold, hard floor.

"You killed my son! You killed my boy!" shouted von Manstein as he produced a silver blade from the inside pocket of his overcoat and lunged once more at Henry who dodged him again.

"I didn't!" shouted Henry, hands outstretched, urging von Manstein to calm down. "I honestly do not know where your son is! I would have told you otherwise!"

Von Manstein stood breathing heavily, holding out the bright silver blade at arm's length.

"Your German accent is horrendous. Schultz was right, you're a really bad agent..." said von Manstein deplorably.

"Schultz?" asked Henry precariously. Surely Dietmarr hadn't tipped off Erich's Father in anger? Why would he do that?

"The very same", said von Manstein gravely. "He told me you shot my son through the head with a single bullet and buried him. Is that true?" His arm was still held out dead straight in front of him, ready to pounce.

"I don't know what you're talking about..." repeated Henry.

"LIAR!" shouted von Manstein, jumping at Henry. This time, Henry could not get out of the way as he was tackled to the ground, hitting his head on the marble flooring as he did. A searing pain shot through his brain, temporarily blinding him. The shadow of von Manstein sat above him, the silver blade reflecting in the moonlight outside.

"Tell me the truth..." von Manstein said periously. "Or I'm going to stab your eyes out..." He held the blade above him threateningly.

"I didn't do it, it was Schultz. He told me to bury him!" said Henry, his heart rate increasing rapidly.

"More lies..." rasped von Manstein. You killed my SON!"

With that, he buried the blade deep into the head of Henry before a strange falling sensation gripped him once more...

...

"There's someone at the door." Brock stood over Henry, confusion in his eyes. The sun was up, once more flooding his bedroom with light.

"Are you okay?" asked Brock, concerned, but Henry merely jumped out of bed, wiped his brow ferociously and put on his shirt.

"I'm fine Brock", he said quickly. "You say there's someone at the door? For me?" He asked with a slight quiver in his voice, remembering the nightmare he had just experienced.

"Indeed lad! Hurry up or he'll get bored of waiting!" Brock strode out of the room, followed swiftly by Henry who waltzed down the staircase. Stood in the hallway, dressed head to toe in grubby clothes yet a brand new leather coat was Dietmarr. He stank dreadfully of alcohol and looked exceptionally tired.

"I'll do it", he said quietly.

A smile spread across Henry's face as he walked up to him to give him a hug, but Dietmarr pushed him away.

"Trust me, inhale this shit, you'll be as ratted as I was last night." He returned a grave smile and made his way for the door. "Meet me at 5pm this evening, usual place." With that, he gingerly walked out of the motel and back up the street. Henry leaned against the same door frame he had last night and watched Dietmarr walk off into the distance.

"I knew he'd come round." Brock had appeared behind Henry, making him jump, startled.

"I didn't." said Henry.

"Breakfast?" responded Brock brazenly, as if he had been expecting Dietmarr all along.

"Sure", replied Henry as he followed Brock through to the dining room where a selection of cereals, cooked meat and eggs were spread across the table. A couple of other people were already tucking in to their breakfasts. An elderly looking gentleman with a crisp white beard and a monocle was pouring over the morning newspaper, dishing fried egg into his mouth via his brazen moustache. Opposite him, a quaint woman sipped tea from her china cup, also perusing the print in front of her. A solitary piece of toast laid on her plate, as the man opposite her grabbed the fork from the middle of the table and stabbed it into the heart of a sausage, causing the woman to wince.

They were both blissfully unaware of the changing shape of their country and what may lie ahead. Henry was pleased that Dietmarr had finally agreed to Brock's idea, but it required a lot of luck and a spotless performance from Dietmarr. Henry was completely aware of Hitler's intelligence. One slip up could cost the whole operation.

At 2pm, Henry joined Brock in the hallway of the motel, rubbing his eyes after catching up on some lost sleep.

Brock was already there, dressed in a thick fur coat with camouflage trousers and sturdy walking boots. He was carrying a huge box over his broad shoulders.

"What's in there?" asked Henry, perplexed.

"A ton of ice", replied Brock simply. My father used to work in the ice trade in the Midwest; he had hundreds of these ice boxes.

Perfect for keepin' heads!"

Henry looked at it, disgusted.

"Come on then sleepy head; let's not keep His Majesty waiting hey!" He strolled out to the front garden as Henry tied up his boots and followed him. The pair walked the now familiar route towards the von Manstein cottage and then through the forest towards the compound where they were due to meet Dietmarr.

"So how did you two come across each other, hey?" asked Brock as they burrowed their way along the forest ground.

Henry remembered back to the time they met in that cramped cellar. Dietmarr was much the same person he is now; living off the land and highly troubled.

"He saved me", stated Henry. "I was a dead man, but he showed me the road out, so I owe him everything."

"Ahh, you're in LOVE!" bellowed Brock delightedly as he ruffled Henry's hair jokingly.

"Shut up you jester!" responded Henry, trying desperately not to give up his true feelings for Dietmarr. It was true, he was in love, but after his outburst to his old bosses, he could not be honest about his feelings anymore. He shoved those thoughts to the back of his mind as the pair continued their journey through the forest. The snow was falling once more, Brock's huge footprints carving out the route as they headed deeper towards the compound.

After a short while, the clearing appeared, the large gazebo cowering over a small fire where Dietmarr was sat huddled over, trying to keep warm. Henry's gaze flew over to the body of von Manstein, still lying motionless next to the oak tree, a light layer of snow covering it. Henry could see Brock also staring at it out of the corner of his eye, before the voice of Dietmarr snapped them out of their daze.

"Try sleeping with that nearby, knowing you're about to decapitate him". Dietmarr stood up from his fire, holding a small metal bowl of soup, pouring some into another bowl before giving it to Henry.

"Thanks", said Henry politely, taking a sip as Brock strolled over to the body, walking round it, examining every angle. Dietmarr's eyes followed him, curious as to what he was doing.

"What are you doing? Imagining him without a head?" asked Dietmarr sarcastically, as he traipsed back to his makeshift bed under the gazebo.

"Yep", replied Brock simply, continuing to peruse the corpse. Henry and Dietmarr resumed their seats in the gazebo, Henry perching on the end of a tree stump as Dietmarr draped himself in the many blankets that were strewn over the ground. It was not long before Brock joined them to outline his plan.

"Hey, so here's how we're gonna go. I'll do the dirty work and cut off the guy's head. My idea, my doing. We're not gonna slice the guy's face off here; we'll let the professionals do it. Could get messy."

Dietmarr looked horrified.

"Fuck, give me a warning before you go into details!" he shouted.

Brock ignored him and continued.

"I've got a plane coming over from the Bureau now the hero over here got himself sacked and we can't use the Brit ones!" Brock gave Henry a slight push as Dietmarr sniggered under his breath.

"You can fuck off!" shouted Henry adamantly. "You're the reason I was fired!" Henry proceeded to slap Dietmarr around the head, but before the former German agent could respond, Brock stepped in.

"Get a grip!" he shouted, breaking the pair up. "Let's concentrate on the job in hand hey, because this ain't gonna be a walk in the park!"

Henry and Dietmarr stopped squabbling and took their seats once more, listening intently to Brock as he outlined each detail in its full gory detail.

"I'm told we can carry out the procedure in London", he continued, looking at Dietmarr who was slowly turning more and more pale at the thought of taking on the face of his dead cousin. "Are you sure you're still okay with this?" Brock added. Dietmarr took a long time to consider his thoughts before he gently nodded.

"Good man", said Brock in an unusually serious tone. He continued to outline the plan, including the impending moment of beheading von Manstein.

"Now, given that I came up with this idea, I'll do the deed", said Brock, casting a brief glance over at the oak tree where von Manstein lay. Henry was still looking over at the dead body, remembering the night it happened and the booming gunshot to his head. A shiver ran down his spine at the very thought of it.

Brock's plan took many hours to convey, with Dietmarr looking more and more horrified with each point. The temperature had dropped as the darkness gathered, the burning fire providing the only light as Henry held a single sausage over the blazing flames before swallowing it whole. It was nearly midnight by the time Brock had finished his plan, laying over the same pile of blankets that Dietmarr had earlier, dozing in and out of sleep. Dietmarr sat on the tree stump in silence, contemplating what he was about to do.

"Might as well try and get some sleep…" said Henry, pulling some blankets off Brock and lying down on the snowy Earth. Dietmarr followed suit, climbing into his makeshift bed at the back of the gazebo. The only noise was the fire crackling and the occasional bird rustling through the trees...

…

The morning sun spread through the forest as Henry awoke the following morning; the snores of Brock and Dietmarr reverberating around the compound. He once more glanced at the dead body, before walking off into the forest to gather wood for the fire that had burnt out overnight. As he collected piles of twigs and branches, his mind went over and over the plan outlined by Brock last night. It was going to be tricky to pull off, but Henry was confident that the outrageous thinking of the American would work in their favour.

When Henry arrived back at the compound, Brock and Dietmarr were both awake, discussing the day ahead.

"I think we should just get it over and done with", said Dietmarr as Henry quickly picked up the fact they were talking about the dead body.

"We should definitely do it this morning…" added Henry, dumping the pile of wood he had gathered at the base of last night's fire. "The worms will get to it otherwise."

Dietmarr threw him a cursed look.

"Thanks, I've got to wear that you know…" he said, displeased. Brock meanwhile had taken a huge meat cleaver out of his rucksack and was walking over to the body. Before Henry and Dietmarr could react, Brock took an almighty swipe at the neck of the corpse taking a huge chunk out of the body. Brock lashed out again at the frozen remains before a third clout saw the head roll away from the rest of von Manstein.

Dietmarr and Henry looked on in horror.

"That quick enough for you hey?" said Brock defiantly, wincing slightly at his actions. He picked up the loose head and quickly shoved it in the ice box he had carried from the motel and closed the lid.

"That's the most fucked up thing I have ever witnessed", said Dietmarr taking a swig of water from his bottle.

"Can't have done a lot in the field then", stated Brock simply as he kicked the ice box and collapsed on to the same pile of blankets he had fallen asleep on the night before. Dietmarr snarled, taking another drink from his bottle.

"Surely we can bury him now?" asked Henry, as he walked over to the headless corpse and began to pile mud and snow on top of it. Dietmarr joined him, eager to get rid of the sight of his cousin. Brock watched on as the sight of the corpse was sprinkled in snow before slowly drifting from sight.

"Come on then, let's shoot", demanded Brock, as Henry used the back of his spade to smooth the large pile of snow and Earth into a barely noticeable knoll. Brock, picking up the box and walking off in the direction of the city, shouted after them as Dietmarr knocked back another swig from his flask, wincing slightly as he did. It was only a short walk to the airfield that was due to pick the threesome up and take them to London.

"Here we are then!" said Brock successfully, dumping the box on to the concrete floor. The threesome had found themselves on the tarmac of a vast airfield, a sole building looking lonely in the distance as the occasional plane took off into the bright sunshine. A short while later, a tiny plane landed a short walk away and without notice Brock took off towards it, Dietmarr and Henry hurrying along after him. The captain, a slight, bespectacled man welcomed them on to the plane that carried just six seats. He cast a suspecting look at the box that Brock was carrying, but before he could open his mouth, Brock had intervened.

"None of your business", he simply noted directing the captain sarcastically back to the cockpit. Henry and Dietmarr had already taken their seats, Dietmarr casting a look towards the attractive female attendant. Henry had noticed him glaring.

"Don't start", he seethed, simultaneously snatching the flask from Dietmarr's hands who turned to him angrily, but Henry was having none of it.

"You're not getting drunk again, especially not before meeting knights of the realm!" handing the flask to the attendant who took it out of sight.

"Bastard..." whispered Dietmarr as he sunk into his seat and glumly stared out of the window.

The short flight was uneventful. Brock was whistling along to an unknown tune as Henry tried to catch some rest. The flight attendant, after trying her best to appease a still disgruntled Dietmarr, had given up hosting and taken a seat in the cockpit with the pilot.

"Are the surgeons meeting us at the airport?" asked Henry, speaking loudly over the roar of the plane's engines.

"We're meeting them at MI6 headquarters, lad!" responded Brock, who laughed at Henry's shocked reaction. "I'm kidding lad, we're meeting at a hotel in Central London! I wouldn't do that to ya!" He laughed at Henry's misfortune, as Henry cautiously grinned in response.

The plane landed, the screech marks of the tyres distracting Henry from gazing around at the familiar landmarks of home. Disembarking the plane, Brock hauling the box down the steps, the threesome walked along British tarmac towards the centre of London.

"So where exactly are we going?" asked Dietmarr, as Brock strolled confidently along the streets of the English capital.

"A hotel", replied Brock simply. Dietmarr shook his head disapprovingly, looking at Henry who shrugged with him.

A long walk later, Brock mounted the steps of Claridge's Hotel in Mayfair, still carrying von Manstein's head with the strength of an ox. The grand exterior of the hotel dwarfed the road it was on, tourists stopping and marveling at its beauty.

"Way to be inconspicuous", said Dietmarr unimpressed, but Brock merely scoffed in his direction.

"That's a big word for such a bimb!" he responded, causing Henry to smirk in Dietmarr's direction.

Bypassing the reception area, Brock hastily made his way up

the royal looking staircase, followed by the others. On the second floor, he made his way along the corridor and knocked on the door of room number 55. A split second later, the door opened to a bald man with a bold, black moustache.

"Sir Harold!" exclaimed Brock, putting down the box and holding out a hand.

"Brock", replied Harold in a deep Australasian accent. "Come in, come in. You must be Henry", said Harold holding out a hand to Dietmarr accidentally.

"Fuck off am I Henry, I'm the better looking one!" exclaimed Dietmarr hastily, holding out a hand. Sir Harold Gillies cast an unimpressed look as he took hold of it, welcoming him into the room. Henry stood behind him, eyes closed in utter shock and disbelief.

"I apologise profusely on behalf of my idiotic friend..." said Henry, embarrassed, throwing an evil look at Dietmarr who had already moved on to introducing himself to the second man in the room, who Henry presumed to be Archibald McIndoe.

"Yes, well..." responded Harold sheepishly. "What else can we expect from a German?" He said it loudly enough for Henry to hear, but not within earshot of Dietmarr, who was chatting to McIndoe, like a schoolboy meeting his idol. Henry ignored the sentiment.

"Settle down, settle down and let's get right to business." Dietmarr sat down next to Sir Harold Gillies, who looked at him as if a court jester had taken his seat at the royal table.

"Now, gentlemen", Brock said, gesturing towards Harold and Archibald, "Thank you very much for agreeing to meet us to discuss our new project. I believe after your escapades in the Great War, you'll be intrigued by what we have planned."

The pair of surgeons listened intently, but Henry wondered if Brock had told them of his plan at all. Before he could wonder any more, Brock opened the box to reveal the battered severed head of von Manstein, drawing a gasp of horror from Archibald and a little scream of detestation from Harold, who stood up alarmed at what was in front of him.

"What in God's name is that?!" squealed Harold, as Archibald stood up and made his way to the door. Henry, noticing what he was doing, stood up in front of him, stopping Archibald from leaving, despite not knowing what Brock had up his sleeve. Archibald stared at him momentarily with fear in his eyes, before returning to his chair.

"It looks worse than it is", stated Brock as Harold was transfixed on the box. "We need you to do a job for us". Brock continued unperturbed. "We're on a mission to eliminate Adolf Hitler. This is the head of one of his closest friends and we want you to cut his face off and stitch it to that man's face." Brock pointed at Dietmarr who waved sarcastically back at the surgeons who continued to look on in disgust. Brock's matter of fact statement had completely thrown Henry who continued to stand by the bedroom door to stop anyone from leaving. Brock continued to beam while Dietmarr tried to stifle his uncontrollable laughter at Brock's methods. There seemed to be a silence that lasted a year before Archibald broke it.

"Are you actually insane?" asked Archibald, almost too politely for the situation.

"Well, yes, but that's another story", replied Brock cheekily before Henry stepped in to calm everyone down.

"Okay, maybe my… friend here… Hasn't explained the situation very well…" Henry was cautious with his words, gesturing towards Brock to elaborate on the plan. The two surgeons continued to look aghast, Archibald still staring at the box and Harold dabbing his forehead with a handkerchief. Brock looked at Henry for a moment, trying to figure out what his intentions were, with Henry staring back at him, eyebrows raised in a motion that suggested Brock should tell the surgeons everything.

"Oh, very well!" shouted Brock. "I was HOPING to get away with telling you the absolute minimum but I suppose if you're going to do this, you might as well know what it's for." This didn't seem to comfort the surgeons, who still looked horrified at the situation they had found themselves in, but after Harold took a sip of his tea, he regained his composure and resumed his seat next to his colleague, followed by another period of silence.

"I don't think I want anything to do with this…" said Archibald quietly, but the nonchalance of Brock kicked in as he poured Archibald another cup of tea.

"Nonsense sir!" he said, almost throwing the china mug in

Archibald's direction. "You're going to be the architects behind stopping one of the most dangerous men on the planet! Let me explain…"

For the first time since the group met, they had all taken their seats and order had taken over. The two surgeons sat next to each other, still looking horribly nervous. Brock sat opposite them, with Brock and Dietmarr seated between the surgeons and the door, in case one tried to make an escape.

"Maybe we should introduce ourselves!" announced Brock, still with the swagger and nonchalance of a king addressing his subjects. "My name is Brock Weston a former American intelligence officer, turned motel owner." He pointed to his right, towards Dietmarr who stood to attention sarcastically.

"My name is Dietmarr Schultz, an estranged Abwehr agent for the German intelligent service!" He resumed his seat, pushing Henry to his feet as he did so.

Henry stood, nodding at the pair of surgeons in an attempt to regain some credibility to the meeting. "Good day Gentlemen, my name is Henry Irthing, MI6 agent for Her Majesty's Secret Service."

"FORMER agent!" shouted Dietmarr, bursting into laughter with Brock as Henry continued to stand, red-faced.

"That is still disputed…" noted Henry, re-taking his seat. It was a few moments until the first surgeon stood up, but placing his tea on the bedside table, Archibald got to his feet gingerly.

"My name is err… Archibald McIndoe. I'm a surgeon." He spoke so fast and with a fear in his eyes, as if something terrible was about to happen to him. Sir Harold Gillies did the same, still offering the occasional fleeting look at the open box that sat menacingly in the middle of the circle.

"Great!" exclaimed Brock, as he poured himself a third cup of tea, splashing in a spot of brandy as he did so. "Let's save the world…"

9.

The box storing the head of von Manstein was still lying open in the middle of the room as Brock sat down next to it, addressing the circle that had formed around him.

"This is Erich von Manstein, one of Hitler's closest advisors and friends. He was taken out by Dietmarr not so long ago, the circumstances of which were particularly violent as you can tell by the huge fucking hole in his head." Dietmarr pointed towards the box, but neither of the surgeons were particularly keen to take a closer look.

"Our ultimate aim is to eliminate Adolf Hitler. All of our intelligence points towards Hitler taking over when Hindenburg dies, using propaganda tactics to take over Europe."

"And what's that got to do with a couple of surgeons?" interjected Harold who jumped to his feet, but as quick as a flash, Brock retorted.

"Patience Sir Harold, patience!" he exclaimed, holding out a pair of hands to usher Harold back into his seat. "Trust me; you'll want to be a part of this." It took a few seconds for Harold to resume his seat.

"Maybe we should hear them out?" Archibald asked, as Henry and Dietmarr looked on sheepishly.

"Fine", said Harold promptly, causing Brock to bow his head as if he were bowing to royalty.

"In response to Sir Harold's intriguing question, the general idea is that we want to stitch von Manstein's face on to this fine young gentleman." Again, Dietmarr waved back sarcastically but the two surgeons look perplexed.

"Sorry, I think I misheard. Did you just say you wanted us to stitch a dead man's face on to him?" Archibald pointed at Dietmarr, who looked on innocently, almost as if he was enjoying the monstrosity of it all.

"That's correct", responded Brock simply.

A silence fell on the room, the shock etched across the face of the surgeons. Henry sat still in his chair, staring at his toes awaiting the response. Dietmarr was trying not to laugh at the whole thing; his original disgust at the idea having vanished to be replaced by humour. It was Brock who broke the silence.

"With all due respect gentlemen, we are on a bit of a time limit here." He pointed at his watch fervently and gestured for one of the surgeons to speak up. Another silence fell, as the surgeons swapped anxious glances.

"I don't know where to begin…" stated Archibald, as he picked up his briefcase and made for the door. Once again, Henry and Dietmarr, like greyhounds out of a trap jumped up to guard the only exit from the room. Archibald stared at them with daggers in his eyes.

"If you don't move out of the way, I am going to swing this briefcase, which incidentally holds quite a lot of weight, straight for your heads. Do you understand?"

Henry and Dietmarr didn't move; in fact it was Henry who burst out laughing.

"We are two of our nation's finest secret agents", he began. "I once fought off three particularly skilled knifemen with my bare hands, while the man stood next to me has the ability to see a bullet coming at him from point blank range. How do you think we're going to react when an ageing gentleman swings a battered box at us?"

Dietmarr let himself snigger under his breath as Archibald took a step backwards. Henry continued to go on the offence.

"Now let me tell you two face-fixers how this is going to go. We're going to sit here and agree that you will do this – for a good price of course - for the greater good, or we can go back to our bosses in Whitehall and notify them that we have discovered two of our nation's finest medical minds splattered across the walls of a London hotel. Your choice."

Henry gestured towards a shocked Archibald to resume his seat. Archibald suddenly looked frightened as he placed his briefcase back on to the marble floor and sat down next to his colleague, who looked extremely nervous and white as a sheet.

"Thank you for agreeing to help Europe", resumed Henry. "I will let my friend Brock here, resume with what will happen next."

Henry re-took his own seat, amazed at his own tenacity while Dietmarr stared at him with a look of admiration.

"We don't have a choice, do we?" mumbled Harold.

"Yes you do", responded Brock. "You can either agree to help us or you can let the maids find you in the morning." Archibald looked up with a face of fire as Harold recoiled into his chair.

"When do we start?" asked Archibald through gritted teeth.

"Tomorrow", responded Brock simply. Dietmarr, who was busy scouring the shelves that contained an assortment of alcohol, looked up sharply.

"What?!" exclaimed Dietmarr. "That wasn't the plan!"

"Well, I've changed my mind", said Brock as he picked himself up from his own armchair and strolled confidently over to the box containing the disconnected head of von Manstein. He picked it up, removing the lid as he did so, and threw the box into the middle of the room into full view of everyone present. The head rolled out on to the marble floor and flew towards Archibald, who flinched in horror and jumped out of the way. His colleague Harold, quickly ran over to the open window and proceeded to vomit out on to the street below. It was the first time Henry had seen the severed head on its own. The pale, ghostly skin had started to rot away, a few maggots crawling in and out of its orifices. His eyes remained closed, but the gunshot wound remained as prominent as ever, as if you could see inside his head. Another maggot crawled its way from inside the wound as Henry managed to avert his gaze away from the ungainly sight. Brock had remained unmoved.

"You have got to be kidding me…" muttered Archibald, as he continued to stare at the head, which had come to rest next to the front door of the hotel room.

"I'm sure you've worked out by now that, no, I'm not kidding you", said Brock nonchalantly as he picked the head up and replaced it back into the ice, face upwards as Archibald was still transfixed. Brock continued.

"This is the point where you tell me that you can slice that fucking face off and put it on him", he pointed towards Dietmarr who had started to look quite unwell himself. Archibald managed to avert his gaze from the head for a moment, as he took his seat once more. Harold was still hovering by the window.

"It's never been done before", said Archibald but he quickly continued as Brock threw him an angry glance from across the room. "But, I suppose we can do something."

"Correct answer", responded Brock. "So, how is it done?"

Archibald looked sadly over at Harold, who had tears rolling down his cheeks as he came to terms with the extreme situation he had found himself in.

"We can't take his face off and put it on another man's face", said Archibald bravely. He continued to speak as Brock looked at him threateningly. "I'm sorry, if that's what you want, then you'll have to kill me now, because it's impossible." Archibald stared at Brock resolutely, before continuing.

"It's not medically possible to transplant a dead man's face on to a living human being. Certainly not one that's been eaten to death by maggots."

"How can he be eaten to death when he's already dead?" asked Dietmarr, as Brock picked up a china ornament and threw it towards him.

"SHUT THE FUCK UP FOR ONCE!" shouted Brock, as the ornament smashed into the wall behind Dietmarr who looked shocked at the angry response from a usually sedate man. Archibald looked unperturbed as he considered what to say next.

"However… If you remember how this German man looked before the maggots got to him, we can work on creating a new face…" Archibald looked disgusted at his own idea, but Brock, who had thought his plan was dead, had a sparkle in his eye.

"Tell me." He dragged his chair next to Archibald's, producing a pen and paper from his bag and placing them into the hands of Archibald McIndoe.

Archibald wavered, placing them on the glass table in front of him almost immediately.

"This is more Harold's area of expertise I'm afraid…" stated Archibald as he turned to look at Harold, who continued to breathe heavily out of the window, looking extremely pale as he did so. It was a long time before Harold walked slowly over to the rest of the group, who stared at him intently.

"I want to place on record that I am not doing this out of choice, but because you monsters have threatened me." Brock rolled his eyes and gestured for him to get on with drawing his plan. Harold's hand was shaking as he picked up the bottle of ink, and placed the pen into it. He began to draw.

"My colleague here is correct, it is impossible to transfer one man's face on to another, however, you are probably aware of a lady called Marie Tussaud who I happen to know very well."

"Of course…" whispered Henry, as Harold continued to

speak.

"Marie Tussaud owns a wax work gallery on Baker Street, depicting notorious figures from history. I feel morose at the idea of getting her involved in a project such as this, but I sense you demons will not vanish unless you reach your ultimate destination."

Harold began to draw. He winced every time he stole a look into the box, but within minutes, he had depicted von Manstein as if he was alive and in the room with them. No maggots, no blood stains and ultimately, no gunshot wound, the figure of von Manstein became more real with each dip of pen in ink. The others looked on in awe, as every minor detail of the dead German became etched in ink on the paper.

It was a couple of hours later when Harold put down his pen. The three dimensional drawing of Erich von Manstein complete, he tore another small piece of paper and wrote down an address on it.

"This is the home of Marie Tussaud. If you utter a single word that I gave this to you, I will make it my own personal mission to have you destroyed. You do not scare me anymore. Take this with you and ask her to create a wax mask. I'm sure you will be able to persuade her to come round to your villainous way of thinking." With that, he picked up his own briefcase before marching out of the room, quickly followed by Archibald, but Brock was not finished there.

"Wait a second…" his arm outstretched across the frame of the door. "How exactly do we attach a wax mask to his face?" It was Archibald who responded.

"Come back to me with it and I will do it. I think you've asked enough of Harold now. I shall meet you in this very room tomorrow. Fifteen hundred hours." With that, he forcibly wrenched Brock's arm out of the way and strolled out of the hotel room.

The trio stood silently in the middle of the room, the original head of Von Manstein innocently sitting on a table staring into the distance.

"Baker Street?" asked Dietmarr.

"Baker Street", responded Henry as he held out the door for his two comrades. "Don't forget the head", he added as Brock scooped up the severed head from the table and placed it neatly back into his briefcase. There was an eerie atmosphere amongst the men, as if the reality of what they were doing had begun to seep into their being. They walked in silence through the hustle and bustle of London's streets towards their next destination.

It had started raining now as the three men sidled out of the hotel and headed north, at a pace that startled the businessmen approaching the hotel, faces buried in their broadsheets. Within seconds Henry had hailed down a horse-drawn carriage, in which he leapt inside followed by Brock and a confused looking Dietmarr.

"I don't think I've ever ridden in a carriage before. You shall now address me as King Schultz."

"You lazy bastards hey, it's literally two kilometers away", stated Brock simply, opening up his own broadsheet, calmly placing the briefcase with the head of von Manstein at his feet.

The short journey was bumpy, with Henry conscious that the briefcase would fly open and release the severed head into the busy markets below them, but within ten minutes, the carriage drew up outside a new building with the large golden letters of Madame Tussaud emblazoned across it.

"Now, we're going to have to come up with a plan. We can't have a repeat of vomiting doctors", whispered Henry as he disembarked but before he could stop him, Dietmarr had strolled to the front door with purpose, only to find it locked.

"Open up!" shouted Dietmarr, pulling furiously at the golden bar that slid across the face of the premises. "We need to speak to the owner!"

Henry sighed as he paid the driver of the carriage and followed Dietmarr, with Brock sauntering behind him, still reading his newspaper.

"Open up!" repeated Dietmarr before he turned to Henry for assistance.

"Maybe try the back entrance?" said Brock, without lifting his head, as the pair quickly shuffled round the back of the building, where they found a door ajar.

"Psst! Brock! This way!" gestured Henry, as Brock finally looked up and followed Henry to the open door. The doorway was rotting away, as the trio blew their way through the dust in the air through to a huge colosseum of unfinished statues, aborted attempts and random masses of wax in large vats, churning in machines as if it were butter in a dairy farm. All three of the men were transfixed by the scale of the operation, a window into a new world of caricatures and figures, before a cunning voice from the top of a stairwell brought them back down to Earth.

"And who, may I ask, are you three fine gentlemen?" The old lady wore a flowing dress, in all black, and wore her hair tied up in an arrangement of colourful flowers. Her eccentricity was only beaten by her stare, her eyes peering finely from behind a netted veil. She looked as if she had just attended the funeral of a high-ranking politician or a member of the royal family.

"I've got a feeling she's going to be a harder nut to crack than our surgical friends…" whispered Brock as Dietmarr, as he was accustomed to do so, went blundering in head first regardless.

"We need to speak to the owner", he stated, as Henry rolled his eyes behind him.

"Well, I'm not the cleaner", replied the lady.

The noise of workmen sifting out hot, molten wax was the only sound as the piercing stare of the lady looked down upon Henry, Dietmarr and Brock who vaguely looked at each other, wondering what to say next.

"My husband is away on business", continued the lady, "You must come back another day", and with that, she twirled around, her dress following her as she went to shut the oak door behind her.

"Then we must speak to you!" shouted Henry, before the opportunity was lost. "You are Marie Tussaud I presume?" The lady stopped in her tracks, slowly turning around again with a cunning smile across her face. She must have been at least 70 years old, but one sensed she was not the least bit frightened by what confronted her.

"And what, pray tell, would one want with me?" she responded courteously.

"We need your assistance making a wax mask", responded Henry, as Brock looked at him with quizzing eyes.

"Do I look like the maker of wax masks? Frederick! Help these fine gentlemen with their masks, and if they try and come up these stairs, shoot them in the back!" With those words, she moved swiftly towards the door, the sound of the oak echoing around the chamber as she slammed it shut.

"How may I be of service?"

All three men jumped as a dirty-faced man stood in front of them, covered head to foot in beige overalls and holding an instrument that resembled a spatula in his hands.

"Erm…" stuttered Henry, aghast that it had been so easy to get to this point. "We need a mask making… Fairly urgently…"

The polite man merely stared back at him, eyebrows raised and attempting to gesture for Henry to continue without coming across as rude or pompous. Henry continued.

"Erm…" Henry looked to his partners for help as he ran out of words but did not count on Brock taking over with such brutality. Brock opened the briefcase, and with a single hand, removed the severed head and held it in his open palm before Frederick.

There was a pause. The colour and the smile from Frederick's face drained in an instant, as he stared into the empty eyes of von Manstein, transfixed.

"We need a wax mask of this dead man's face", added Brock, as Henry once again stared with menace in response to Brock's frank nature.

"You could at least try and break it to people gently…" added Dietmarr, before Brock broke ranks and continued.

"We don't have time to play games!" he gesticulated, seemingly letting out his pent up anger at the typically British way of doing things. "This is of the utmost importance. Will you do it or not?"

Frederick had not taken his eyes off von Manstein, and had a similar shade of putrid in his face as Harold had at Claridge's hotel a mere hour ago.

"Who, or what, is that?" asked Frederick, still staring through the eyes of the dead strategist.

Brock sighed, as if he was bored of explaining why he was carrying round a severed head.

"This used to be the mind of Erich von Manstein, the chief strategist of Adolf Hitler", he said simply, before gesticulating for an answer from the workman.

"Who's Adolf Hitler", asked Frederick, looking aghast at the situation in front of him.

"We don't exactly have time to explain his life history", said Brock curtly, but Henry, noticing the look of disdain on Frederick's face stepped in to appease him.

"Look, we are on a bit of a time limit here, but in short, Adolf Hitler has plans to invade the entirety of mainland Europe. We need a mask of this man to help with our plan to eliminate him before he does any more damage."

There was a slight pause before Frederick turned back to the waxwork he had been interrupted from.

"Not interested", he said simply, turning his back on the three men, but before he could pick up his tools, Brock had dropped the suitcase and grabbed the man by his neck and pinned him up against the nearest wall.

"I don't know what it is about you Brits, but you're all rude, stubborn bastards", he began, as Henry and Dietmarr took a step back. "I don't think we made ourselves very clear. We need a wax mask of this dear man's dead face hey, and you ARE going to make it for us. Is that clear?"

"Put me down and I'll do it", said Frederick, squirming under the weight of Brock's hand. Brock obliged.

"It'll cost you", added Frederick, but he recoiled quickly as Brock raised his hand once more. "Okay, okay!" he squealed. "I'll do it".

"Well, that was easier than I thought", exclaimed Brock as he playfully threw the head at Frederick who let out a little scream as he caught it and instantaneously dropped it on the floor. He was looking around the chamber for assistance, before realising he was the only workman in the room.

"How long will it take?" asked Brock, as Henry and Dietmarr looked on in amazement.

"It will take at least 24 hours…" whispered Frederick. "But please, can you place that thing on my table over there. I don't want to touch it."

"Certainly can hey! And make sure the eyes and mouth are empty, this guy needs to see and speak without looking like a rag doll!" shouted Brock, pointing at Dietmarr with one hand and slapping Frederick on the back with the other. Frederick wretched slightly as Brock picked up the head and carried it over to the workstation as if it were a bowling ball. He placed it in the vice and secured it in place, before turning to Frederick.

"Thank you Frederick", said Brock genuinely. "You might well be saving Europe." And with another slap on the back, he left a shocked and bedraggled Frederick to get on with his work as he strolled past Henry and Dietmarr. "I think I need a drink", he added.

With a final look back at the startled figure of Frederick, Henry followed Brock out of the building, swiftly followed by Dietmarr who took a swig from his hidden hip flask that he kept inside his coat pocket.

The sun was beginning to set as the three men sat down in a tavern a few doors down from the back doors of Madame Tussaud. Brock ordered three ales as Henry sat down next to the window, staring out at the continuing hustle and bustle of the city he had called home for a number of years.

As Brock set down the tankards, Henry turned back towards them.

"Do you ever wonder how we have ended up here?" he asked questioningly, as Brock raised an eyebrow and Dietmarr took a huge gulp of the free ale on offer.

"What do you mean, hey?" asked Brock, as he took his own drink and offered a simple toast, in which Dietmarr accepted followed by Henry, slowly tipping his tankard into Brock's with a tiny clunk.

"I mean... Here we are, on a secret mission that we're not officially on anymore, a British man, an American and a German. The most unlikely trio imaginable, and everyone else is carrying on without a care in the world. Completely oblivious... Don't you think it would sometimes be better to be one of these drunks?"

Dietmarr looked up at this point, but swiftly returned to his drink when he realised that Henry was not talking about him.

"Nope", responded Brock simply.

"Why so certain?" replied Henry.

Brock took another sip of his drink as he contemplated his answer.

"I've been one of these men myself", he said. "Only a few years ago I was helping build one of America's greatest monuments and overnight, it vanished. Everything vanished. No job, no home, no money. The only solace was the liquor we stole, and I wouldn't want to go back there in a million years."

Brock now turned around to stare out of the window, at the same spot Henry had simply moments earlier. Just outside of the window was a beggar, bedraggled in rags, scratching away at his unkempt beard and walking around aimlessly with his hands outstretched.

"That was me three years ago, hey…" said Brock taking yet another sip from his drink. "Three years ago…"

The trio continued to sit in near silence, the only movement being to get another drink from the bar that slowly started to become quieter and quieter as the night drew in.

"I escaped to Germany after being discharged from the US air force. I stole a plane from Pennsylvania air base when loaded up one night. After that, I was court martialled but never turned up. I'm still wanted by the authorities now." Brock sighed and drank another shot of whiskey before getting up from his seat.

"I'm going to call it a night. Sleep tight gents hey. It's going to be a day and a half tomorrow…" And with that, he sidled off towards the back of the building and up the stairs towards his room.

"Good night", added Henry. Dietmarr merely grumbled, slouched in his seat.

It had been a while since Henry had stopped and taken stock of what he had been doing, taking a few moments to remember his admiration for Dietmarr, who had been drinking by the gallon since they had sat down a few hours earlier.

"I have a confession to make". Dietmarr had gone to get another drink, while Henry continued to stare out into the evening.

"What…?" asked Henry inquisitively, as Dietmarr stumbled back across the bar and slumped at the table, head bowed and in his hands as the audible sound of crying came from within them.

"What's wrong?" asked Henry again, placing a hand on Dietmarr's shoulder but Dietmarr jumped and threw the outstretched arm off and continued to cry into the wooden table.

"Everything is wrong", sobbed Dietmarr. "Do you have any idea what it's like working against a country you've dedicated your entire life to defending?"

Those words struck Henry. Not only did he resonate, but he had not taken a moment to appreciate all that Dietmarr had done to help against the country he had spent years working for. Regardless of sides, that must take a toll on anybody.

"I'm an alcoholic", added Dietmarr.

"That is your confession? This is common knowledge my friend." Henry merely shrugged, not surprised by an admission he already knew.

"It numbs the pain of the treachery I feel", added Dietmarr.

There was a moment of silence as Dietmarr's words emanated around the bar and began to sink in.

"I never thought to ask. Why are you helping us?"

The reddened eyes of Dietmarr looked up into Henry's as he took a further swig from his latest tankard of ale.

"It all started in the winter of 1931", began Dietmarr as he wiped the tears from his eyes with the dirty handkerchief he kept in his jacket pocket. "I had been with the Abwehr for over a decade, and was Germany's best secret agent following the Great War. I had vowed when I joined up that I would not allow my country to be fooled into another Battle of the Marne. Our country was better than invasion."

Dietmarr downed the rest of his ale, signaling in one swoop to the barman for a top up. The barman quickly obliged, putting down his cloth and pouring a fresh tankard in one foul swoop.

"Bring over a bottle of whisky as well", demanded Dietmarr with a wrap of his knuckles on the table. The barman doubled back, bringing the bottle over with two glasses as Dietmarr continued his story.

"I thought I was doing the right thing", he said, pouring a glass of his own. "I had been at the last days of the Marne, I didn't want us going down the same path again. I joined the agency with the sole purpose of keeping an eye on the Weimar." He began to cry once more.

"I did my duty for the republic, and I was punished for it. Made a scapegoat by Hindenburg and imprisoned for a crime I did not commit, banishing me to the outskirts and to a life of destitution."

His words became sharper as he looked up from his tankard, straight into Henry's eyes. He could feel the stare of the German burning his skull.

"You ask why I am doing this", he whispered. "I want revenge. There is no such thing in this world as rewarding loyalty."

He poured a further glass of whisky and downed it, and went for another one before Henry's hand shot out from under the table, reaching the bottle before Dietmarr. Dietmarr's hand was on top of Henry's, falling just short of grabbing the bottle first. They held their positions for a few seconds before Henry drew back his hand.

"I think we've had enough for one night", said Henry simply.

His hands were shaking and he could feel the sweat dripping down his back and his heartbeat pounding through his chest.

A few moments of silence passed, with the odd clink coming from the bar top as the sole barman began putting glasses away for safe keeping. It was soon to be closing time.

"And what about you?" Dietmarr broke the silence with a question aimed at Henry.

"What about me?" replied Henry quickly, fearing his moment with Dietmarr had been clocked by his friend.

"Everyone has a secret. What's yours?"

Henry could feel the eyes of Dietmarr on him once more as his mind whirled in the vagueness and certainty of the question put before him. Did he know? All those nights spent together in the woods outside Potsdam, had he said something in his sleep that Dietmarr had clocked? What if he knew all this time and was just waiting for him to say it? What if Dietmarr was also like him?

"Life has always been about the fight", responded Henry. More silence filled the room.

"No idea what you mean with your abstract nonsense", responded Dietmarr.

"Not just in the field or in boardrooms. Life has just got in the way of me being happy", added Henry, with an air of solemnness.

"You should take up drinking", said Dietmarr with a laugh, taking another large helping of whisky. "It makes everything somewhat easier…"

Henry looked at Dietmarr. Here they were, locked away in an empty pub, the odd squeak of flannel on glass the only noise emanating from the bar, as the bedraggled barman continued to clean his solitary glass. The scene outside had drifted away into the night. If ever there was a time to be honest, now was it.

"I remember when you asked me, all the way back in the forest, as we were digging that grave, whether I'd ever fallen in love", started Henry, staring into his own empty glass, as if he was expecting a spirit to appear from it and whisk him away from the situation. "The thing is… I have."

He stopped in his tracks once more; as he could feel the alcohol take a grip of his senses. They had come so far, done so much and gone through unimaginable things together that honesty seemed to be the only way forward. Even if it ruined all of their hard work.

Dietmarr didn't say a word. He continued to look deep into Henry's eyes, almost as if he was staring into his very psyche; almost as if he knew and he was waiting for Henry to say the words.

"Dietmarr... I think I am in love with you."

"Why the fuck is there a bear in the hallway?!"

A scream then filled the silence, as Henry snapped out of his self-made trance and Dietmarr looked around in confusion.

"This is Dagger sir; my dog..." responded the barman. "Away Dagger!" he added, before he could be heard dragging the dog down the stairs and out into the bar area. What appeared was a huge dog with mottled fur and paws the size of boulders. Before Dagger could pounce at the agents, the barman tethered him to a pole by the back door using a thick rope and tape.

"Stay there!" he demanded, pointing an authoritative finger at the dog, who was now whining at being tied to the pole.

"Jesus, I'm sure he was supposed to be the sensible one out of us three!" said Dietmarr, wiping the tears of laughter out of his eyes. He paused for a few moments, as if contemplating what to say next. Henry waited with baited breath. "I'm sorry, I didn't hear you before he screamed! What did you say?"

Henry was not laughing. His mouth hung open in shock, for that was the first time he had ever talked about his loving feelings for his comrade.

"No, no, it's nothing", said Henry, as he rushed to his feet. "I think we've had enough for one night don't you!" and without a moment's hesitation, he deposited his glass at the bar and quickly strode up the same staircase Brock had moments earlier. The less time he spent in Dietmarr's company this evening, the better.

"Good night..." whispered Dietmarr, taking a final swig of whisky.

...

"In love with me? What the fuck?"

Dietmarr stood over Henry, with the sun shining through the barely-attached curtains of his hotel room, holding a carving knife calmly by his side. Blood was dripping from his cheek, flowing out of a deep gash across his face as the crimson dripped on the floor from the blade.

"Why did you never tell me? After all that I've been through, why didn't you just tell me?" Dietmarr was unsteady on his feet, the blood from his face now flowing on to Henry's face and into his eyes as he struggled to see the figure before him, frantically wiping it away only for more blood to appear…

"Jesus!" Henry jumped awake, his hotel bedroom empty and the early morning sunshine lighting up the room before him. Henry was covered in sweat; the bed sheets all over the place signaling an uncomfortable nights rest.

Henry quickly got showered and dressed and made his way to the same table he had sat at just hours earlier, waiting for Brock and Dietmarr to appear from their own rooms. An hour passed before Brock appeared with an enthusiastic and wholesome greeting.

"Great beds here hey!" he exclaimed, slapping Henry on the back and taking the seat opposite him. "Eggs?"

"Hmm sure", replied Henry tiredly, taking a sip of water.

Footsteps from the nearby staircase became audible before Dietmarr soon appeared, looking bedraggled and tired from the night's exploits.

"Eggs?" asked Brock a second time, with an over enthusiastic gesture towards the kitchen.

"I feel sick", responded Dietmarr, slouching in the last remaining chair.

"Get some breakfast inside you hey, you'll feel much better", responded Brock.

The trio sat in near silence as they ate varying amounts of breakfast. Brock's plate was stacked high with eggs and bacon, as Dietmarr worked his way through a single slice of toast. Another important day lay ahead.

"We need to arrange getting to Munich within the next few days", stated Brock, as Dietmarr looked up for the first time that morning.

"When for?" he asked, taking an immediate interest in proceedings.

"Presuming we have our mask ready, we need to stitch it on to you today and send you packing", responded Brock. "I've been given intelligence that Hitler is meeting with his top team on Friday morning, meaning we have 72 hours to get you prepped and there, ready to go in."

"Might take him 70 of those 72 to sober up..." Henry added, as Brock sniggered. Dietmarr didn't respond.

They continued to eat their breakfast, slowly but surely, weighing up the challenges that lay ahead. Henry felt nervous for his friend, for he was the one putting himself in danger to confront his countryman in Munich, wearing someone else's face. He had not stopped to consider the magnitude of their escapade throughout their journey, but looking at Dietmarr, Henry could sense something was making him uneasy, other than his hangover.

The bright sun bathed the bar in light, much to the disgust of Dietmarr, as the traders outside set up for another day of bargaining. The barman, the same man from the night before, was sat sipping coffee reading the morning newspaper as the trio quietly finished their breakfasts and spent a few sparing moments in silence. The only noises came from outside, where the occasional crash of a wooden pallet was met with a curse of a disgruntled market stall trader.

It wasn't until near midday that Henry, Dietmarr and Brock left the guest house, making the small journey through the now bustling streets back to the factory where Frederick worked to collect the mask.

Brock took the lead, banging with a heavy fist against the corrugated iron door. Unlike yesterday, the door was locked, but it wasn't long before a tired-looking Frederick greeted them.

"Don't draw attention to yourselves and just follow me", he stated, turning around. The threesome followed him in earnest all the way through the factory and to a small, dank room where the suitcase lay open with the head of von Manstein sitting in it, face down. On a plinth behind it, sat the mask.

The likeness was uncanny; almost creepy in its solemn appearance. Henry was instantly bewitched by the cunning eyes, open and full of life and the skin tone matched that of the German when he was alive, even though Frederick only had the pale, maggot-infested shell to work from.

"Jesus Christ..." whispered Dietmarr, as the realisation he would have to wear it dawned on him.

"That is far too good..." added Brock as Frederick carefully lifted the mask from its stand and placed it into the hands of Brock who stood admiring it for a few seconds before handing it over to

Dietmarr.

"I don't ever want to see you three ever again", stated Frederick before he ushered them out of the smaller room back out on to the factory floor. "Get out", he added as the trio drifted out, still under the spell of the mask that gazed blankly back at them.

Once they were outside, they all spent a moment with the mask in their hands; the first time they had seen a physical result from their journey. It was Brock who broke the silence.

"We need to track down Archibald quick fast and get this on your head", he said, looking at Dietmarr who winced at the very thought.

Brock took off at the pace of an athletic sprinter as Henry and Dietmarr broke out into sporadic jogs in order to keep up with him. They were heading back to the hotel and had ten minutes to get there. They didn't want to give Archibald a reason to leave by being late.

They arrived a mere couple of minutes before 3pm, and raced up the staircase, Brock still holding the mask in his hand. Knocking on room 229, he opened the door and entered before its occupant had time to answer, and was greeted by a seated Archibald, sipping a cup of tea and huddled over a newspaper.

"You know, part of me was hoping you'd just not turn up", he said, placing the tea on the table as he gingerly got to his feet, eyes fixed on the mask in Brock's hand. "Is that it?"

"Yup", replied Brock. "As real as the real thing hey!" Archibald merely shuddered.

"I've been thinking about how to attach it to your face", he said, turning to Dietmarr who was growing paler by the second. "I'm afraid, in order for it to be secure and believable, it's going to hurt."

"I had a funny feeling it would…" said Dietmarr.

Archibald continued.

"Now the wax has dried, I am able to penetrate it with four holes, all around the cheek and jaw line. I have special screws here, that I would need to secure to your face and then screw the mask on."

"Won't the mask just fall off at the top?" asked Brock. Archibald looked at him menacingly.

"I'm getting to it…" he said, with an air of annoyance. "As your American friend states, the mask would fall at the top and I cannot drill into the skull, so I have enlisted the help of a man called Harry Coover, who is working on patenting the use of a chemical called cyanoacrylate." Archibald stopped in his tracks, taking a moment to consider his next actions.

"Cyanoacrylate is completely untested. We have no idea what it could do to you. It could poison you, it could burn your skin off, we just don't know."

Dietmarr, who looked queasy at the beginning of the conversation, looked as if he was about to pass out, but Brock gestured for Archibald to continue.

"Cyanoacrylate is essentially a super strength glue. Once we secure the top of the mask to your forehead, it will not fall off. In fact, when the time comes for you to take the mask off, you will need it surgically removed."

"Excuse me…?" asked Dietmarr. "SURGICALLY removed?" Archibald nodded.

"You've got some of this "cyano" stuff with you I take it?" asked Brock, as Archibald took a small metal bottle from his bag and placed it on the table in front of him.

"I'm ready to do it now", said Archibald as Dietmarr made an almost inaudible noise of discomfort at the idea.

"Okay great, do you need the room? Shall Henry and I fuck off?" added Brock, holding out a guiding arm to Henry.

"Woah woah, wait a second" said Dietmarr with alarm. "Now?" He looked as if he was about to vomit, but Brock was insistent.

"We need to be in Munich inside 48 hours, it's now or never".

"It's now or now", said Archibald insistently. "The quicker this is over and done with the better and I'm not waiting another day."

"We'll leave you to it!" said Brock, leading Henry out of the room, leaving Dietmarr with Archibald, both of whom looked as scared as each other.

It was three hours later that Archibald came down the stairs to greet Henry and Brock in the reception area, his shirt sodden with sweat.

"It's done", he said simply. "Follow me."

They went back up to the hotel room and walked inside to

find Dietmarr sitting on the bed facing out towards the city. Henry could notice two tiny metal screws on the side of his cheeks.

"So?" asked Brock. "Let's see!" Dietmarr took an eternity to move but finally slid round the bed and faced Henry and Dietmarr, with Archibald remaining by the door, as if he wanted to make a quick escape.

The work was remarkable. Dietmarr was no longer Dietmarr, the wax mask molded to his face with ease. Henry was taken back to that night in the enclosure where Dietmarr had shot von Manstein, except he looked alive. He looked as real as the advisor himself, except the eyes behind the mask were crying. The sobs of Dietmarr, audible.

10.

(20th January 1933. Hitler is gaining in power as Hindenburg fades)

Brock and Henry looked at one another, both as reluctant to speak as the other. Dietmarr was facing them now; dried blood stains on either side where the screws had been secured to his neck. Except the face looking at them was not the shaggy, bearded, tired-looking face of the former Abwehr agent, but that of the fresh faced young, but dead, strategist. Henry could see Dietmarr's eyes through the mask, teary and full of dread.

"Holy fuck…" said Brock quietly. "That is remarkable…"

Henry was still looking into Dietmarr's eyes, the eyes he had fallen in love with the very first time he had been dragged down into the cellar to be greeted with the man who sat before him, looking completely unfamiliar.

"Are you okay…?" asked Henry tentatively. He could see Dietmarr's eyes through the mask give him a searing stare that suggested he was not. Archibald stood by the window, looking out on to the streets below, attempting to come to terms with what he had helped facilitate.

A few moments of silence passed as the four men digested the scene in front of them. It was raining outside now, as if the weather attempted to match the mood of the room.

"I understand this is difficult, but I must insist that we get going…" said Brock carefully, as Henry nodded along. Dietmarr was still in shock and did not respond.

"I'll leave you all to it then", said Archibald as he picked up his briefcase and his sodden surgical gown and made for the door.

"What about your fee?" asked Brock, but Archibald did not stop.

"I don't want your blood money", he snapped back. "What you have just made me do is not just unethical, but illegal and frankly disgusting. My fee is that I never want to see any of you ever again." With that, he threw open the door to the hotel room and disappeared from view, leaving the three men alone again.

"Right, we need a plan", said Brock, unperturbed by Archibald's outburst and trying to overlook the clearly distressed Dietmarr. "I understand you may need time to adjust, but we're on a time limit here", he added as Dietmarr's tears began to roll out from underneath his mask once more. Brock however, ploughed on.

"I've been linking in with British intelligence services and they have been feeding me as much as they can about Hitler's schedule leading up to the elections in March, but noise is that Hitler is the clear favourite to win the Chancellorship."

Henry listened intently but Dietmarr was still in a world of his own. Brock continued.

"We need to land in Munich by the 24th, set up camp in Ostfriedof, just outside the city and get our bearings before infiltrating the Reichstag on the 26th. I am told Hitler will be in the Goetz Room meeting with his advisors at ten hundred hours; this is the meeting you will make a magical reappearance Dietmarr…"

Dietmarr looked up as he began to regain some element of composure.

"We need you to get into as many meetings as possible", continued Brock. "Come back to base every evening to update us and we can decide from there when and where the best point of attack is. Is this fair?"

Henry nodded. Dietmarr took longer to do so, but nodded in agreement also.

"Good!" triumphed Brock. "And again, thank you Dietmarr. I know this is difficult for you."

Dietmarr merely nodded again, wiping away the tears that had managed to escape the mask that was screwed into the sides of his neck with care, but glued to the top of his head rather clumsily by Archibald.

"Have we actually thought about whether this disguise is good enough?" questioned Henry, but he was immediately shot down by Brock and also by Dietmarr, who had all of a sudden found a voice.

"Are you fucking serious?" he seethed. "Don't be asking stuff like that NOW", as Henry saw the error of his ways and backed down.

"I guess this is as good as it gets", he admitted, finally taking a seat in the comfy armchair in the corner of the hotel room.

"We have all of von Manstein's old belongings including his passport so that will help us with the image", confirmed Henry.

"And actually getting into the country…" added Brock.

Neither Henry nor Dietmarr laughed.

The rain continued to pour outside, mixed in with an abundance of sleet, as if the atmosphere knew of the bleak intent the trio had planned for the next couple of weeks. The traders down below, oblivious of the events upstairs, cowered away under tarpaulins as they attempted to fill damp paper bags with fruit and vegetables for the increasingly frustrated punters, dodging the increasingly large puddles as they jumped from stall to stall.

…

It was forty eight hours later that Henry, Brock and the masked Dietmarr landed in Dachau, in a helicopter provided by Brock. He was the one man left who still had official connections with intelligence services, and throughout the whole journey, he had reminded both Henry and Dietmarr of that fact, although neither were highly amused by Brock's japery.

They had a twenty kilometer walk before landing in a small enclosure in a wooded area, eerily similar to the campsite Henry and Dietmarr had spent weeks living just outside Potsdam. The snow on the ground was gathering and the winter sun setting as everyone dumped their belongings on the sodden ground; Dietmarr scratching at the edges of his mask, still clearly uncomfortable with the setup.

"I'll go on the hunt for some wood", said Dietmarr as he traipsed off into the woodland, as if he was desperate to get away from the company of his peers. Brock began assembling the tents as Henry stared after Dietmarr; still concerned for the welfare of his friend.

"Don't worry about him!" piped Brock cheerfully, as he lay out an ensemble of poles on the ground. "He's an agent at heart, he'll get used to it". Henry wasn't so sure, but merely shrugged and began to help Brock.

It was a full two hours before Dietmarr returned, carrying an assortment of logs and branches that he threw into the middle of the enclosure. Within moments, he had managed to get a spark despite the damp weather and the fire was up and running as Brock made the final adjustments to the trio's tents.

Dietmarr fell asleep almost instantly by the fireplace, clearly emotionally drained from the events of the past few days, as Brock and Henry tucked into the sausages they had roasted over their camp fire.

"It must be so difficult for him…" said Henry, quietly. Brock merely nodded in agreement, scoffing large helpings of sausage and downing it with ale. It wasn't long before both of them were wrapped up in multiple blankets inside their respective tents, bidding goodbye to the day.

The following morning was frosty, with all three in reflective moods sipping on their coffee. Only Dietmarr had a task for the day, to reintroduce himself as von Manstein to the top brass of German politics as Henry and Brock waited in the wings for updates.

It was another two hours before Dietmarr changed into his best suit and reluctantly left the camp to make his first visit into the city. Henry and Brock could do nothing but wait for his return, making an occasional trip into the village to buy food and coffee. There was occasional snowfall to greet the pair. It was well after sunset that Dietmarr returned, carrying a smart briefcase.

"Well?" asked Brock eagerly, barely giving Dietmarr a chance to sit down. "How did the mask play?"

"Didn't even question it", responded Dietmarr. "Didn't even ask where I had been! Clearly didn't miss von Manstein very much!" He set his briefcase up on a dismembered tree trunk and opened it to reveal a smaller suitcase. Upon opening the smaller case, a few pages blew out on to the snow covered ground below.

"This is Hitler's personal diary for the next three months", began Dietmarr, a fluttering smile emanating through the mask for the first time since it had been glued to him. Henry and Dietmarr both peered at it, examining its contents before turning to each other and then simultaneously to Dietmarr in surprise.

"Victory parade on February 15th?!" said Henry. "There hasn't even been a vote yet!" but Dietmarr interrupted, merely placing a finger on the appointment above it.

"This is when we should surround him", he said menacingly. "A one to one appointment with myself in Brown House to finalise the arrangements for this parade. I think it's the easiest plan we've had to date. I can merely sit down with him, excuse myself to go for a shit, and then bring you two bastards in from outside. No one will question Hitler's chief strategist, will they?! I even have his ID now", he said, flashing his wallet to show the old face of the real von Manstein. "Three on one", he added.

"So, 4th February is the date", confirmed Brock. "We'll kill Hitler on that day." Henry nodded to confirm his approval. Brock continued.

"In the meantime, you need to gather as much information as possible on what his next steps are going to be, who else is involved, the condition of Hindenburg. Anything and everything we can take back to our superiors to help them."

All three nodded in approval, with visual excitement. Finally they had a plan set in stone and by all accounts, it sounded too good to be true.

The threesome spent the next week swapping anecdotes from their previous travails as full time agents, with Dietmarr leaving the camp in order to keep himself acquainted with the powers that be at the Reichstag, bringing back rafts of information to the camp about Hitler's plans for Germany and the rest of Europe.

Henry was feeling the most relaxed he had in weeks, enjoying the camping life with two other men he had grown to trust. Dietmarr had seemingly adjusted to his new life behind the mask while Brock continued to be his boisterous, brash self but making Henry laugh more than he had done in the past year.

…

The morning of 4th February came round far too fast for Henry's liking. The snow had continued to fall throughout their stay, and the ground around them was now covered in snow a foot deep, the only colour in the enclosure coming from the flickering flame of the camp fire.

Henry and Brock left the campsite at the crack of dawn, leaving behind their camping gear and taking a simple light backpack between them. Dietmarr, more nervous than he had been recently, remained behind, reminding the other two of the exact location of Hitler's headquarters as they headed off through the woods.

"For the hundredth time, we know…" said Brock, waving cheerily as the pair walked out of sight.

It was only a short walk to the centre of Munich, and it wasn't long before Henry and Dietmarr were in their agreed meeting place, a grand orchestral stage used for outdoor music just outside Brown House, where Adolf Hitler had based himself. It was still early in the morning, but the city was full of people, some dressed in smart suits, some stumbling through the streets begging for money or food.

The morning dragged as the pair waited for the now familiar masked face of Dietmarr to appear by the entrance of Brown House, but just before midday, as Brock was distracted by a fight happening nearby, Henry gave him an almighty shove towards the building as Dietmarr appeared by the huge golden doors, beckoning them in his direction.

The atmosphere was tense as the trio all nodded courteously to each other.

"They're with me", Dietmarr said simply as the security guard made a move towards Henry and Brock. The security guard, alarmed at his apparent mistake, took a step back.

"Of course sir", he added bashfully.

The threesome walked in complete silence, through the building and to a room at the back, where two golden horses on their hind legs welcomed them to the office of Adolf Hitler. Before they got to the door, Dietmarr broke the silence.

"Remember. I go first, and straight for him, while Henry goes right and you go left", he said quietly, aiming a nod at Brock who returned it. "That way we surround him. No one else is in there. My pistol is in my right pocket, but as discussed, we will try and get as much information as possible before I blow his brains out."

"Right", said Henry.

"Right", added Brock. He looked nervous, which simultaneously made Henry nervous. The trio made for the door, led by Dietmarr who crashed through and made straight for the winged armchair behind the mahogany desk. Henry went right, picking up a china ornament as he did so; the first thing he saw he could use as a potential weapon. Brock went left, and pulled a small knife from his pocket, clutching it in his hands so hard his knuckles turned white.

Dietmarr was quick to get behind the armchair, holding the pistol in his right hand as Hitler dropped his pen and put both his arms up slightly in the air.

"What is this?" he asked, looking around at Dietmarr. "Erich? What are you doing? Who are these people?"

"Henry Irthing. British intelligence service", stated Henry with a wry smile. This is my friend Brock, American intelligence service. I'm afraid the game is up."

Hitler looked confused, continuing to look around at Dietmarr as if he was silently demanding answers.

"Erich?" he asked. "What are you doing?" Dietmarr remained silent, running his thumb along the grip of the pistol. Henry continued.

"I'm afraid you've been infiltrated", he said confidently. "You find yourself in an enclosed room with three enemies, one of whom happens to be one of your own countrymen. We know your plans. We know what you want. We know you are a monster."

Hitler's eyes lost their spark, as he slowly drew his arms down to his side. Dietmarr rose his pistol up slightly in anticipation.

"You're going to tell us what you have been doing in this country and why you want to invade Europe", said Brock forcefully, now pointing his knife in the direction of Hitler.

"And why would I do that?" asked Hitler, the smallest hint of a smile trying to find its way through. "You are indeed… Outnumbered", he added.

Henry and Brock looked at each other confused, as Dietmarr continued to give his full attention to Hitler, his pistol slowly rising further towards the German politician.

"WACHEN!" boomed Hitler, as two fully armed guards burst through the door. Brock, with the reflexes of a man half his age, jumped at one of the guards, planting his knife into his neck, as Henry grappled with the other one, easily taking him down and pinning him to the floor.

Brock withdrew the knife from the neck of the first guard, as blood seeped out on to the marble floor and plunged it into the neck of the second who collapsed to the ground. Blood flowed across the room, but Dietmarr had not moved as Henry and Brock recovered their positions and returned their focus on Hitler, who seemed unperturbed by the gruesome death of his security guards.

"Oh well. I guess it makes it more fun if it's an even fight", he said, smirking. Henry and Brock's confused looks returned.

"There's nothing even about a three on one hey", said Brock, continuing to point his pocket knife at Hitler.

"True", he responded simply. "But there is something even about two on two. Wouldn't you agree, Mr. Schultz?"

"I would say that was correct, sir", responded Dietmarr, turning the pistol away from Hitler towards Brock.

Henry's stomach dropped. Dietmarr's pose seemed to take on a more aggressive form, as he pointed the gun at Brock, the booming laughter of Hitler resonating around the marble and echoing through the air.

"I always had an inkling…" said Brock quietly. "There was something not quite right about you from the start…" A gun shot rang out, making both Henry and Hitler jump, as Brock collapsed to the floor, a clean bullet hole through his head.

Brock was dead.

With merely a pause, Dietmarr turned the pistol on Henry, staring right into the whites of his eyes.

"Now it's not very even, is it?"

There was a menacing pierce to Dietmarr's eyes, as if he was a completely different person to the one Henry had spent the last year with.

"Who are you?" said Henry, with a quivering fear to his voice.

"My name is Dietmarr Schultz. Agent for Germany, agent for Adolf Hitler and agent for the National Socialist German Workers Party" he responded, as if he was reading from a pre-prepared script.

Henry had so many questions, but was wary of Dietmarr's gun, which was pointed directly between his eyes. Henry put down the china ornament whilst simultaneously holding his other hand up, imploring Dietmarr not to shoot him too.

"I don't understand?" asked Henry, not sure where to begin.

"It's quite simple", replied Hitler. "You Brits are a gullible bunch", as he let out a searing laugh once more. Dietmarr was not laughing; his eyes fixed solely on Henry.

"But you killed von Manstein?!" asked Henry.

"Ah yes, a shame", said Hitler. "Erich was once a very good advisor and a friend to me but then he became… expendable…"

"I want to hear it from him", said Henry, nodding towards Dietmarr.

There was a long pause before Dietmarr spoke.

"Adolf is right, Erich was a fine asset", he began. "However, I know how good you Brits are". Hitler scorned at the last sentence, but Dietmarr continued uninterrupted.

"I had worked out what you were up to when I watched you running from those guards all those months ago. There was only one place you could have been and that was trying to get close to this man." He waved his pistol in Hitler's direction.

This seemed like news to Hitler, who was looking inquisitively in Dietmarr's direction, but nothing was going to stop Dietmarr in full flow.

"When I dragged you down into that basement, it was the start of my repatriation", he continued. "The German state had let me down but I was no traitor."

It seemed Dietmarr had been desperate to let out his speech for a long time, pained by the emotional stress of his own personal covert mission. His eyes were manic, and he kept pulling on his now lengthy beard and scratching at the edges of his mask, laughing sporadically but loudly at certain intervals.

"The German state lets no German man down!" boomed Hitler, but Dietmarr was quick to respond.

"Oh but it did, sir. It did! Hindenburg stitched me up!" he replied loudly. "Saw me as a liability and made sure I was punished for it. Everything that has happened Adolf; everything, has happened because of me. This man – admittedly a man capable of stopping you – is stood before us, begging for his life. The other one capable of such is dead", he added pointing at the lifeless body of Brock. "I even made sure Hindenburg died before his time. Slowly but surely. The more pain the better…" Dietmarr continued to scratch away at his beard and the edges of his mask for he was unable to take it off.

"I still don't get it…" whispered Henry. "I don't get why you killed von Manstein?" Dietmarr laughed and put the gun down on Hitler's desk.

"Oh come on my dear Henry, keep up. I thought you were more intelligent than this?" mocked Dietmarr. Henry looked on, bemused.

"How else was I to get you to trust me? I had to convince you I was the real deal. Admittedly, the idea of wearing a mask of his face freaked me out a bit, but I will do whatever is necessary to regain my rightful place!"

"And you applauded him for this did you?" Henry asked, looking at Hitler. "Murdering your chief advisor against your wishes?"

"How do you know it was against my wishes?" asked Hitler. "He was a liability, I couldn't care less if he lived or died."

"But it wasn't your order?" Henry responded, with a new found confidence. If he were to survive this, he would need to appear confident and ready for anything.

"I trust Mr Schultz's judgment," replied Hitler curtly but Henry was on the attack.

"His judgment? His judgment is diabolical. He's a raging alcoholic and clearly a maniac, why on Earth would you trust his judgment?!" asked Henry. Hitler paused, but it was Dietmarr who responded.

"It takes a maniac to know a maniac", he said, with an almost ghostly aura.

"What does that mean?" asked Henry.

"Aren't all agents maniacs? I mean… What kind of human being do you have to be to do what we do?" asked Dietmarr. Henry, bemused by the cryptic response, turned his attention turned to the politician in the room.

"So, given I'm probably about to die, how about you give me my last supper and tell me what you have planned for this place?" asked Henry.

"My view for Europe is one of cleanliness", replied Hitler. "German blooded. No blacks. No Jews…" but before he could continue, Dietmarr interrupted.

"No homosexuals…" he said, with an evil smile across his face.

Henry's eyes turned to Dietmarr, who looked as though he had struck gold.

There was tension in the air as Henry tried to remain calm. For the first time, he was convinced Dietmarr definitely knew his secret, but he wasn't about to confirm his suspicions. Henry turned and made for the door, attempting to open it and dash out into the corridor. As he opened it, he looked up and ran straight into a mountain of a man, holding a rifle and wearing a number of badges on his huge chest. The impact caused Henry to fly back across Hitler's office, crashing on to the marble floor. Opening his eyes, he saw Dietmarr directly above him, the same menacing grin across his bearded face.

"No. Way. Out." said Dietmarr, letting out another maniacal laugh. Hitler joined him.

"Just kill me now…" said Henry, not seeing a route to

freedom. He was scared of admitting his secret, and ashamed he had let himself fall in love with a man who was ultimately the enemy. Nothing mattered to him now. He knew the game was up.

Henry lay on the floor helpless, breathing heavily as Dietmarr stood over him, pistol drawn and aiming right between Henry's eyes once more.

"I heard you", said Dietmarr, quietly enough for Henry to hear. "In the motel the night before I got this damned mask... You remember what you said... I heard you..."

Henry lay still, a single tear coming from his right eye as Dietmarr looked on, almost as if he felt sorry for the former British agent. He continued.

"Is this why they sacked you? The high command of Britain couldn't have a bugger in their ranks! Is that the right word? Bugger?" Dietmarr lifted his right shoe and placed it against the throat of Henry.

"Do you like this?" asked Dietmarr. "Does it turn you on?"

Henry struggled under the weight of the foot, finding it difficult to catch his breath as the weight increased. "Have you dreamt about this moment too?!" asked Dietmarr, returning to laugh in his own evil way. The force was so high, Henry found it difficult to breathe under the weight until he managed to grab Dietmarr's leg with both hands and bring him to the ground next to him. They both lay there next to each other for a few moments, catching their breath.

"To be honest... I always knew..." whispered Dietmarr, jumping to his feet with superior agility, as Henry continued to lie on the floor, helpless. Dietmarr picked up his pistol again, pointing it at Henry for the third time. Hitler continued to look on from behind his desk, as if he was watching a play on stage, personally performed for him at his bequest.

"But why?" continued Dietmarr. "Why did you have to fall in love with a German MAN? You may think I am a monster, and maybe I am, but what sort of monster are you?" Dietmarr drew back his size eleven boot and kicked Henry in the side of the head, knocking him out cold.

…

Henry awoke, tasting his own blood as it run down the side of his cheek. He was tied to a chair as Dietmarr and Hitler were speaking in strong German accents behind the desk. Henry could only hear bits and pieces; his ears ringing from the impact.

"Good morning…" said Dietmarr. "We're just discussing how we're going to dispose of your body". Hitler laughed, as if the roles of superior and servant had changed, and Hitler was doing all he could to appease the masked Dietmarr.

The pair continued to converse, knowing that Henry could understand their every word, for the next ten minutes before attention returned to the Brit.

"We've decided to keep you alive", said Hitler, as Henry let out a sigh of relief. "However, we need you."

Henry wasn't surprised.

"What for?" he said, knowing what the answer was going to be.

"Mr. Schultz there happens to think you English are actually quite good at what you do, and he has convinced me you need keeping in line. Therefore, you're going to do all of our bidding. We need someone on the inside…" Dietmarr had strolled around the back of Henry, keeping his eye on him at all times.

Henry's expectations were confirmed.

"I would rather you killed me now", he said, as Hitler withdrew a pistol of his own from his desk drawer and pointed it at Henry.

"As you wish", stated Hitler, as Henry closed his eyes anticipating the worst, but before Hitler could pull the trigger, Dietmarr shouted to stop him, at the same time the door burst open.

"WHAT IS IT?!" screamed Hitler, as the aide stopped in his tracks, shocked by the scene that he had been greeted with.

"Erm… Sorry, sir, but your presence is requested in the charter room", the aide said quickly, before performing a little bow.

"Why are you bowing?!" screeched Hitler again. "Very well, Schultz, remain here, I shall be back shortly. Make sure he goes nowhere", he added, throwing the pistol on to his desk and leaving the room with a brisk walk.

As the red-faced aide left behind Hitler, there was an eerie and almost poetic silence, as the echo of the slamming door rang around the room. Dietmarr was slowly wandering around the room in perfect circles as Henry merely stared into the distance.

After ten minutes of circling, Dietmarr had found himself by the entrance, seemingly entranced by the lock on the door. After a few tense moments, he reached for the key and slowly locked the door, before letting out a sigh. A few more moments passed, Dietmarr's gaze fixed upon the lock, as he turned back towards Henry.

Dietmarr stuttered slightly before getting his words out.

"I'm so sorry..." he said. "I'm so, so sorry..."

Henry didn't respond, another look of confusion spread across his bloody face.

"I'm in way too deep..." continued Dietmarr. "I could have saved Brock, but I didn't... I'm so, so sorry..." he said, punching himself in the face as he finished.

"Wait, stop punching yourself, what on Earth is going on here?" asked Henry, squirming to get out of the chair but unable to. Dietmarr took a seat behind Hitler's desk, a tear coming out from under the mask once more.

"I was forced to", he started, his voice quivering. "I was forced to abide by their rules." Henry looked as confused as ever.

"What do you mean? What is going on?" he repeated. "Dietmarr, what is going on?!"

Dietmarr was stroking the barrel of the pistol that Hitler had thrown on the desk, seemingly being very careful over what he said next.

"The trial", he said. "The trial forced me to, they knew what they were doing. Hindenburg, Hitler, all of them." Henry could hear Dietmarr audibly crying below the mask now as he implored him to continue speaking.

"And I was happy to", he continued. "I was happy to, I was just serving my country, and it's all I ever wanted to do." He then buried his head in his hands, but Henry shouted at him to continue talking.

"Dietmarr. I'm confused as Hell right now, what is going on?! Tell me!"

Dietmarr closed his eyes, and took a deep breath.

"I was court martialed by my friends; stitched up by my colleagues", he began. "I was due to go to prison, but evaded it by agreeing to Hitler's proposition of being his eyes and ears. I was under his supervision and I had to do everything he said." Henry listened on intently.

"We knew you were tracking Hitler. We knew about the

meetings you had with Pursey and his crowd; we knew everything. You were sitting ducks, and Brock and I led you here to either join us or be eliminated." It was at this point Henry interjected.

"Wait, you AND Brock?" he asked.

"Yes. Me and Brock", replied Dietmarr. "Brock was a double agent. He was working for the Germans. Our intent was to get you here to surrender and join the Germans. An American and a British double agent would have helped the Germans immensely in Hitler's quest for domination…"

"So why did you shoot him dead if he was on your side?" asked Henry, his mind going a million miles an hour, trying to keep up with who was doing what work for whom.

"Because I love you."

Another silence spread through the room. Dietmarr sat deflated at the desk, as if all of the air he had been built up over the months had been let out of him. Henry, at first amazed by what he had heard, began laughing.

"I'm sorry, what did you just say?" he asked, a smile beginning to flitter across his face.

"Because I love you", replied Dietmarr once more. "I thought I had to hide it", he continued, as signs of life began to reappear in his eyes through the holes in his mask. "Then I heard you say it in the motel and I knew."

"But why didn't you stop it then? Why did we have to go through all of this?" Henry asked, his heart beating faster than it had ever done before.

"It was too late. I had this mask on, the plan had been made and I was still scared. I lay awake all night, repeating that scene in my head. At first, I thought I'd misheard but I knew I hadn't. I just didn't know what else to do, but go ahead and hope it worked out for the best."

"But surely Hitler would have done something when you shot him?" asked Henry, pointing at the pale face of Brock who still lay motionless on the floor of the office.

"Hitler didn't know he was on our side", said Dietmarr. "At first he wasn't, but I convinced him it was the right thing to do one night when you were asleep. We paid him well… Hitler didn't need to know…"

Henry sat, still tied to the chair, completely aghast at what he was hearing. He couldn't quite get his head around the state of affairs.

"So let me get this straight", started Henry. "You had intended to betray me all along, but fell in love with me, while Brock had started out to defeat Hitler with me but had been talked round by you?" Dietmarr merely nodded in response.

"That makes no sense!" shouted Henry, his emotion had gone from amazement to relief to frustration in a flash. "Why have you done all of this?"

"I had no choice", responded Dietmarr desperately. "At least up until the last couple of weeks, I thought my destiny was to fight for Germany, no matter what, but you opened my eyes Henry. I didn't know there was someone else like me out there. I didn't know that person was you. I didn't know I could live a different life to the one that had been given to me."

Henry paused once more, trying to digest what he was hearing.

"And how am I supposed to believe you?" he asked. Dietmarr seemed ready for the question.

"I locked the door… And left the key in…" he replied. Dietmarr got up from behind the desk and slowly made his way over to Henry. Time seemed to stop, as Dietmarr lent d circled around him and back to the desk.

"In a moment, Hitler is going to come back in", he said, switching from romantic to professional in an instant. "I'm not going to mess around. I have his pistol, and I will shoot him immediately." He then rose up from the desk, and went to take the key out of the door before returning to his desk, opening one of the drawers and stealing a gulp of vodka from Hitler's stash.

The pair sat in complete silence for almost half an hour before Hitler's booming voice could be heard getting nearer and nearer from outside. Henry held his breath as Dietmarr braced and steadied his hand, aiming straight for the door.

Bang. The door opened and a bullet was fired almost immediately. Hitler fell to the floor, clutching at his stomach. Dietmarr pulled the trigger again as another bullet pierced the air. A third, fourth and fifth bullet sound echoed around the room, Henry jumping at each shot, and all of them ending up resting in the abdomen of Adolf Hitler.

"Dietmarr…" he squirmed, before he collapsed on to the floor, a fresh swathe of blood seeping across the floor, covering the now dried blood stains coming from Brock's body. Hitler was dead.

Both Henry and Dietmarr sat and stared at the still open eyes of Hitler for a moment before Dietmarr leapt into action. Taking Brock's discarded knife from the ground, he slashed away at the rope tying Henry to his chair, as Henry tried frantically to get free, kicking the chair to the wall as he did so. The pair stood face to face together, as the blood trickled on to their boots, as Dietmarr gently stroked Henry's face with his forefinger. A mixture of relief and euphoria briefly flowed through Henry's body before Dietmarr grabbed his hand.

"Run", he said. They bolted towards the door, and veered off to the right, the sounds of more security guards getting closer from the front of the building. "It's lucky I've been here for a few weeks; I kind of know my way around now!" shouted Dietmarr, still dragging Henry by the hand as they swerved in and out of corridors, past well-dressed officials and men in suits until they reached another golden set of doors leading out into perfectly maintained gardens adorned with similar statues that stood outside Adolf Hitler's office.

Before they set off outside, the sound of an alarm blared through the corridors, signaling both men to run through the golden doors and make for the high security fence that protected the building.

"This way!" shouted Dietmarr once more, as he guided Henry towards the solitary gate where all but one of the security guards were sprinting towards them, aiming for the commotion inside.

"He's with me!" he shouted, as one of the guards gleefully greeted who he thought was Erich von Manstein with a friendly wave before running past, rifle drawn. Henry and Dietmarr reached the gate and without a pause, Dietmarr was speaking to the lone guard.

"You need to go inside and help, there is a major security alert", he said.

"Yes sir!" responded the young-looking guard, as he picked up his own rifle and sprinted after his colleagues.

"That was easy…" said Henry, as he and Dietmarr jumped

the barrier and sprinted off into the distance towards the city, the sound of the alarms becoming quieter and quieter as they did so.

The pair had ran for about a kilometer before they came to a halt, Dietmarr wiping the sweat that had got caught between the mask and his face.

"I need to get this off..." he said, but he didn't get the response he had wanted from Henry.

"I don't know where or how this is possible unless we get back to London?" questioned Henry, much to the disappointment of Dietmarr. "I think you're going to have to manage a little while longer..."

...

"Don't you think we're a little too old to be going off to fight? Plus, they know who you are..."

Henry and Dietmarr were sat outside in the garden, sipping at their morning coffee and reading the newspapers; all of which were peppered with news about the Prime Minister's announcement the night before that the country was going to war.

"This is all I have ever known, my love", replied Henry. "I don't think I could live with myself if I sat here and watched my comrades do battle..."

The sun was out and the day was already getting hot; the songs of the birds filling the skies around Henry's cottage, the only building in the middle of lush green fields filled with cows and sheep, grazing at the grass below their feet. The wooden furniture sat at the top of a long garden, with two cats chasing each other, dodging between the water feature and a clumsily built shed that Henry had erected a few months earlier.

"We aren't allowed to fight", said Dietmarr, "and besides... I have to keep you safe. We only have each other in this world, I don't know what I'd do without you here."

Henry continued to peruse the paper, reading about his country going to join America in a war in Asia.

"You are right. Even if I wanted to, I couldn't..." he lamented, placing the newspaper on top of the pile and laying back in his chair, shielding his eyes from the bright sun.

It had been 21 years since that day in Munich, both Henry

and Dietmarr granted with military clearance due to their bravery. Neither of them were allowed to re-join the forces, choosing instead to live in solitude, tending to the animals and living the farming life in the English countryside. Both men were in their mid-50s now, barely seeing another soul, preferring each other's company in quiet existence.

The world around them had not changed. Despite receiving thanks for their efforts during the mission to defeat Hitler, neither of them received any official praise with Commander Pursey, in his final year in MI5, asking for Henry to receive chemical castration due to his homosexuality. Henry however, had escaped to join Dietmarr, who had already fled to the countryside and they had not been found since. The pair would like to think they had been left alone, the British Secret Service forgetting about them and letting them get on with their lives, but Henry would keep a keen look out for official looking vehicles coming up the dirt tracks regardless.

"One day, our world will change for the better…" said Dietmarr, quietly, as if he did not truly believe the words coming out of his mouth, Henry's binoculars strapped around his neck.

"One day…" confirmed Henry, with more authority, helping himself to another cup of coffee. Dietmarr was smiling, and Henry responded in kind. They had escaped, and they were happy, all that Grandad Joe had wanted for his only grandchild.

Printed in Great Britain
by Amazon